RULES OF THE ROAD

Mike Manson

First published by Tangent Books 2011

Tangent Books, Unit 5.16 Paintworks, Bristol BS4 3EH

www.tangentbooks.co.uk

Tel: 0117 972 0645

ISBN-10: 1906477493
ISBN-13: 978-1906477493

Cover: Gillian Marles
Map: Adrian Barclay
Boz's Rules of the Road: Matt Manson
Print management: Jon Lewis, Essential Print Management

For Hannah

www.rulesoftheroad.co.uk

What's her name?
Her name is Gloria
G . L . O . R . I . A.
GLORIA
Gonna shout it every night
Van Morrison

I am on a lonely road and I am travelling
Looking for the key to set me free
Joni Mitchell

Much have I travelled in the realms of gold,
And many goodly states and kingdoms seen;
John Keats (1795-1821)

the Rules of the Road.

1. You only get a lift where there are cars.
2. Each spot has its own karma.
3. Hitch at a bottom of of a hill that way you look smaller. *
4. Stand under a lamp post when hitching in the dark.
5. Respect men with Rubber stamps.
6. Be patient, Be flexible, Be friendly. (Be clean)
7. Go with your instincts.
8. Remember the Road doesn't lead from A to B But A to Z
9. A lift in the wrong direction is better than no lift at all.
10. Pray, Sometime you are very close to God.

* Turn towards the oncoming traffic - its the your face the Driver wants to see, not your arse. unless your a chick.

4

RULES OF THE ROAD

Boz's Rules of the Road

1. You only get a lift where there are cars.
2. Each spot has its own karma.
3. Hitch at the bottom of a hill, that way you look smaller.*
4. Stand under a lamp post when hitching in the dark.
5. Respect men with rubber stamps.
6. Be patient, be flexible, be friendly. (Be clean.)
7. Go with your instincts.
8. Remember, the journey isn't from A to B but from A to Z.
9. A lift in the wrong direction is better than no lift at all.
10. Pray, sometimes you are very close to God.

And a couple of my own:

11. Don't try out your jokes on immigration officers.
12. Don't get arrested for looking like a freak.

*Turn towards the oncoming traffic – it's your face drivers want to see, not your arse. Unless you're a chick.

'Europe. It's a big place.' The route to Matala.

INTRODUCTION

I'd been packing some unwanted books to take to the Oxfam shop when my attention was grabbed by an old paperback with a yolk yellow cover called 'I, Jan Cremer'. As far as I can recollect it was the autobiography of a Dutch painter. Other than that, thirty years on, I can recall very little about the book. I flicked through the pages and a lost photograph fell out. The photograph shows a smiling young man standing on the gravel drive of 27 Laurel Close, Ruislip. The colours are faded to brown and red.

I seem to remember the picture was taken with Dad's Kodak Instamatic. The young man is about twenty years old, he's dressed in a fudge brown crew neck sweater and black cord trousers with a denim flare sewn into the side and is carrying a brown holdall with fake leather handles. Not a rucksack - that was for youth hostellers or Canadians. He's wearing gleaming white plimsolls. New footwear seemed like a good idea at the time but those plimsolls were to prove a mistake.

Look at that face. So young, and keen. The smile is nervous. A panama hat is sitting on clean, wavy blonde shoulder-length hair. A panama hat! The sort of hat worn by old geezers at the bowling club down our local park. Mum had brought it back from a recent holiday in Majorca. I threw it in the bin as soon as I got to London.

Dad was tearful and gave me a hug; we didn't normally even touch each other. He looked older and vague, as if he'd lost something. This was one of the few occasions when he gave me advice. For a moment he seemed to have trouble speaking, he gave me a long searching look and then he said, 'Felix, when you go travelling you'll have some good times and some bad times. The bad times are all part of the experience.' Thanks, Dad. What did he know? He'd never been further than Dunkirk in the war when he'd popped over the Channel for an ice cream.

Mum said, 'Do be careful Felix. In Italy the Mafia fill train carriages with gas and rob everybody.'

I couldn't even begin to argue with that. 'I'll keep away from the Mafia. I promise.'

'Make sure you write. At least send us a postcard.'

I was planning to visit the great galleries of Europe, I was going to sample the finest beers, chill with the most far out freaks[1] and smoke the best shit. I wanted to be the coolest dude in Ruislip. But that hat! I knew the truth; on the coolometer I rated perhaps only four out of ten. But that wasn't going to stop me. In Matala, I'd promised to meet that sweet, sweet girl Gloria. And if everything went according to plan the coolometer would ping right off the scale.

'Don't go and do anything stupid and get arrested,' was Dad's parting shot.

I'd got a long summer ahead of me. I'd got rides to hitch, I'd got freight trains to jump. I wanted to get on with it.

---

[1] Freak is a compliment, not an insult.

ONE

I stood under the portico waiting for Boz. I'd arranged to meet him on the steps of the National Gallery. I looked across Trafalgar Square under low clouds. It was as if all the colours had been sucked out of the world leaving just grey. No wonder London needs red buses to brighten the landscape.

I'd got some news to tell Boz. I wasn't sure how I was going to break it to him. Okay, it wasn't that bad, but it was important that Boz didn't use this as an opportunity to insist that we change our plans.

As this was the beginning of our cultural journey I thought we'd set the tone and get our eye in by taking in a couple of rooms. I went into the gift shop and looked at the postcards. The early Renaissance would be a good start - Leonardo, Michelangelo, Rubens. We'd come across those guys in all the major European galleries.

It was just after one o' clock when Boz arrived; he was two hours late.

'Sorry Felix, I had some last-minute business to attend to. Bixby sends peace and love.'

'Bixby? What were you doing with Bixby?'

'Stocking up on some essential supplies.'

'Boz, I wasn't able to get the Eurorail tickets.'

'What! Why not? What are we going to do?'

'How old are you?'

'Twenty-three.'

'And I'm twenty.'

'So?'

'You've got to be under twenty-one to be eligible for Eurorail. You're too old.'

'I'm twenty-three and I'm too old. That's ridiculous.'

'Never trust anybody over twenty-five.'

'We'll have to go to St Ives as we originally planned.'

'No, no, no. You don't understand. It's better NOT travelling by Eurorail. It'll give us more flexibility. It means we can also go by bus and boat. And hitch. It'll be much more fun. And it'll probably work out cheaper.'

'Are you sure?'

'Yeah, positive.'

'But St Ives would be easier.'

I had to stop these thoughts immediately.

'No Boz.'

'But...'

'I've already booked the train to Venice.'

*

Boz and I had spent many evenings planning our summer. We agreed we were heading to Cornwall. Although Boz had never visited St Ives, I'd holidayed there the previous year. You turn a corner and there it is before you, golden beaches, turquoise sea and a cluster of fishermen's cottages. 'It's the Big Sur of the West Country,' I told Boz.

During the winter we would talk for hours about St Ives and what we would do. 'There's something miraculous about the light there. The crystal-clear Atlantic air has a luminosity that makes the atmosphere sparkle. It's a little bit arty, a little bit existential. Even the fishermen are painters.'

We'd hang out in cafes reading Jean-Paul Sartre and Kafka. If I caught the creative vibe I thought I might even knock up some oil paintings myself. Maybe write some poetry or scribble a few short stories.

'There's some weird stuff going on. There's this artist who has her town garden filled with monolithic sculptures. Her old man's a painter as well - does brown cubist stuff. He's a drinking buddy of Picasso, apparently. There's the lighthouse that Virginia Woolf wrote about, you can see it across the bay. And D.H. Lawrence hung out a couple of miles along the coast. The walk through the ancient landscape along the coffin path to Zennor is like going on a spiritual journey. The old straight track was used by funeral processions to carry their dead to the parish church from the remote outlying farms. You can feel the primeval vibe, it's so strong it's tangible.'

I know Boz feared St Ives would be like other West Country seaside towns: a broken-down dump. He was also concerned that there would be too many soft southerners. 'It's cosmopolitan, there are people from the Midlands there as well,' I said, 'and they make Cornish pasties in three different sizes.'

Over the weeks I found my descriptions of St Ives becoming increasingly vivid.

'There'll be parties on the beaches. Wild dancing round driftwood fires. Free love, gorgeous bohemian chicks who'll take you behind the rocks for a head job. And in every pub hippies rub shoulders with crusty old fishermen; there's always some foot stomping Cornubian playing a fiddle.'

'And that's a good thing?' Boz asked.

'There's a little hut on the cliff where you can watch for shoals of pilchards. At the right time of year you can swim with them. Have you ever swum with pilchards, Boz? You've got to swim with the pilchards. It's a life-changing experience. You're at one with nature. Buoyed up by thousands of these beautiful fishes, it's like floating on mercury.'

'Have you done this Felix?'

'No, but I intend to. This summer.' Boz appeared excited by this. 'Boz, are you up for it?'

'Sounds alright to me.'

I saved the best bit for last. 'I haven't checked this out yet, but I reckon we could probably sign on while we're there.'

TWO

S o that was it. We were going to stay in a little house behind the
beach in St Ives. We would crash on the golden sand by day and
drink, smoke and shag by night. We'd probably shag in the day
as well. Our summer plans were sorted. Sorted, that is, until I spoke to
Gloria.

'Eurorail?' Gloria's blue eyes were wide with excitement. 'You're
Eurorailing?'

'That's exactly what I'm doing,' I felt bad saying this, but a summer
Eurorailing was suddenly a much better idea than going to St Ives.

'Felix, why didn't you tell me this before?'

'It didn't seem important.'

'It could be important. Where are you going?'

'Europe. By rail!' I laughed.

'But where, Felix? Europe. It's a big place.'

'All over.' I looked at her and guessed. 'South.'

Her face lit up. 'That's brilliant! My friend Blodwyn and I are going
south. And we're going to make a detour. We're going to Crete. It'll
cost more but it'll be worth it. There's this place on Crete called…'

I was enjoying this. 'Don't tell me, it's called…'

'Matala!' Gloria said.

'You've spoilt it, I wanted to guess. But what a coincidence. You
won't believe this, but that's exactly what I was going to say. Matala.'

'The Matala with the caves?' Gloria asked.

'Yes, with the caves.' I once remember looking at a picture of
troglodytes living in white cones of rock. Was that Matala? Was that
Crete?

'They all live in the caves,' Gloria sighed. 'We're going to live in a cave and be self-sufficient.'

'Yes! Caves in white conical hillocks.'

'And they wear little white conical hats,' Gloria added.

We were both laughing. I loved Gloria's scatty humour.

But then Gloria stopped giggling and a frown wrinkled her enchanting forehead. 'Felix, I don't think the caves are in white conical hillocks.'

'No,' I said, 'and I don't think they wear white conical hats either.' I must have been thinking of somewhere else. 'But they ought to!'

'Yes they ought to!' agreed Gloria. I leant over and hugged her. This was heaven. And then we laughed some more.

Ten minutes ago Eurorail had never even crossed my mind. But now Boz and I were going to travel round Europe and live in a cave - in a white conical hillock or not - with the hottest, sexiest babe in town. Yabba dabba doo.

I was sure Boz would understand and, who knows, maybe he'd get it on with Blodwyn?

*

I watched traffic lights shining through thin nylon curtains. I didn't know what time it was. Boz was slumped with his arm hanging loosely over the side of his chair, his mouth slightly agape. I reckoned this was as good a time as any to update him on our holiday schedule.

'Boz, we've got a change of plan.'

I waited but there was no reaction.

I said it louder. 'BOZ, WE'VE GOT A CHANGE OF PLAN.'

'Uh.' Boz stirred. A muscle in his cheek twitched. 'No need to shout,' he muttered.

'I thought you were asleep.'

'I heard you. We've got a change of plan.'

'Yeah. Good news. It's all coming together.'

'What good news?'

'We're going to live in a cave.'

'I didn't think there were any caves in St Ives.'

'We're going somewhere much better than St Ives?'

'Where? Morecambe?'

He could be such a prick. This was like talking to Benny from *Crossroads*.

'No, not Morecambe. We're going to stay with some chicks…'

'Yeah?' Boz sounded interested. His eyes flickered open - but then closed again.

'…in Crete.'

'That's a long way from St Ives.'

'We're not going to St Ives.'

'Oh.' Silence. I was losing him. I picked up a dirty fork from the dinner plate on the floor by his chair. Maybe I could gently stab him. Too late. Boz's jaw had slackened and he was breathing heavily as if he was asleep.

I drew closer and shouted in Boz's ear. 'Crete, it's a big Greek island. We're going to hang out in Crete. With a couple of chicks.'

'Which chicks?' Boz was still conscious. I put the fork down.

'Gloria and Blodwyn.'

'Blodwyn's a bitch.'

'She comes from Lancashire.'

'She's a liability,' Boz mumbled.

'You don't know Blodwyn.'

'I do. She stole a frozen duck from Fine Fare. I hate her.'

'That's a bit harsh. We all make mistakes.'

'How do you forget to pay for a frozen duck?'

'Blodwyn's a free spirit. And they have moussaka in Greece. It's a Greek pie.'

'I know what moussaka is. It's not a pie.'

'It's a kind of pie.'

'What about the pilchards?'

I thought it best to ignore this. 'It's going to be an adventure. You and I, on the road. Go with the flow. We're going to take hospitality where we find it. Freaks and Greeks. No hurry. No worry. Are you up for it, Boz?'

Boz was silent. I reckon we'd gone as far as we could. Well, at least he hadn't said 'no'.

It had been a long night. I could hear birds twittering outside, and the *wrrrr* of a milkfloat. I was suddenly feeling hungry. 'I've got to go, I need some ice cream,' I said, struggling to stand up. I knocked a bottle off the table and onto the carpet. 'Sorry about that. Red wine. It was almost empty.'

For a moment I couldn't find the door handle.

I could hear Boz mutter. 'I've got my own plan, Felix. There's something I want to check out on our travels. You're not the only guy who knows about art and culture and all that shit.'

I think he was talking in his sleep. I opened the door and stumbled out.

I hoped Boz would remember our conversation when he woke. I was sorry after all I'd said that Boz wouldn't be cavorting with fishes this summer. To make up for his disappointment I felt duty bound to arrange some other memorable experience. I owed him that. I needed to find out the sort of pies we might come across on our travels. I was surprised he didn't like Blodwyn, especially as she came from Lancashire. I'd been hoping she could surprise him with a trick behind the rocks in Matala. I'd have to come up with something else.

I lurched along the road in the grey of the early morning. A street light clicked out as I walked past. I wondered what time the corner shop opened. It was too late to go to bed now.

*

Meanwhile, Plank told me some surprising and unwelcome news.

'Yeah, I'm heading to this place in Greece,' he said. 'It's the end of the road, the edge of Europe. Next stop Africa. Hippie Shangri-La.

There's old caves there that the freaks live in. Most people walk about starkers. Free love. Makes Sodom and Gomorrah look like a chimp's tea party.'

I had an uneasy feeling about this.

'Sounds cool,' I said. 'Where is it?'

Plank continued. 'Do you know the real coincidence? That little chick, that angel with big tits Gloria, well, she told me she's heading that way as well. She said it with a glint in her eye. With any luck our visits will coincide and who knows we could well have ourselves a love in.'

I could feel my gut tighten.

'Anything wrong, Felix? You look a bit tense.'

I was rapidly going off Plank. We'd been introduced at a party a few months before and although I hardly knew him, whenever we met he would greet me like an old friend. At first he had seemed nice enough, but on further acquaintance his veneer of charm wore thin. I was particularly concerned by his dated, and now unacceptable, attitude to women.

'I'm not tense,' I snapped. 'So what's this place called?'

'I don't know… it's Sex-on-Sea as far as I'm concerned.'

'Yeah, but what's its real name?'

'It's on Crete, Malta or something.'

'Matala?' I suggested.

'Yeah, something like that. Matala. AKA Sex-on-Sea.' Plank gave a grotesque primeval howl; anthropologists would recognise this lascivious cry as being similar to the howl generated by a cave man as he clubbed some poor maiden unconscious prior to non-consensual sex.

'Like Bexhill-on-Sea then,' I added lamely, trying to ignore his horrible outburst, 'but without the De La Warr Pavilion.'

'I wouldn't know about that.'

'That's a coincidence, because that's where I'm going.'

'Far out! We're going to have a gas. You, me and little miss love bumps, we're all going to Matala.'

I didn't like Plank calling Gloria that.

Plank continued, 'I've got an idea, we could travel together. We'd have a great time.'

'That might be difficult. I'm going with Boz.'

'You're going with Boz? Boz doesn't travel. He's never been further south than Watford Gap. People don't understand his Lancashire accent.'

'He told me he once met someone from Brittany and they could understand each other perfectly. They were both speaking the same dialect.'

'So people from Bolton are Celts?'

'Yeah, maybe.'

'Forget Boz. Just you and me. We'll be like Jack Kerouac and Neil Cassady. On the road.'

'Two people hitching together is difficult, three people is impossible.'

'Ditch Boz. He doesn't want to go anyway.'

'He does. Boz and I have been planning this for ages. We're going to visit art galleries and museums.'

'You pretentious git. Anyway, that's not what Boz told me. He said he was going to Cornwall to swim with the mackerel.'

'Boz is my best mate. I couldn't dump him. Anyway it was pilchards.'

'It's up to you. But don't say I didn't warn you.'

'Warn me about what?'

'I can tell you now Boz will be excess baggage, you'll have to carry him. He's a dead weight.'

'He's got a smattering of the lingo.'

'You don't need languages for travelling! That's a fallacy about going abroad.'

'It helps.'

'The language of love is what I'm going to use. C'mon Felix, let's be honest. Basically, Boz is a bag of shite.' Plank sniggered. 'A bag of shite with arms and legs.'

'Hey! He's my mate. You can't say things like that about my mate.'

Plank shrugged his shoulders. 'Okay then. I'll make my own way to Matala. I'll see you there, Felix. Unless you get arrested on the way for looking like a freak.'

'You sound just like my old man.'

He punched me on the shoulder in what was meant to be a friendly manner. 'Last one there's a loser.'

THREE

Let me tell you about the first time I met Gloria. It was when I was at University. We were in the students' union. She was sitting on a low-slung chip-greased sofa in the George Davis is Innocent Okay Bar. I couldn't stop looking at her. She had blonde shoulder length hair, slightly wavy. I sat opposite her. Those big eyes. Her pale luminous face and those big denim blue eyes, accentuated by smudges of mascara. Even when I looked away, I was aware of her in the corner of my eye. She was like a film star from a silent movie. I wanted to rescue her from the tracks of an on-coming train. At the top of her notebook, she had written in a rounded female hand and underlined the word 'Cunt'. She saw me looking at her doodled obscenity and smiled unapologetically.

No, now I think about it, this wasn't the first time I'd seen Gloria. I was at a party a few weeks before sitting crossed legged in a smoky room full of stoned strangers. Some dude had pointed her out and told me something interesting about her. I remember thinking, how remarkable. The thing is, I was so out of my head that the next day I couldn't for the life of me recall what it was. Like the contents of a once vivid dream, the details had vanished into white space. It was so annoying.

*

Boz and I were listening to *Revolver*.
'So tell me, how exactly are we going to get to Crete?' asked Boz.

As yet, I wasn't clear about our itinerary. I was aware of a little problem: there was a big blob of communist countries in Eastern Europe that we would have to circumnavigate.

'Easy, Eurorail. And ferry. We may have to hitch as well.'

'Yeah, but what's the route?'

'Look, I've got a map.'

The previous Christmas my Grandmother had given me a pocket diary. With its leatherette cover and gilt-edged pages it was an attractive present, but what use did I have for a diary? It also contained several pages of information I could never envisage consulting: Imperial to Metric conversion tables; a world temperature guide; international shoe size comparisons; and a chart indicating time zones. More handy, however, was a map of Europe spread over two pages.

When examining the map I was shocked to realise how little I knew about Europe. I'd enjoyed geography at school but we only studied far away continents like South America and Australia. Sure, I knew where the three Guyanas were and could recite the names of the six states of Australia. But what use was that?

'It's a small map,' Boz said. 'We need a bigger map to plan properly.'

'We've got to keep things flexible. Neil Cassady didn't have a map as he gunned the Hudson getting his kicks along Route 66. We need to make space for the unexpected. We might stumble across a bar which it is imperative to check out. And things might develop, and lead to another bar. And maybe a club. And then back somewhere else. And then we might wake up by a beach with a beautiful girl. You can't put that sort of stuff into a schedule. We've got to build in a flexibility factor. Maps are for straights.'

'I understand all that. But what's the route?'

'Okay, I think this is what we need to do: Paris, Venice, down the Adriatic, round to Athens and then jump a ferry to Crete. It's a bit of a roundabout route but the communist countries get in the way. To enter those we'd need visas, and visas cost money. Basically, we just keep heading south and east until we hit the sea. Man, I'm excited just thinking about it.'

Boz gave me a questioning look. 'Isn't Yugoslavia communist?' he asked.

'Yeah, but I don't think they're aligned with the Soviets. They're liberal, they have nudist beaches.'

'What about this country here?' Boz pointed to a little black spot abbreviated to 'Alb'. 'I've read about Albania,' he said, 'they've got an extreme dictator; there are labour camps in every town and they've outlawed religion. The president, Enver Hoxha, is so totalitarian even Stalin thought he was too hardcore.'

'I've never heard of him. Albania's a tiny country; I don't think we need to worry about Albania.'

I didn't want to plan too much. Apart from meeting Gloria in Matala I wanted this trip to be spontaneous. 'We don't want to get hung up on the details. Let's see how it goes. And of course on the way we'll come across some interesting pies.'

'So where are we going to stay?'

'We'll camp. We'll buy tents and we'll camp. The remoter the place, the easier it is to find somewhere.'

'That's certainly not my experience of the Yorkshire Dales.'

'You'll see, we'll be fine.'

'But what about the languages? I can only speak a smattering of French and German.'

'Questions, questions, questions! Take it easy. We'll cope just fine. Body language is what we're going to use. That's how we'll communicate. Everybody speaks body language, it's international.'

'Okay. So we know how we're going to get there and we know where we're going to sleep. There is still one not so unimportant thing we need to talk about. Namely, we've got no money.'

I was getting bored by Boz's almost obsessive attention to detail. Where I saw a groove, Boz would always see hassles.

'You are such a downer,' I said.

'I think you mean realist.'

'Well, as it happens, I have already thought about this.'

A couple of days before I had thumbed through a volume in W.H.Smith called *Work Your Way Round the World*. It had some useful suggestions.

'We could work our passage. There's lots of jobs you can do abroad: au pair, underwater modelling, chalet assistant.'

'Yeah, those are all jobs that we won't be doing. Those are girls' jobs.'

'Steady. Germaine Greer would have you strung up by the nuts if she heard you say that.'

'Look, we're the disadvantaged gender here.'

'Maybe those aren't the best examples. We could do bar work, pick grapes. Europe's cheap. The weather's good, we won't need much dosh.'

Of course there were other, more hardcore, ways of raising money that didn't come within the scope of *Work Your Way Round the World*. I'd recently read in *OZ* magazine about the international trafficking of blood, spare organs and body parts. While I didn't feel I had any inessential organs or superfluous body parts, I did think if the going got tough I could spare a few pints of blood. You could get a tenner a bottle in Turkey. That was a week's money. I wondered how frequently I could donate. Every week? If so, our financial problems were sorted.

'If the going gets tough we could sell our blood.'

Boz jerked upright in his chair. 'Whoa! Heavy! Where did that come from? I don't like the sound of that. I don't like the sound of that at all.'

'I didn't realise you were so squeamish.'

'I'm not.'

'We'll only give a little blood.'

'The amount isn't the issue - it's what goes with it. Rusty needles, hepatitis, stuff like that.'

'Some people sell their kidneys.'

'I'm not selling any organs just for a holiday. Look Felix, why don't we forget about all this and go to St Ives. It's so much simpler. We can sign on and keep our blood.'

It was clear that I needed to get Boz more emotionally engaged in this trip. I needed to get him involved in the planning process.

'Okay so what's your answer? There's got to be a way. We need to do a bit of lateral thinking.'

We were both silent for a while. I looked at Boz expectantly. It was his turn to come up with something; so far I'd done all the hard work.

'Roll another one. I can't think straight,' he said.

Eventually Boz cleared his throat and said: 'Can't you borrow some money? You must have some connections; your family are well off. In fact, you could borrow money for both of us.'

'I'll ignore that.'

Boz's unhelpful attitude was beginning to depress me. I studied Klaus Voorman's psychedelic drawing of the Beatles and then turned over the LP cover. *Taxman!* I had a flash of inspiration.

'I've got it. It's obvious.'

'What?'

'It's under our noses.'

'Yeah? I haven't seen it.'

'We're going to have to get a job.'

'Isn't that what we're discussing?'

'Yeah, but what I'm thinking about is a real job, a proper job, here, in Bristol.'

'Oh a real job. Proper, nine to five job, in Bristol?'

'Yeah, in the tax office or something. They've always got vacancies in the tax office.'

Boz seemed shocked. I could hear him involuntarily drawing in his breath. For a moment I thought he was hyperventilating.

'Felix, I'm astounded that you've come up with such an idea. I don't want to become a straight and have my soul sucked out of me.'

'Radical situations require radical solutions.'

'But the tax office? Wear a shirt and tie. Push a pen. Work in silence. Only have a piss when you are allowed to. Is that what you're proposing?'

'Just for a while.'

FOUR

I'd had to take a year out from University. Initially I'd chosen to study sociology as it seemed a good way of delaying any serious decisions about my future. But after giving the course a try for a couple of terms it became clear that even sociology didn't fit my requirements. I found the discipline of study too restrictive for my free-thinking mind. I was looking for something a bit more spontaneous and was keen to experience the new progressive 'free learning approach' to education, whereby you learnt what you wanted when you wanted. I yearned to cut through all the educational bullshit of formal lectures at 9.00 am and three-thousand word essays churned out every month. I was interested in the sharing of knowledge, not just having it pumped down my throat. The university timetable was so old fashioned. It shouldn't have been like this in the age of the 'sit-in'. If we were able to storm the administration building, squirt glue in the locks and set up a disco in the vice-chancellor's committee room as a reaction to the perceived mal-treatment of, and discrimination against, Stan the porter's pet bull mastiff, who had been banned from the campus for running amok after being fed LSD by some misguided student; surely we could sort out the curriculum? I found myself thinking that I didn't want to be complicit in supporting such a reactionary establishment. So I took a year's sabbatical to give me time to reflect. It was a difficult decision as it meant renouncing my generous student grant, but sometimes you have to be true to your principles. I promised Mum and Dad that after twelve months I'd have my future plans sorted.

Let's face it. I had no idea what to do with my life, let alone my career. At school I had asked the careers adviser what I should do?

She said the decision was up to me; 'it was far too important to be left to anybody else'. What a cop-out. What sort of help was that? I thought it was her job, she was being paid, to TELL me what to do. She suggested I write a list of the sort of things I was interested in. So I drew up an inventory of my basic needs. It got me thinking. I was looking for something creative, non-routine, nothing that involved heavy lifting but also not too sedentary, reasonably well paid and with a good opportunity to become acquainted with beautiful women.

Once, at school, we'd had a careers talk by an architect, and for a while I thought that that was a job that might meet my needs. I'd always liked the art deco curves and colours of the Hoover Building on the A40 going into London. There was one problem, though, architecture appeared to be a male-dominated profession with a low female/male worker ratio. In the end it didn't matter as I failed my 'O' Level maths and had to lower my expectations.

'Keep your options open' was the careers adviser's parting suggestion. So that's what I'd started doing, studying sociology and keeping my options open. Indeed, sociology was very much an options open subject. It didn't seem to lead anywhere.

Boz had had a similar problem. That's how we met. I saw him in the dole queue. I can remember it now. He must have been a couple of years older than me: slightly simian, with a beard as thick as a hessian doormat, he cut a hirsute image. He wasn't what you'd call good looking, but he had good straight teeth and a big wide smile. He was wearing a red sweater and red cord trousers. I thought he looked interesting rather than taking this as a sign of mental instability.

'What were your expectations of University?' I once asked Boz.

'I'd already spent a couple of years working in the family firm so my expectations were the highest,' Boz replied. 'I'd come to University anticipating plentiful narcotics, quality pies, and hot monkey sex. Though, not necessarily in that order. Unfortunately, it didn't quite work out like that. I fell in with a bad crowd. It was my first term and I was allocated a room in a house by the University Accommodation Officer. I had no choice. My new roommates got up at the crack of dawn to go to lectures. They were leaving the house as I was going to bed. They drank pints of PG Tips and consumed Rich Tea biscuits. The clarity of their vision did my head in. Careerist over-achievers. I was at that stage in my life when I needed to be bit more soft focus, a bit more floaty. I couldn't cope.'

So, that's how we'd both dropped out.

'So what about you?' asked Boz. 'What's your story?'

'There's not much to tell.'

'Yeah?'

'Get born, keep warm, short pants, romance…that sort of stuff.'

'What's that mean?'

'My life is so normal. I don't come from an interesting place like you. I come from Ruislip, the epitome of suburbia. I was brought up in a 1930s box. My mum goes to work doing I know not what, my Dad catches the train into London and then returns in the evening. Do you know, some of the men on that train still wear pin striped suits and bowler hats?'

'What are you complaining about? They've got jobs, haven't they? It's better than seeing your uncle queuing outside the dole office.'

'But it's stifling. A cosy artificial middle class cul-de-sac of gabled mock beamed houses; *Semi Detached Suburban Mr Jones.* The ordered life, housewives with nothing to do but twitch net curtains, the neat lawns, the rules. The rules! Laurel Close is run by all these unwritten rules: washing on the line on Monday; cutting the privet hedge on Saturday; no mowing the lawn on Sunday. It does my head in. It's so respectable; it's so *petit bourgeois.* I don't want to be respectable. There's no room for creativity. We're the generation of youth culture. Not in Ruislip though. Kensington Market, with its Afghan coats and freak stalls may be an hour away by tube; but for all I know it could be in another universe. It's as if the Rolling Stones had never written '*Street Fighting Man.*'

Boz looked at me with a pitying incredulity. 'So why did you choose to move to Bristol?'

I thought for a moment.

'Do you know what? I can't remember. I just went with the flow. I think I liked the sound of the name.'

'And Bristol isn't suburban?'

'I'm sure it is in parts. Patchway, Downend, dead places like that. The thing is, I don't feel like I'm living a suburban life.'

'Maybe not at the moment, but that's because you're dossing in a squat and drawing the dole. Even you don't want to be doing that forever.'

'Suburban is a state of mind. We all like to feel that we're different, that we're pushing the boundaries. I don't get that feeling in Ruislip. It's just... it's just so complacent. It's a town for losers.'

'What about your future plans?' asked Boz.

'I have no idea. When I went for my university interview I was asked where I saw myself in five years' time. I can't do that. I can hardly think about next week. Five years! Does anybody think five years ahead?'

'I think they're thinking about cars, families and a house.'

'There are too many options. If you can think five years ahead you've got no imagination.'

What was it about Boz? He was so relaxed, and this wasn't just to do with his habit of having a spliff for breakfast. Of course this relaxation could translate itself into extreme lassitude which at times could be annoying, but I came to love him like a brother. He had an inner calm, a self belief, which, he once explained, came from the sure knowledge that you were born and bred in Bolton.

As far as I knew Boz wasn't particularly religious. We never spoke about religion anyway. If I didn't know, I'd put him down as a Buddhist. I recall him taking an interest in *The Dharma Bums*, but even then I couldn't see Boz bothering with meditation or the seven paths to enlightenment. 'Seven paths? That's six paths too many,' I remember him saying, 'It's all a bit too poncy for me, I don't see Buddhism catching on up north.'

Although Boz would often appear to act like an idiot, he was remarkably well informed about current affairs and politics. He was surprisingly well read in a northern sort of way; *Kes*, and the works of Alan Sillitoe, Bill Naughton and D.H. Lawrence, were all to be found on his bookshelf. He also had an encyclopaedic knowledge of the social and economic history of Lancashire. Get him started and he would talk for hours about radical politics and solidarity with the workers. Being a 'soft southerner' he said I wouldn't understand what he was on about. But when it came to doing anything like going to a political meeting or protest march he'd run out of energy. He did, however, once join the miners on the picket line outside the power station. The comrades weren't as appreciative of his support as he had expected. 'The last bloody thing we need is a load of hippies supporting us', they'd said. The miners wanted solidarity with the workers, not the workshy.

FIVE

It was at about the same time as I'd started my sabbatical that I met Gloria again. I remember it was a drab, muted February day. I'd been sitting at the back of a coach heading to London when I spotted Gloria getting on the bus. She hadn't noticed me. I waited until the twenty minute break at Membury Services to buy a cup of tea and casually say hello.

'Hello Gloria!'

'Felix! What are you doing here?' She seemed pleased to see me.

'I'm on a coach.'

'So am I,' she laughed. 'Are you going to Victoria?'

'Yes.'

'I didn't see you.'

'I'm sitting at the back.'

'Why don't you join me?'

'Are you sure?'

Gloria patted the seat. 'There's a place here.'

I sat down knowing that I'd got at least an hour and a half of Gloria's company. Whatever she said I found fascinating. We sorted out the world. She would lean towards me and drop her voice as if she was about to tell me her most intimate secrets. We agreed on everything. Swindon was a dump. Leonard Cohen was brilliant, though probably wasted on Suzanne. I pointed out a motorway sign that said 'Hard Shoulder'. 'Soft thighs,' she countered immediately. We both laughed. I was entranced. I just wanted to sit there and listen to her sweet, soft, slightly posh voice and look into her Gloria Swanson eyes. That's all I ever wanted to do.

We were so close. She smelt of that expensive perfume with the aroma of carbolic soap. I put my arm through hers as if to keep warm. She didn't object. We discussed the big issues of the day. How incredible were the Incredible String Band? Was Bob Dylan's *Tarantula* a work of genius or just a babbling stream of consciousness? Were Strangely Strange oddly normal? And were tea and oranges a good combination? I didn't think so. Gloria laughed. 'Leonard Cohen is not talking about Typhoo Tea. This is Darjeeling, the champagne of teas. Without milk, of course.' I snuggled closer. 'Was small really beautiful?' she asked. 'Was the geometric simplicity of Buckminster-Fuller's geodesic dome the future?' In the Nevada Desert they were setting up self-sufficient communities in geodesic domes, with hermetically sealed environments. She talked about such interesting things. Even if much of what she said I didn't understand. I'd never come across anybody like her. She was like some sweet wild child. She said she wanted to lie in a meadow while sky larks flew overhead, she wanted to walk in the woods at night time and listen to owls. She wanted to make love in a haystack. And then as we hurtled along the M4 we kissed; long, deep and wonderful. I couldn't believe it. I was kissing Gloria in broad daylight on the Bristol to Victoria coach. Something was happening and I wasn't going to fight it. I wanted the journey to last for ever. I prayed for the coach to break down. If only we could be stranded at Heston services. That's how much I loved her.

From Victoria coach station we walked along the road to the Underground. I was floating. I felt as if somebody had anaesthetised me with chloroform. I was afflicted by a kind of tunnel vision myopia. I could see only Gloria.

'Wait.' She looked in her bag for some paper and hurriedly wrote out her address. 'Come and see me sometime. Just drop in. Anytime.'

'Yeah, if I'm passing, I will,' I said.

I had to lean against a wall and steady myself. There was a ringing in my ears from a fanfare of trumpeting angels. These emotions were strong and potentially dangerous. I looked at the bit of paper. Pembroke Road. I couldn't afford to live there. It was the posh bit of Bristol just by the Downs.

'It's near the Zoo, she said. 'At night time I can sometimes hear the gibbons. And before a thunderstorm the lions will roar.'

At the top of the page a word had been heavily scrubbed out. I held this ticket to my dreams up to the light. The writing that had been blanked clearly said 'Wanker'.

SIX

Boz and I agreed to view a couple of rooms of the National Gallery before we caught the train to Dover.

'A cultural odyssey. This is what this trip is all about,' I said.

'Definitely,' said Boz. 'But first I must get some liquid down me before I suffer from an adverse reaction. I've been travelling on a coach for six hours. I have to have a clear mind to appreciate art and stuff like that.'

'Good idea,' I agreed.

We started walking towards Soho under the dull London sky. Boz said he had heard of a drinking club that stayed open all afternoon. I was excited; this was the beginning of our grand tour, the whole world was opening up.

'We'll come back to the National Gallery, eh? In an hour?' I said.

'Try stopping me. I just need to uncork some lunch, and then I'll be right up for it. I have to warn you, Felix, that I can get emotionally involved with art. For me, looking at some of those masterpieces can be an intensive and mentally draining experience. But first of all we need to get our feet on a brass rail.'

We walked through Leicester Square. I hadn't taken it in before now, but I realised that Boz had a rucksack on his back.

'Rucksack, eh?' I didn't approve of rucksacks.

'Yeah, it's a bit scouting for boys, but it does the trick. This aluminium frame distributes the load and makes carrying stuff easier. The frame is hollow so it's really light. It has other uses as well.' Boz gave me a weird knowing wink.

Although Boz had told me about nocturnal trips from Bolton 'up t' moors', invariably for a shag with some mill worker in the back of the pie shop van, I hadn't expected him to be so knowledgeable about outdoor survival techniques. My own attempts at sleeping under canvas had never been successful. At the age of eleven I'd been drummed out of the Scouts on account of my left-handedness and was consequently ignorant of Baden-Powell's dark arts. I'm sure camping can be a wonderful, life-affirming, back-to-nature experience, but whenever I pitched a tent, and this was before the invention of the built-in ground sheet, it would rain relentlessly and I would be woken in the cold hour before dawn by a puddle of water creeping like oil up a wick towards my sleeping bag. By first light I was invariably huddled in the toilet block attempting to dry off. For this reason I didn't have any camping equipment.

The previous week I'd seen a little blue tent in the window of Millets that at £4.75 looked suitable for our trip. The salesman was apologetic. Unfortunately they were currently out of stock of that particular item. He also told me that the tent I wished to buy was a child's play tent. (I didn't have the heart to admit that I intended to take this tent round Europe.) He could, however, offer me, a wigwam or a Wendy House. While I quietly liked the idea of using a Wendy House with a window and floral curtains, and I'm sure Gloria would have approved, it wasn't big enough to accommodate two adults even if they were sharing a sleeping bag. In the end I lashed out ten pounds on a reliable tent with more practical features to meet my needs.

'What's that for?' I asked Boz, pointing to a scout badge sewn onto the side of his rucksack that depicted what looked like a steaming pastry.

'Pie making.'

'I didn't know you could get a pie making badge.'

'You could in our troop.'

'What troop was that? The Bolton Bakers?'

'Something like that.' I could feel that Boz didn't want to say any more. I felt embarrassed for him.

Meanwhile Boz was looking at my shoes. It was his turn to quiz me.

'What are those? What happened to your desert boots?'

'Plimsolls. I bought them in Woolworths.'

'Far out. Why?'

'They make me feel free.'

'They're a bit white.'

'They're new.' Thin-soled plimsolls seemed like a good idea at the time. I could feel every stone through them. They made me feel grounded. Ideally I would have been walking barefoot, but these were the next best thing.

We settled down in a corner of the Coach and Horses as Boz embarked on his emergency rehydration therapy. The trip from Bolton had been more gruelling than Boz had anticipated. After an early start and a long journey Boz said that he was dangerously dehydrated. He insisted he would need to quickly drink several pints for his body to regain its equilibrium.

'Here, I bought you this...' Boz handed me a small tin the size of an old thrupenny bit.

'Thanks. What is it?'

'Tiger Balm. It might come in useful.'

'Brilliant!' A present from Boz; this was unprecedented. It made me nervous. I wondered if he was going to ask me for a loan.

'What do I do with it?' I asked.

'You rub it on various pressure points. It comes from the Far East. It's an ancient Chinese remedy for unblocking the chi and clearing the mind. '

'Useful.'

'Yeah, when the going gets tough, the tough use Tiger Balm. But that's not all that it's good for. It stimulates the chakra. It can be used for heightening sexual experiences. You've got to be careful. If you don't know what you're doing you can orgasm quite violently.'

'I think I can handle that.'

Boz drew in his breath and sucked in his cheeks as if I hadn't understood the seriousness of the problem.

'A ruptured urethra. I wouldn't wish that on anybody, not even Ted Heath.'

'When you put it like that I see what you mean.'

'Just read the instructions. This tin contains the extra strong version.'

Five pints of beer later, Boz appeared to have made a full recovery.

'I now need to settle my stomach with a vindaloo,' said Boz.

'Good idea,' I said. 'We've still got a couple of hours before the National Gallery closes.'

'We're on holiday. We've got all summer. There's no need to rush.'

'You're right Boz. We've got to slow down. We must break away from capitalist-driven rushing.'

'Agreed, comrade. No bourgeois anxieties on this trip. Go with the flow. We must trust in fate. No hurry, no worry. That's our mantra.'

I held up my glass. 'To our trip.'

'Yeah, to our trip.'

'We've got to do this.'

'Of course we have.' Boz raised his glass 'To culture - with a capital K.'

'That's what this trip is all about.'

'Yeah, wake up and smell the patchouli.'

SEVEN

Boz and I were on a train travelling through the north Kent countryside. In the distance were the Medway towns and the brown sludge of the Thames Estuary. We were already running late.

'That Lucien, he was an interesting guy,' I said.

'Yeah. How many people have you met who know Francis Bacon?'

'It's a shame we never got to the National Gallery.'

'That pub was just as good. Rather than looking at art, we were talking to an artist.'

'An artist's friend,' I corrected Boz.

'Some of those other guys in the pub were artists. The guy with the Borsalino hat and pink cravat was. '

'Definitely.'

'Where did he say we ought to go in Paris? The museum with the Impressionist paintings?'

'The Jeu de Paume?'

'We'll do that on our return journey,' said Boz. 'It was probably best not to start with the National Gallery. I don't think I would have been ready for it. It could have freaked me out at the first hurdle.' Boz gave me a quizzical look as if he was trying to tell me something.

'Yeah, we can do the National Gallery on the way back.'

'It'll be a good way to end the trip.'

'Meeting those guys in the pub was an opportunity not to be missed.'

'So what have you brought to read?' I asked.

'Bixby gave me Bob Dylan's *Tarantula*.'

'What did he say about it?'

'Something about nuggets of truth hidden deep.'

'Far out! After you with it.'

'What have you got?'

I pulled out of my bag a book with a bright yellow pop art cover. It featured a photo of a hip young man in a denim jacket engaged in an uncomfortable looking clinch with a girl pressed up against a wall.

'I bought this at the station. *I, Jan Cremer*. I like the yellow cover.'

'Yeah, that is an attractive cover,' Boz agreed.

In the end we missed our cross-channel ferry and spent the night crashed out on benches at the Dover ferry terminal. The next day as we went through customs Boz appeared surprisingly edgy. I noticed he was perspiring and swallowing a lot. He said he was still suffering from the after-effects of severe dehydration, though in truth, although he was an experienced hitch-hiker, I think he was nervous about going abroad.

It was while thumbing lifts from Bolton to Bristol that Boz had developed his ten rules of the road. Most, like Rule 1: you only get a lift where there is transport, were obvious. Some, such as Rule 3, contained a nugget of psychology: hitch at the bottom of a hill, that way you look smaller and less threatening. As Boz explained, 'you have just a split second of eye contact, when the driver sees you, and makes that decision to share their ride with you and puts the brakes on'. Rule 4 was also useful. If you're hitching in the dark stand under a lamp post, but hold your head up. Otherwise the shadows on your face make you look like an axe murderer. Some were a bit metaphysical. Best of all I liked Rule 8 which said, 'the journey isn't from A to B but from A to Z'.

In Paris I'd hoped that we'd stroll down the Boulevard St Michel, visit the Sorbonne and hang around with left bank activists drinking Pernod and smoking jazz cigarettes. I'd particularly wanted to see where the '68 riots had happened. Maybe we'd join a workers' demonstration, show solidarity with some street-fighting radicals and get in our fair share of abuse. As it was, we had just a couple of hours to traverse the city. At least, as we rushed across a wide and busy boulevard, I caught a glimpse of the Eiffel Tower through a break in the streets. The Metro, with its airy and spacious un-tube-like stations and rubber wheeled trains, was interesting though.

From the Gare de Lyon we journeyed south through the night.

I had a seat by the window. I shaded the reflection on the glass with my hand and looked out onto a silvery moonlit landscape. We travelled through wide countryside, past vineyards and then deep forests. I'd never realised how rural France was. At first, the scenery had been all very recognisable; green fields and rolling chalk downs. But the features slowly morphed into the different and then the exotic. I slept. Occasionally I'd be woken by the shudder of the train, shouting and the bang of doors as we stopped at a seemingly deserted station. The moon disappeared; all I could see were the yellow lights of isolated farmhouses. Then there was torrential rain and hail. The towering rocks of the Alps were lit by flashes of lightning. I wanted to see more, I wished we were travelling in the daylight; I'd never seen mountains before. As dawn broke I looked out on a flat green landscape of ditches and poplar trees.

At Milan we changed trains. It had been a long night and I was feeling jet-lagged from lack of sleep. I looked around the station, feeling spaced by its ecclesiastical proportions. With its high arches it could have been a cathedral. Shafts of early morning sunlight were cutting through the massive passenger hall. I half expected to hear the heavenly chanting of a choir.

'Look at that,' said Boz, pointing at people sitting on stools round a cosy little bar selling small cups of coffee and beer.

'What?'

'They're drinking coffee and alcohol.'

'So?'

'It's breakfast time. In England we don't drink alcohol with our breakfast. The pubs aren't open at breakfast time.'

'I see what you mean. We need to adapt to this continental lifestyle.'

'Yeah, I don't want to get dehydrated again.'

We were on our third breakfast pint - continental lager has a surprisingly low alcohol content - when Boz said, 'Hang on. What's that?'

I followed Boz's line of vision. At first I couldn't be sure. I caught just a glimpse though the early morning crush; a flash and it was gone. Was the light playing tricks on faces in the crowd? But then a couple of seconds later I saw him again. Thrusting his way through the commuters like a snowplough. Horrible, white and unshaved. Surely this wasn't a coincidence? It was Plank. Plank was in Milan.

'Let's go and say hello,' said Boz.

I felt sick. I knew where Plank was heading. He was on his way to Matala. We were in a race, and the sweet sacrificial lamb Gloria was the prize. I had to get to Sex-on-Sea before him.

'No, we need to hide,' I said, pulling Boz behind a pillar.

EIGHT

We arrived in Venice to a grey dawn and walked down the steps of the railway station to catch a water bus. We were cocooned in an early morning shroud of mist. The fog was so dense I could only guess the direction of the canal from the putt-putt of boat engines, the slap of water and the smell of drains.

As we travelled by ferry down the Grand Canal I could hear the muted ringing of ships' bells and anxious shouts from gondoliers. I was later told that fog is common in Venice but it was unusual at this time of year. It was caused by the air from the mountains to the north condensing when it hits the warm Adriatic. The polluted Venetian air makes the city particularly susceptible.

After a while I felt we were in open water. As the vaporetto moved across the pallid lagoon, every now and again, for a few seconds, I glimpsed the sun as it burnt its way through the fog. But then the fog would swirl and thicken and the world would turn to a damp grey. There were unfamiliar sounds. The deep vibration and clap of a pile being driven into the silt, perhaps. During the forty-minute journey to the Lido all I saw of Venice through the evanescent light was the occasional, and alarmingly close, flash of a motor launch.

After all that railway grime Boz and I needed beach time to unwind. From the campsite it was a three minute walk to the shore. By now the miasma had lifted. We climbed over a breakwater of concrete blocks the size of trucks to get to the water.

Boz stood looking out to sea. 'It's not quite how I imagined Venice.'

'You're looking the wrong way. This is the Adriatic. Venice is on the other side of the island.'

'Oh,' said Boz. I don't think he believed me.

Did I mention, like Boz, I'd never been abroad before? For the first sixteen years of my life our family spent summer holidays in a guest house in Weymouth. I loved it. The Grosvenor House B&B was a couple of streets back from the beach. You walked round the corner and there was the sea - sparkling and blue. I never got tired of that first sight of the sea.

And the air. After life in Ruislip with the fumes of the A40 and, when there was a southerly breeze, the slight taste of kerosene from the planes at Heathrow, the sea air was so clear and full of ozone. 'This sea air is strong stuff', Dad would say. 'Breathe it in, it's like wine, it makes you sleepy.'

We'd spend our two weeks on the beach. We had a striped canvas wind break and would huddle under blankets when it got cold. But most days I would be in my sagging woollen bathers, running in and out of the sea, digging holes in the sand.

In the evening we would walk along the promenade, admiring the illuminations and spending our pocket money on the penny machines in the amusement arcade. Amusement arcade. I liked that. Towards the end of our second week, we'd go to the summer show in the theatre at the end of the pier. They had well known comedians who I'd seen on TV, like Harry Worth and Charlie Drake.

When I was sixteen, and my sister eighteen, Dad said that we were too old for family holidays. After that Mum and Dad went on package trips to exotic places like Majorca and Ibiza while Big Sis and I were left to sort out our own holidays. It didn't seem fair.

I walked into the water of the Adriatic. I'd never swum in a warm sea before. I remember a school friend describing swimming in the Mediterranean. He said the sea was as tepid as dishwater. In England I was used to inching my way in, holding my shoulders, hyperventilating as the cold water came up to my waist. On Chesil Beach the water was glacier cold. But this was like easing into a bath. I looked along the shore to the distant cream-coloured hotels with their private beaches. Call me an old-fashioned socialist, but I reckon beaches are public spaces and should be open to everyone.

I swam and yelled with delight. I lay in the warm water, suspended, weightless. For the first time since I'd left England I felt relaxed. I closed my eyes and floated on my back. I could feel the sun's heat on my chest and the warm push of water on my shoulders. All I needed was a beer and a pizza and I'd be in paradise. The long journey to get here had been worth it just for this.

Our tents were pitched about 50 metres away from the campsite entrance. I watched the travellers come and go. It was a busy place: mostly backpackers, with the occasional German biker on a roaring BMW, or Aussie camper-van.

We hung out in the campsite bar eating pizza or spaghetti. The only spaghetti I'd eaten before was out of a Heinz tin. This tasted so different. A thick rich sauce of fresh tomatoes, sweet onions and some Mediterranean herbs topped by a monticule of parmesan cheese. And the pizza! Soft and doughy, smelling of hot buffalo cheese and sweet oregano. Oh man, I'd never eaten anything like it.

It was easy to meet travellers and swap tales. I felt a novice at this but Boz would talk to blue-eyed Swedish girls with great enthusiasm. Fuelled by cheap Italian wine from plastic bottles we had long earnest conversations. Boz would talk with ecstatic intensity and great authority about the North of England. Again and again his conversation would return to Bolton. He would compare Bolton, with its municipal parks, memorial fountains and Pennine backdrop, to Geneva or Vienna or any one of the great cities of Europe.

One day, a beaten up VW camper-van with surf boards strapped to the roof drove in. It was bursting at the seams with people and energy. Three hippie guys and half a dozen laughing chicks spilled out of the doors. Judging by the shrieks and yells they seemed to be having a good time.

Outside the campsite office there was a notice board. Torn pieces of paper asked for, and offered lifts.

'Anybody going to Istanbul and beyond? Two girls seek lift.'

'Room in campervan heading to Spain. Help needed with gas costs.'

Europe felt like an enormous vortex with everybody spinning round and visiting the same places. Paris, the South of France, Spain maybe, Rome, Athens, Munich and then, if Boz had his way, Bolton.

Among these requests there was a more enigmatic message:

Nicola, I've gone ahead. I'll see you at the train station. Sorry about last night. Bruce.

I wondered what Bruce had done. Whatever it was, every traveller in Europe would soon know.

Time drifted by. The unfamiliar heat and warm resinous air multiplied the soporific effect of alcohol. I spent the middle of the day dozing under the low mimosa trees that provided the campsite with shade. I settled down to read *'I, Jan Cremer.'*

'How's the book?' Boz asked.

'Jan's an important and influential Dutch artist. He writes like Nelson Allgren but with more gratuitous swearing.'

'Sounds interesting. What's it about?'

'He was bought up in a number of reform schools. He's a tough guy. I'm hoping that it contains a critical analysis of the Dutch underground arts lab and agitprop movement. But I haven't got to that part yet.'

Jan Cremer's writing was fast and crude and he swore like a bastard. His autobiography portrayed him as loud and bombastic with a swaggering sexuality; everything I wanted from a role model.

I read out the blurb. *'Lock up your wives, girlfriends, mistresses and mothers! This book was designed to shock and make the author a lot of money. It has.'*

'So not exactly high culture then,' said Boz.

'I think something might have been lost in translation.'

'How's *Tarantula* coming along?' I asked.

'It's deep. Trippy.'

Boz was silent for a while and then said. 'You know what. When I write my autobiography I'm going to call it *I, Jean Creamer.*'

'Boz, a bit of advice. If it's not worth saying, don't say it.'

In the campsite I picked up a postcard. I'd been travelling for so long I hadn't had the time to take in my surroundings. So this was Venice. Until now it hadn't quite sunk in that this is where I was. As I stared at the picture of St Mark's Square, with its pigeons and its tall tower and its funny looking cathedral, this was the first time I fully realised that I was abroad. Bristol felt like a universe away.

Those were idyllic days. But as I soaked up the sun, the smells and the new food of Italy there was one annoying niggle interrupting my reverie. Where exactly was Plank? I'd been worried ever since we'd seen him in Milan.

Why didn't I like Plank? It certainly wasn't anything to do with him studying engineering. Boz once said he thought I felt threatened by Plank. That was rubbish. What I didn't understand was that most people thought Plank was okay. But they didn't know the real Plank, the great prognathous Neanderthal that I'd seen. Plank was on a different wavelength. He wasn't a straight; but he was straight, if you get what I mean. He was a bit serious, yeah, that's right, even when he was having fun he was serious. The way the Plank talked was strange. He used unusual archaic sounding words; it was probably due to his public school upbringing. Maybe it was his lack of irony, I don't know.

We did share one thing in common; we both had the same taste in girls. Whenever I met a new woman and hoped to be heading for the sack, sure enough Plank would appear over the horizon sticking his bloody great mandible in where it wasn't wanted. He thought of himself as a bit of a shag artist. I couldn't understand it, women seemed to find him attractive. They must have felt sorry for him.

Maybe Boz put his finger on it. 'It's obvious, he's a prog rocker.' Progressive Rock! Loved by all those clean and clever public school boys. I liked the down and dirty American blues based music: Jimi, Janis, Jim; they'd suffered, you could feel their pain. Their music came straight from a bruised and broken heart. Yes and Genesis, pretentious English bands, came out of the repressed sexuality of a mattress munching public school dormitory.

'We've got to stop Plank,' I said to Boz

'I don't know what you're worried about,' Boz protested.

'You saw him. Even from that distance I could see that he was up to no good. He's a monster. He looked possessed. Did you see that look in his eyes?'

'Similar to yours.'

'Whose side are you on?'

'I'm not on anybody's side.'

'I thought you were my buddy.'

Boz shrugged. 'Well...'

'He's about to deflower my girlfriend. Doesn't that concern you?'

'Felix, your so-called girl friend was deflowered a long time ago. She's been deflowered so many times she could set up a chain of florists.'

'What's she see in him? He's studying engineering.'

'He's not that bad.'

'He's got the jaw of early man. An anthropologist might be interested in him, but not Gloria, surely?'

'He's got a good physique and he's heading for a First.'

'Women hate that sort of smug self satisfaction.'

'Well, he's got a good sense of humour.'

'I've never found him funny. But what does she actually see in him? So he's good looking, and clever and funny. That doesn't add up to much does it? I just don't get it.'

'I don't know what you're worried about. I thought you and Gloria had spent the night together.'

'We did. I struck lucky.'

'She wouldn't have slept with you if she didn't like you.'

'We haven't really got a solid relationship going yet.'

'But she promised to meet you in Matala. That's got to be a good sign.'

'Yeah, we arranged to meet.' But now I wasn't so sure. How many other people had Gloria promised a rendezvous with?

'Don't worry, Felix, there are plenty more fish in the sea.'

'Well, thank you. It's all right for you. You've got that easy charm that girls fall for. When somebody like Gloria gets the hots for me, I've got to get in there and keep the flame stoked up.'

I didn't know how to do the romantic stuff. I'd watched Boz and people with girl friends; they were so relaxed and natural. But as soon as I got to know somebody, really got to like somebody, I'd tense up. I'd write a poem or something stupid. It's the kiss of death to a relationship. No woman wants some serious guy hanging onto their every word. So, as soon as I was really into somebody the whole thing would fall apart.

'Okay, so what can you do about Plank?'

'There could be an accident,' I said.

'Oh, come on.'

'Nothing bad. We could get somebody to mug him.'

'Get somebody to mug him?'

'Yes! Steal his passport, rough him up a bit, and leave him destitute.'

'Who's going to mug him? You? Not me, I can tell you.'

'We could pay somebody. They could take him down an alley and show him the error of his ways. This is Italy, for God's sake?'

'We don't know anybody,' Boz said.

'Anonymity is what we're after.'

'We haven't got enough bread.'

'We've got to think of something.'

NINE

I next met Gloria in Corn Street market when I was thumbing through the boxes of LPs searching for Bob Dylan bootlegs. I felt a tap on my shoulder, turned round and there she was in her long cotton country-girl dress and flippity-floppity hat.

'Hi, Felix.'

'Gloria!'

'I thought you were coming to see me,' she said.

'I lost your address,' I said. In truth I was afraid of breaking the spell. 'What are you doing here?'

'Going for a drink with you.'

She took me to a curious establishment, a cellar bar, its entrance tucked down a narrow lane. It was full of market traders and old ladies in head scarves drinking sweet white wine. We stayed till closing time and she told me about her Quaker up-bringing. In the war her dad was a conscientious objector so they put him to work in the Post Office; his job was delivering telegrams. Telegrams from the War Office. Wives, mothers, and children would tremble at the sight of him in his Post Office uniform as he got off his motorbike and walked down the garden path. He never knew how they would react. Some would be mute, some would cry, some would hug him and hang on for dear life. Others would shout or even hit him. At first he saw this as part of the job and was happy to comfort. But you can only handle this level of despair for so long. 'Eventually he had a nervous breakdown which is, I suppose, what the authorities wanted.'

'Downer,' I said.

'I don't tell this to everybody.'

By now it was raining, so we bought a bottle of Hirondelle and caught a bus back to Gloria's place. As we passed the Zoo I could hear the monkeys whooping. Gloria lived in a bright house with big windows in a wide tree-lined street near the Downs. We lay fully clothed on her single bed listening to *Tea for the Tillerman*. She felt so warm and soft. I was in a bubble; the world outside her room didn't exist. I listened to her every word with intensity.

'This is what I want to do.' Gloria showed me a book called *Self-Sufficiency*.

'What's this about?'

'I want to buy a plot of land with a pond and ducks. I'm going to grow strawberries and become self-sufficient.'

'Is that possible?' I'd not come across this idea before.

'According to this book it is. You live off the land.'

'Ducks and strawberries are nice, but I think you'd grow tired of eating just that.'

'There's loads of food for free in the fields and hedgerows.'

'Really?'

'You've got to look for them. Mushrooms, berries, leaves.'

'Stinging nettles?' I remembered my Gran talking about eating stinging nettles in the war.

'I don't think I'll be eating stinging nettles, Felix.'

'It sounds brilliant. I don't know why everybody doesn't do it.'

'And to earn money for those little extras like Laura Ashley dresses, I'm going to make macramé baskets to sell.'

I loved her idealism. She was going to save the world, and in the process I hoped she was going to save me. But I was worried about getting enough to eat. Maybe we could barter our foraged food for smoky bacon crisps and Fry's Peppermint Cream chocolate bars.

'Does it say anything about growing marijuana?'

'Felix!'

'Okay, I could brew beer. We could sell that as well.'

'That would be useful.'

I gave her a hug. We kissed.

'What have you got to offer our new utopian society, Felix?'

'I'm sure I could do something.' For a moment I couldn't think clearly. 'I'm pretty handy with a spade.'

'You could do the heavy digging.'

I liked the thought of that. It sounded a bit sweaty, a bit macho. I'd spend half an hour digging in the fields, build up an appetite, and then, for the rest of the day, we'd shag ourselves brainless.

'I used to do the edging of my parents' lawn.'

'You'll have to do more than that.'

'I can do a sharp edge. You'd be impressed.'

'This isn't a suburban garden with herbaceous borders and gnomes.'

'I understand this stuff. My parents have friends with allotments, you know.'

'This book tells you how to do it.' We flicked through the pages. The illustrations showed a plot of land, about the size of my parents' garden, neatly divided up into vegetable beds, a pig enclosure and a composting area. 'It doesn't look that difficult,' I said.

'You could look after the pigs. You could be my pig man.'

I gave a little grunt. 'I think bees would be more my scene.'

'I love honey. Yoghurt and honey are my favourite.' Gloria turned the page. 'Look at this. It tells you how to make your own muesli.'

'Muesli?'

'Nuts, raw oats, fruit.

'Are you sure it's not rabbit feed?'

'It's good for you.'

'My flatmate Boz has some useful skills. He makes pies.'

'That would be good. I'm sure we could do with a pie maker.'

'He's inherently lazy though,' I added. I didn't want Boz getting in there before me.

*

'Take your socks off,' she said. By now we were nicely pissed.

'What?'

'I want to have a look at your feet.'

'Do you have to?'

'I want to see them. You can tell a lot about a person from their feet.'

I was glad I was wearing my favourite rainbow socks. I got a lot of envious looks when people saw those.

'I don't take my socks off for everybody, you know. My mate Boz sleeps with his boots on.'

'How do you know?'

'I once knocked on his door; he answered it wearing just his Y Fronts and his cowboy boots.'

'I don't like the sound of that.'

'No, he looked cool.'

'He should have been wearing a Stetson.'

'Knowing Boz it would more likely have been a flat cap.' We both laughed.

I also told Gloria all about Boz's extreme lassitude. How he once went to the doctor who examined him and then scribbled a note to take to the pharmacist which simply read KITA. The chemist laughted. 'I don't think I can dispense this.' 'Why not?' 'Don't you know what KITA means? It means kick in the arse.'

'Boz sounds funny. I'd like to meet him.'

'He's okay.' I didn't think I ought to be speaking about Boz when I was trying to get off with Gloria.

'We wouldn't have room for slackers. Everybody has to carry their own weight. I'm worried enough about your lawn edging skills.'

I wrote the name of the book on self sufficiency in my notepad. Gloria watched me and said. 'Oh, how funny.'

'What?'

'You're left-handed.'

'Yeah. So?'

'I love left-handed people.'

'That's good, because I like right-handed people. We should get on okay.'

'Left-handed people are so different.'

'I don't think so.' Before then I'd never thought about it.

'They are. They think differently. They have a different perspective on the world.'

'We write differently. I don't know about the different view, though.'

'Left-handed people are more creative, I'm sure they are.' I liked Gloria saying this. 'Think of Paul McCartney or Jimi Hendrix. I'm sure Cat Stevens must be left-handed.'

'I'll tell you one thing,' I said. 'When I first started using a pen I couldn't understand why my writing was smudged. I remember looking round the classroom. Nobody else's pages were smudged. I think that's the only time I've ever thought about being left-handed. In Arabic, they write right to left. I wonder in the Arab world if there are more left-handed people.'

'I don't think so.'

'Oh, and opening cans with a tin opener can be a hassle.'

We snuggled up closer. 'You smell nice,' she said.

'What do I smell of?'

She pressed her face against my neck.

'Warm skin, clean hair.'

'Is that it?'

I liked the feel of her nose against my ear.

'I don't know. Let me think. A slight metallic odour?' She licked my cheek. 'The taste of rusting iron railings?' We both laughed.

I went to buy more wine and ice cream. It was still raining. I was so happy I jumped in the puddles. When I returned I told her she was beautiful. She laughed and said don't be silly.

That night we slept together. In the afterglow, as I lay in her arms, I could hear the monkeys from the zoo whooping. For a moment the world felt pretty damn perfect.

TEN

Bristol, with its hilly topography, deep gorge and charming suspension bridge, is rightly known as one of England's most attractive cities. Where Boz and I lived, however, was a dump. Here, in Victorian times, row upon row of red brick houses had been quickly constructed to accommodate the expanding population of factory workers. One hundred years later, these jerry-built houses were now unfit for habitation and were being demolished to make way for the construction of an urban expressway. Whole streets were evacuated and the residents were put into temporary accommodation while they waited to move into their new flats in high rise blocks.

Fortunately for us there would be a time lapse of months, years even, between the residents leaving their old crumbling homes and the demolition of their property. These streets of empty houses were too good an opportunity to be missed.

Myself, I could never get my head around the tenant/landlord relationship. I remember visiting one of Bristol's notorious slum landlords to enquire whether he had any available accommodation. Mr Zimbler lived in an architect designed house in the prosperous suburb of Sneyd Park. It didn't seem right. Here was Zimbler in his plate glass home overlooking the Avon Gorge, while his tenants were living in damp slums. It was then that I formulated the belief that all landlords, however nice they are, are bastards.

Let me give you an example. Once, for a reason that I now forget, I asked my landlord for a waste paper basket. Not an unreasonable request and one that showed a certain amount of tenant responsibility. The next week he arrived with a yellow plastic bucket. 'I thought the handle would be useful,' he said. See what I mean? The thought of it still makes me laugh. Or there was the landlord who would empty the electricity slot meter and lay all the 10ps out on the kitchen table. He'd then give us a pound and tell us to buy a bottle of wine. Patronising bastard!

Anyway, I'm getting distracted. So Boz and I moved into our squat, Pancho Villa, on Hallowe'en. The house had a not unpleasant autumn woodland smell to it - the odour of rotting wood, fungus and mushrooms. During the first few weeks we'd wipe the mould off the kitchen walls, but eventually gave into the unstoppable forces of nature and learnt to live with this black fur. We worked hard to cover up these damp odours with the bitter smoke of Lebanese Gold.

Pancho Villa, which fronted onto traffic lights, was a typical red brick Victorian two up, two down, with an extension to the rear and an outdoor loo in the back yard. There was no bathroom; we'd use the baths at the university.

Our first night in Pancho Villa was suitably spooky. As we hadn't yet worked out how to jump the electricity meter our first task was to buy candles. These candles were to stand us in good stead during a long winter of miners' strikes and power blackouts.

From my bedroom at the back of the house I had a view of the yard and the outside toilet. I could also see beyond to the street at the back and watch the working girls going about their business. At first I thought I was viewing the express checkout side of the operation. I soon realised that five minutes was the gold service.

Boz's bedroom was at the front of the house. I don't think he slept well. He told me he was prone to nightmares; sometimes I would hear what sounded like shouting in the middle of the night.

The neighbourhood had a largely transient population of arty bohemian types, prostitutes and refugees recently arrived from Uganda. I liked the cosmopolitan feel of the place. We still had a neighbour on our left-hand side who was a dental surgeon. 'Hear that?' said Boz, referring to the dentist's drill next door, 'the day that drilling stops is the day we leave.' Because of the nature of his business, the dentist had been allowed to stay behind after the area was evacuated. The dentist had told Boz that the demolition men had promised to give him a week's notice before they knocked his walls down; they wouldn't bother to tell us squatters.

So we never knew when the wrecker's ball would swing through our living room wall. At least we didn't have any furniture to worry about. I didn't have much stuff: some LPs, books, a bit of clothing, that was about it.

I'd got a few posters that I used to decorate my room: Bob Dylan at the Isle of Wight, a Toulouse Lautrec and a map of Middle Earth. Boz took the 'Buddhist minimalist' approach to interior design. Apart from a black and white drawing of Ho Chi Minh his walls were bare. 'Posters are too petit bourgeois for me. I like to look at the cracks, endless free entertainment. It's all in the mind,' Boz would say.

The one thing I did value was my music system: Garrard deck; Sinclair amplifier and Denton speakers. Buying that had taken up a big chunk of my student grant. I often imagined I would turn the corner to find a pile of rubble where our house had once stood - my stereo buried deep underneath the bricks. They were unsettling times. As a Taurean I needed a safe place to rest my head. I never did get used to eating Corn Flakes to the distant sound of the dentist's drill.

You learn a lot about a person when you share a squat with them. Boz was a no-nonsense sort of a guy. He wouldn't take any crap and was self-contained to the point of selfishness. I noticed Boz was frequently afflicted by extreme lassitude and appeared to be satisfied with a very low level of intellectual stimulation. A full day consisted of sitting in an armchair with a warm tea pot beside him and the test match on the radio. He always wore his 'roach crushers,' calf high boots - a cross between cowboy and biker boots - that he'd bought from the head shop in the arcade by the market. Sometimes he'd get up in the morning, only to go back to bed half an hour later. Sometimes he wouldn't get up at all. At certain times of the month every ounce of energy seemed to have been sucked from his body. 'It's lunar,' he'd explain. He was quickly exhausted by routine tasks such as filling the kettle, doing the washing up or cleaning the cooker. He once told me that he couldn't be bothered to get out of the shower to take a piss. I now know illnesses like M.E. can be a dreadful debilitating curse. But Boz was physically fit. Admittedly, a nutritionist would say that he had too much pastry in his diet which would generate a certain amount of lethargy. But Boz's formidable torpor was attributable to a severe psychosis. According to his Dad this severe psychosis was called 'being a lazy git.' As such, the cure was simple. In the words of his father, all he needed to do was to 'get up off his bleedin' backside'.

Nevertheless this fatigue didn't stop a constant stream of overnight visitors. It was as if Boz's doormat beard had 'Welcome' written on it. Boz's languid manner and lack of emotional commitment seemed to be particularly attractive to feminists and women aligned to the extreme left, none of whom liked to have the door opened for them. I quickly learnt not to say 'ladies first.'

Sure, we all have our foibles but some people's quirks can be particularly annoying. In Boz's case it was his allergic reaction to washing up liquid. And when I suggested he might like to use rubber gloves he patiently explained he had an allergy to those as well. 'Sorry Felix, no can do.'

So we stripped down our crockery requirements to the bare minimum. We soon found that most food could be eaten out of a pint mug - cornflakes, soup, even bacon and eggs.

Boz also wouldn't allow any lettuce in the fridge. He had an aversion to it; he said it made him feel uneasy. He'd had a bad childhood experience. He wouldn't say exactly what it was, but hinted that he'd once eaten something alien and unexpected that had been hidden on the underside of a leaf.

Boz taught me a number of things. Have you ever been into the gents and found there's no light or loo paper? I can tell you why. For people like Boz any visit to the pub is an opportunity to stock up on bulbs and bog roll. Boz also showed me that you didn't necessarily need to take your boots off to go to bed.

I should point out that Boz isn't his real name. Back in Bolton, Boz is just plain Bobby. I found this out the hard way. Why he's called Boz, I've no idea. Of course, it's a popular name. In fact I've got another mate called Boz; it can get confusing.

Perhaps I should also have mentioned before that Boz comes from the Scaggs Lancashire pie-making dynasty. In Lancashire Scaggs' Pies are legendary. Scaggs have a chain of shops and make the award winning 'Bolton Growler.' For a few years in the 1950s the local football team were known by many as the 'Growlers' due to a sponsorship deal with Scaggs' Pies. 'We had to sell a lot of pies to pay for that partnership.' Boz was passionate about his pies. 'Pies, peas and gravy, in a tray with a fork. What more can a man ask for? Scaggs' pies are what the North is all about. Good old-fashioned grub. The Growler is made in exactly the same way as when great grandfather Ebenezer Scaggs first made it - apart from the electric ovens. We tried a chicken pie for a while. But our customers can't abide change.' [2]

'If you're ever in Bolton and need a bite to eat go into a Scaggs' Pie Shop and mention my name. They'll see you right.'

And sure enough, one chill winter's day I did find myself in Bolton with an empty stomach. And there, on Market Street, was a Scaggs' Pie Shop - warm, brightly lit and as welcoming as the food counter in a motorway service station. Without hesitation I went in and introduced myself.

---

[2] Boz has asked me to put this bit in. I know it's shameless advertising but it's the least that I can do for him.

'SCAGGS USES ONLY THE FINEST, FRESHEST INGREDIENTS, SOURCED IN LANCASHIRE WHEREVER POSSIBLE AND AVOIDS PRESERVATIVES AND ARTIFICIAL ADDITIVES IN ITS PRODUCTS.

SCAGGS ARE PART OF THE LANCASHIRE PASTRY FEDERATION SUPPORTING THE PROTECTION OF THE LANCASHIRE PIE. IN 1966 SCAGGS'S *GROWLER* WON THE GOLD MEDALLION IN THE BRITISH PIE AWARDS - THE BIGGEST AND MOST SIGNIFICANT PRIZE IN THE INDUSTRY.'

'I'm a mate of Boz's. We're at university together. Boz said if I was ever in Bolton I should drop in and ask for a bag of pies?'

'Fook off, you scrounging little tyke,' snarled the lardy-armed woman behind the counter.

Later, I told Boz of my embarrassment. He laughed.

'I forgot to tell you. Back in Bolton I'm known as plain old Bobby Scaggs. They wouldn't have known Boz from Nat Lofthouse.' Whoever he is.

What did Boz see in me? Who knows? Companionship, maybe? Somebody who would put up with his funny ways? I suppose I offered him a window into the world of the 'soft Southerner'. I was keen to dig the world and find out how it all fitted together. We both had that in common. It just worked - we both shared a relaxed chemistry.

I never did get used to the cold in that house. It was a long freezing winter. I'd pile all my clothes on my bed to add extra insulation to my two flimsy blankets. I'd wake up to frost on my window and have to urinate on the ice in the outside loo to get it to flush properly. It took so long to get up in the morning. Luckily there was no shortage of wood to burn as a hundred yards down the road was an abandoned shoe manufactory. We systematically stripped out all the shelving and pigeon holes for storing the cobbler's lasts. Once, on a particularly cold night, Boz didn't have the energy to leave the squat, so he burnt some of the floor boards from our front room. The following morning, as we balanced on the remaining joists to get to the front door, we regretted this. Next time we'd take out alternate planks.

ELEVEN

Gloria and I met for coffee at the Swiss Cottage, an alpine themed coffee shop at the top of Park Street. It was a place Boz and I would occasionally visit to ogle the waitresses in their strangely erotic Heidi uniforms. Gloria handed me her Eurorail schedule. At the top of the paper she'd written 'fuckwit'. This time she hadn't even bothered to scrub it out.

'Why have you written that?' I asked.

'Just ignore it. It's nothing.'

'Is that what you think of me?'

'Of course it isn't. Don't be stupid.'

'Don't be a fuckwit, you mean.'

'Don't take it personally.'

'Well, who else is this note for?'

'It's just something I do.'

'What? Write obscenities on paper?'

'Well, yes. Something like that.'

'But why?'

'I've got this little ... problem.'

'What's that?'

'You've heard of Tourettes Syndrome?'

'Fucking right.'

'Keep your voice down Felix. That's such a predictable response, I've heard that so many times.'

'Sorry.'

'I have a written form of Tourettes Syndrome. I can't help it. Before I know it I've written something that I shouldn't have done.'

'How long have you been doing this?'

'As long as I can remember. My parents thought I was messing around, but I couldn't stop myself. And even before I could write I was drawing pictures of turds. It got me into lots of trouble. One of my earliest memories is of spending time drawing this neat little mound of steaming poo. I'd spent hours on it, it was coloured in, it had texture, everything. The play leader in the nursery class went mad. 'We can't pin that on the wall,' she said. She tore it up. She made me cry. That was the start of it. I got into even more trouble when I started to write.'

'How did you know how to write obscenities, where did you learn the words at that age?'

Gloria leant forward and spoke in a whisper. 'I can remember it quite clearly. We were on holiday in Devon, I think it was Torquay, and I needed to go to the loo. I went into the public toilets and there were all those words on the wall. I was learning to read. I asked Mummy what they meant. I thought they were nice words to say. I liked the sound of them. Mummy was horrified. Within days I was copying what I'd seen on that wall. While everybody else was writing 'the cat sat on the mat' I was carefully drawing out the words 'wank', 'fuck' and 'cunt'.

Even though Gloria was speaking quietly I could see a couple at the adjoining table both turn and give her a shocked look.

I laughed. 'But why did you write these obscenities?'

'It's not funny, Felix. People were truly shocked. Imagine how you would react if a five year old girl with hair in bunches had written a load of swear words on the blackboard. But I couldn't help it. It drove everybody mad. I couldn't see the problem. I thought everybody did it. I had to be moved to another school. Eventually I was sent to a shrink. He was a creepy old man with flecks of toothpaste, or maybe it was shaving cream, round his mouth. I didn't like him. He said that I was very interesting from a psychiatric point of view. As far as I was concerned he was the weird one. He told my parents I did it as an attention seeking device when my little brother Gabriel got ill. I was only about three or four when Gabriel was rushed to hospital with polio. Apparently, it was at that time that I started drawing the pictures of poo. I can't remember it, but that's what the shrink said. He said I was doing it to attract attention. I think he might have been right. Secretly, I liked the power of the reaction. Anyway my third appointment had to be cancelled. The shrink had hung himself.'

'Far out!' I said.

'My new shrink, Dr Pimperton, was more helpful. She told me that we all have a little switch in our head that censors what we write. In my case the inhibitors in my brain malfunction; the switch has been turned off. There's even an official term for what I do. It's called copralexia[3]. It made me feel better knowing there's a name for it.

'Dr Pimperton helped me cope with it. Basically, I was encouraged to become more aware of what I was doing. Sometimes I'd forget and find that I'd just drawn some obscene doodle or written a swear word.'

'That's weird.'

'So, Felix, when I call you a fuckwit, please ignore it. Unless you ARE being a fuckwit. And then I mean it. Otherwise I'm totally fucking normal, if you'll excuse my French.'

'Who's being predictable now?'

The couple at the next table got up to leave. The man, smartly dressed in a tweed jacket, with a stiff military bearing, stood by our table and said:

'How dare you swear like that in front of my wife.'

'Sorry, I didn't know it was her turn,' I said. It was a lousy joke but I couldn't stop myself.

---

[3] Greek: Kopros 'dung' + lexis 'speech'.

TWELVE

B ristol isn't the sort of place you can live comfortably without a good income. By now it was becoming increasingly important that Boz and I got a job. I needed to be saving money for our trip, and besides we were running low on floor-boards.

But with the economy on the rocks, and the unemployment numbers surging to one million, jobs were scarce. With my qualifications, all the brawny, manual, sod-busting jobs were obviously out of the question. Sure, I could have worked crating up cigarettes or as a sweeper in the tea bag factory but I felt I might be taking someone else's work.

So, when I received a letter with details of my job interview at the Tax Office in Unity Street, I thought my financial problems would soon be over. To be honest I was expecting the interrogation to be more of a formality; I'd negotiate my salary, terms and conditions and agree on a starting date and that would be that. I'd obviously not mention that I'd only be with them for a couple of months. On the day of the interview, however, things didn't go according to plan. I have to say I was disappointed with the calibre of the man who interviewed me. I can only put his confusion down to the fact that I was over-qualified for the job - a situation I would probably have to get used to. And so what if my application form had coffee mug stains on it? These civil servants are so hung up on trivial detail they miss the wider picture. I suppose that's what comes of spending your life scrutinising tax returns. The guy interviewing me, a thin, sallow-faced bed-wetting mummy's boy, asked, with unnecessary sarcasm, if I possessed a shirt and tie and whether I had any plans to visit a barber in the near future.

Anyway, as far as I was concerned, it was their loss, not mine. I never wanted that soul-sucking job anyway.

Boz also set about looking for work. Unfortunately Boz made the mistake of telling the Job Centre clerk that he was the heir to the Scaggs' pie empire and was knowledgeable about the manufacture of pies and other pastry-based products. 'Ah, we might have something for you here. Meat processing. How's that sound?' Meat processing was a job that frequently appeared on the Job Centre notice board. It didn't sound good at all. Boz had failed to mention, however, that his experience was limited to the back office rather than the production line. The clerk read out the details. The work involved the 'extraction of ocular, oral and anal extremities'. Boz showed the clerk a white scar on his left hand. 'I'm not very handy with knives I'm afraid. I'm more interested in the management side of pie making.' The Job Centre clerk remained undeterred. 'Don't worry about that, they provide chain mail gloves and a protective helmet in case of seepage.' 'What might seepage be?' asked Boz. 'Maybe this job is a bit too technical for you,' the Job Centre clerk conceded.

*

Boz pointed to an advert in the *Evening Post*.

West of England Transportation Survey. Roadside interviewers required. Must be willing to work shifts. 50p an hour. To start immediately.

'We could do that.' It turned out to be good money too. At 50p an hour I could make £20.00 a week. This time there was no messing and I was interviewed by an astute young man who offered me the job straight away. And it got even better. For some inexplicable reason our future gang leader, John Stoner, had a strategy that positively encouraged the recruitment of hippies. Why, I don't know. Maybe he was looking for sociology students. He wasn't even deterred by Boz's chronic ennui.

I'd already heard of John Stoner; he was a friend of a friend and had a reputation as a bit of a maverick. He was one of those effortlessly charming people that women find strangely attractive. He had a twisted Salvador Dali moustache. It was a good look which must have taken him at least half an hour every morning to achieve, though he claimed it curled naturally.

There were six people in our team: me; Boz; John Stoner; Mohan, a Malaysian guy over in England to study accountancy; Dave, a Jethro Tull lookalike, and Jacqui, a sulky art student who wore diaphanous cheese cloth shirts and no bra.

On the first day Stoner explained the rules.

'We work as a team, we get the work done with minimum fuss, we attract as little attention from HQ as possible. That way they leave us to get on with things, they don't interfere. Got it? Low profile, that's the name of the game. All queries with HQ have to come through me. If you have any problems about terms and conditions you discuss them with me. Never, ever contact HQ about wages. I deal with all that. You got questions, you come to me. Just remember what happened to Sanchez's team.' Stoner hesitated for effect and scanned our faces. 'That's an example for all of us.'

I'd no idea who Sanchez was or what had happened to his team.

Stoner continued. 'We're going to start with urban hardcore and then, if everything goes according to my plan, HQ will move us to the rural evidence-based work.'

'Excuse me, but what's that mean?' Jacqui asked.

Stoner gave Jacqui a big charming smile. 'Don't worry. I'll personally take you through the technical details again later.'

Mohan, who had done the same job the previous summer whispered in my ear. 'It means we'll work hard for a month - and then it's a doss.'

Stoner then broke the news that made me nervous.

'We'll be accompanied by a policeman.'

'Riding shotgun in bandit land, huh?' said Boz.

'Something like that. His name is P.C. Bixby. I've already briefed him on his role. His job is to stop the traffic. It is essential that fraternisation with Bixby is kept to a minimum. We need to keep him at a discreet distance. We don't want him disturbing our groove.'

'Got it, boss,' we replied in unison. We were already working as a team.

Later on, on the first day, Stoner took me aside. 'I've been watching you and I've set up a special deal. I think you'll like it. I'd be grateful if you don't tell anybody else though.'

'Thank you, I'm intrigued.' I felt pleased to be singled out like this.

'I've arranged for you to get paid in dope rather than cash.'

'What!?'

'Yeah, I knew you'd like that. I'll get the shit delivered to the van on Friday. I buy it in bulk, that way you'll get more than your twenty quid's worth.'

'John, this might sound weird, but I need the cash.'

Stoner looked at me if I'd pissed on the Holy Grail. 'I've gone to a lot of trouble to sort out this arrangement for you.'

'I appreciate it, but I need the money to go travelling.' This didn't seem to make things any better. He looked at me appalled. I could see what he was thinking: 'bread head'.

'Remember,' Stoner said, quoting loosely from that colossus of 1960s philosophy, Freewheeling Franklin, 'dope can get you through times of no money, but money can't get you through times of no dope.'

'I realise that. But I'm only working to get some additional cash.'

In the end we came to a compromise. Every fourth week Stoner would pay me in dope.

'But what about the policeman?' I asked.

'I can cut him in on the deal if you think it's a good idea.'

That wasn't what I was thinking.

THIRTEEN

So where next?' Boz asked.

We'd been so busy relaxing at Venice Lido, drinking red wine, eating pizza and a black liquorice-flavoured ice cream called James Bound (sic) that we hadn't got round to deciding the precise details of our next destination.

It was another foggy morning and yet again we passed along the Grand Canal to the railway station in a dense miasma that blanketed out all Venice's features.

'In the spirit of our cultural odyssey our next destination is obvious,' I said.

'It's not obvious to me,' said Boz.

'It's written in our destiny. Michelangelo, the Medicis, E.M. Forster,' I said.

'What are you on about?'

'Our next stop is Florence.'

I got the diary out of my bag and looked at the map. There wasn't much to see: Venice, Milan, Turin, but no Florence.

'Florence, where is it?' asked Boz.

We sneaked a look at a map which we borrowed from a news kiosk. I still couldn't find it. 'Maybe it's further away than I thought,' I said.

'What about Turin?' suggested Boz.

'What's there to do in Turin?' It sounded a bit industrial to me. Fiat with its rooftop race track wasn't the sort of cultural experience I was seeking out.

'The Turin Shroud.'

I thought of Gloria in her cave. A stained old cloth or fantastic sex with Gloria? It wasn't a difficult decision.

'Turin is west. We'd be heading backwards. We haven't got time to do that.'

'Where else, then?' Boz pointed at the destination board. There was a train leaving for Trieste in fifteen minutes. According to our map Trieste was near the border with Yugoslavia.

'Yeah, let's go to Trieste.' I said.

'Pity about Florence though. I love those little biscuits.'

'All Italian cites have their own culinary speciality; I expect Trieste is famous for its salami or something like that.'

'Maybe Trieste has a speciality of a pastry-based savoury?' Boz said hopefully.

I looked at the map again. 'There's no time to waste. We've been away a week already and we don't seem to have travelled anywhere.'

'We're in Venice,' said Boz. 'That's not bad. Anyway by my reckoning we've been away ten days.'

'No. Eight, maybe?'

'Work it out Felix, it's ten.'

'We need to get moving.' I was hoping for at least a month in Matala. 'Two tickets to Trieste it is.'

I held the ticket in my hand and looked at the unadorned sans serif typeface and the flimsy puce paper. It was the little details like this that made me realise I was abroad.

The train rumbled along the causeway to the mainland as the morning vapours lifted. I pressed my cheek against the gritty window, trying to catch a last look at Venice. For a second, through a break in the mist, I caught sight of a slender brick tower crowned with a gilded cross, burning like a match in the milky sun. It was over so quickly. Venice was now behind us. I later wondered if I'd really seen this glorious sight.

*

We never did get the opportunity to investigate whether Trieste had any specialty dishes. Earlier in the day we'd been told that a ferry sailed twice a week from Rijeka, a port down the Adriatic coast in northern Yugoslavia. If we were to catch the evening boat to Dubrovnik we had to leave Trieste by coach immediately.

Trieste coach station had the bustle of an early morning market. Before we boarded the bus that was to take us across the border to Yugoslavia, a man in a black leather jacket, Elvis sunglasses and an imposing, almost threatening manner, approached me:

'My friend, you want to wear extra trousers?' he said.

'Pardon?'

'Extra Levis. I pay you 100 Kuna.'

I couldn't understand what he meant.

'100 Kuna. I see you in toilets.'

I didn't like the sound of this. I'd already noticed the man in the black leather jacket talking earnestly to a Japanese, or maybe Korean, tourist, and handing him a cardboard suitcase.

'No.'

'My friend, we have no Levis in Yugoslavia. You help me.'

'No.'

'See, lots of people help me. Why not you? What's so special about you?'

I looked around the waiting room. At first I couldn't see what he was talking about. But then I noticed that many of the young men and women seemed to be stouter round the waist and chunkier about the legs than the usual snake hipped local. Could they really be wearing extra trousers?

'No, it's too hot,' I said.

The man scowled and with an intimidating grunt walked away.

It was only a two hour journey by bus to Rijeka through a landscape of neat farm houses and small yellow fields backed by distant blue mountains. The Slovenian countryside seemed so different from home. Not just the geography, but the farmers. In Britain you rarely see people working directly with the soil, tilling the earth. They tend the fields from the seat of a tractor or perch on a harvester. Here, labourers were bent double pulling vegetables out of the hard ground. Horses and oxen pulled the type of plough that I'd seen in school history text books.

While we were having our passports stamped at the Yugoslav border I noticed the Japanese tourist being ordered to open his suitcase. I could see him give a big, toothy, nervous smile.

This brings me neatly to an additional rule to add to Boz's list - let's call it Rule of the Road number 11. I'm sure it's obvious to frequent travellers but I'll tell you anyway. Don't try out your new jokes on immigration officers. They won't laugh. Don't even try sarcasm or hyperbole. They won't get it; they are programmed not to get it. When you are going through Immigration only speak when you are spoken to and be as polite as if you were speaking to your new girlfriend's parents. In other words, agree with every fatuous thing they say, but preferably, just read a book and shut up. Believe me this is an important rule - especially if you are a freak.

As our Nippon friend lifted the lid I heard him give a squeal of surprise. I could see the case contained not Levi jeans but hundreds of pornographic magazines. I don't think I will ever forget the look of horror and shame on that poor man's face.

*

Rijeka was a largely unattractive port. Immediately behind the docks, concrete tower blocks spread up a steep hillside. Apart from one notable building belonging to an Adriatic shipping line, an impressive commercial citadel adorned with muscular statues of Atlas and Neptune, there was little to see. We found a bench under the shade of a plane tree near the gateway to the docks and settled down to read our books.

'Have you finished *Tarantula* yet?' I asked Boz.

'You can't rush quality writing like this. There's a lot in it.'

'You've been reading it for a while.'

'The narrative's a bit disjoined. It's the kind of book that's best for dipping in and out of. I'll let you have it soon.'

*

It was a perfect evening. I leant against the railings at the back of the ferry and watched the port of Rijeka recede into the purple dusk. The Adriatic was as still and as flat as mercury; the air felt warm to the skin.

We'd explored and found a place to settle at the back of the boat away from the judder of the funnel. Apart from the cross-channel ferry I'd never before been on a boat this size. We'd climbed up and down staircases and looked through the doorway to the restaurant with its starched tablecloths and waiters dressed in black and white. On the lower decks there were long corridors of cabins but the artificial lighting and the thrum of the engine made me feel nauseous. I was glad to be travelling 'Deck Class'.

'So what are you going to do with your life?' I asked Boz. The bottle of cheap red Bosnian wine was nearly empty.

'Get shacked up with some like-minded soul, have a couple of nippers.'

'Really?' I couldn't imagine Boz as a family man. I thought it would be too hard work for him.

'And a Border Collie. It's inevitable, isn't it? The family want me to marry Jennifer Rutley.'

'Who?'

'I've told you about her: a feisty little red-head. Her old man owns a brewery.'

'So?'

'Pies and pints. A reet canny marriage, if ever there was one. Her parents are loaded.'

I couldn't believe Boz was saying this. 'That's like an arranged marriage?'

'So? It's common sense. A financial and domestic arrangement made in heaven.'

'It's depressing.'

'Look, I've got some heavy responsibilities in my life.'

'Like what?'

'The secret ingredient of the Growler for one thing. The hundred-year-old recipe written by my great grandfather Ebenezer Scaggs and secured in a box, which I'll inherit when the old man dies. He's very frail, the doctor says any big shock could kill him. So that's generations of knowledge resting on my shoulders.'

I held the empty wine bottle up to the stars.

'Is the bar still open?' I asked.

'Yeah, I think it's open all night.'

'What are your parents like?' I asked.

'They're normal decent people. The old man wears a cloth cap and braces and keeps whippets. Mum smokes like a chimney, wears a hairnet and has false teeth which she only puts in at weekends and Christmas. And on Friday we all have a bath in a zinc tub in front of the fire in t' back room.'

'That's amazing. That's exactly how I pictured them.'

'Don't be daft. Of course they're not like that. I don't live in bloody Coronation Street you know.'

'But what about your university education?'

'Jennifer Rutley wouldn't marry me without one.'

'It seems so old fashioned. What happens if you fall for some cute honey that isn't in the licensed trade?'

'It all depends what her parents do. Now, suppose they had a fish and chip shop, that would be okay.'

'What about love?'

'Love? I've experienced love. Several times, in fact. Love at first sight on the late night bus. But after thirty seconds I've come to my senses.'

'Boz, you have a weird perspective on the world.'

'I think of myself as a realist.'

'After all this?' I waved my hand at the sea and the sky. 'Look around you, there's a whole world out there beyond the Bolton Chamber of Commerce.'

'Yeah, you're right, there's Bolton Rotary Club as well.'

I couldn't be sure, but I hoped Boz was winding me up.

I slept well, woken only by the occasional slam of a door. Once in a while I'd think about the carnal delights that lay ahead in Matala, though mostly I was enjoying the very act of travelling; I wanted to concentrate on what was around me now.

Next morning, I watched the coast slide by. The bare limestone mountains went straight down to the sea; there were no beaches. It was as if a whole mountain range had been submerged. Every two or three hours the boat would stop at a small fortified town. In between these towns, apart from the occasional deserted farm, the wide and empty mountainsides showed little sign of habitation.

Boz was scanning the sea.

'Beautiful isn't it,' I said.

'Yeah, the water is so clear. We'll be able to spot pilchards easily.'

'They call them sardines here.'

'Are they the same thing?'

'I'm sure they are.'

'I can't wait to swim with them.' Boz looked at me, his face as keen as a young lad on his first visit to the zoo.

I didn't want to disappoint him.

FOURTEEN

On impulse we stopped off at the small Dalmatian port of Hav. We weren't planning to do this, but as the boat sailed round the corner of the bay and we saw this walled town with its castle on the hill, church tower and palm lined quay, we looked at each other and said 'why not?'. We were free spirits, travelling where we wanted, when we wanted. And for a brief moment I'd even forgotten about Gloria.

We walked down the gangplank alongside old ladies carrying boxes of figs and men with gallon tins of cooking oil. On the quayside we were surrounded by a horde of black-robed women. One of them grabbed Boz's arm with a talon-like hand and pulled him through the narrow, dim alleys of the old town. We had no option but to go with her.

We were hurried along brown cobbled back streets smelling of fish and wine, past archways that led into courtyards with women talking and children fighting. At last, the old woman pushed Boz up the front steps of a substantial stone built town house. From a dark, marble floored hall, we climbed a further three storeys up an impressive staircase with a sweeping mahogany handrail and cast iron banisters. Two young boys were playing hide and seek in the dark. This previously grand house, with an odour of dust and fried fish, was now divided into apartments.

Once in her shabby flat the old woman took us to a small ill-lit room and proudly pushed open the shutters to reveal an uninterrupted view of a honeycomb coloured wall just feet away from the window.

'The walls!' the woman said.

I put my head outside the window and could see a patch of blue sky above and the street below. Otherwise the view was of unadorned stone. No direct sunlight had ever penetrated this room.

'Impressive,' Boz said charitably.

As I wrote my name in her registration book I could hear a sharp intake of breath from the old woman. I looked up. Shaking her head she touched the small gold crucifix round her neck. She waved her hands and made a pushing gesture for me to leave.

I turned to Boz. 'What's up with her?'

'You've upset her.'

'I didn't do anything. I just wrote my name.'

'Maybe there's something about the name Radstock in these parts. Have any of your relatives visited here recently?'

I looked at the old woman. She appeared to be pointing at the Biro in my hand.

'She doesn't like me using a Biro. Maybe I should have used a pencil.'

'Biro not good?' I asked.

She was making a clucking noise.

'I think she's about to lay an egg,' I said.

I put the pen down. She pointed at my hand. What was wrong with it? Four fingers and one thumb. No horrible warts. Okay, the nails could have been cleaner. I was once told by a girl that I had nice hands. I quite liked my hands. They were one of the few parts of my body that I did like.

'I dunno,' I said.

'I've got it,' Boz said. 'She doesn't like you because you're keck handed.'

'What?'

'Left-handed.'

'Oh man, that is crazy.'

Boz took the pen and attempted to complete the register, but the woman was having none of it.

'No room. No room,' she repeated.

'But we've just seen it. We've seen the walls!' Boz protested.

'*Nien zimmer.*' The woman was adamant.

'Let's go,' I said. 'There wasn't much of a view anyway.'

It didn't take long before another crow black woman grabbed Boz's arm and with equal insistence offered a *zimmer*. For some reason the widows of Hav seemed to be drawn to Boz. Perhaps his sailor's beard reminded them of long lost husbands.

We were taken to another dingy room, empty apart from two iron bedsteads separated by an up-ended orange crate which served as a bedside table. On the crate was an old crab shell overflowing with cigarette ends. While the sheets on the beds had been smoothed, it didn't look as if we were going to be the first people to have used them. We followed the woman down a dim corridor to a cupboard that contained a squat toilet with a shower next to it. As she opened the door I heard the unmistakable scuttle of cockroaches. The old lady proudly demonstrated the flush mechanism. 'Good,' she said as she patted her hands together and rubbed them on her black dress. Back in the room she opened the shutters with a flourish. And sure enough, just three metres away from the window were the massive hewn city walls. The walls! I was getting pissed off by these walls. They felt like they were sucking the air out of the town. They were always there, giving Hav a tight claustrophobic feel.

'You like?' said the woman.

'Good,' we said in unison.

This time Boz did the registration. 'Keep your hands in your pockets,' he said.

Once the woman had gone, we lay on our beds. I was pleased to see Boz had taken his shoes off. It was only then that I noticed the dark red splots on the wall from squashed mosquitoes.

Boz gave a contented sigh. 'This'll do fine. I wonder if we get breakfast.'

We needed to buy something to eat for lunch. As we walked along the streets it was difficult to tell the private houses from the shops. We walked into a large unlit room. On the wooden counter were jars of jam, and giant pickled gherkins and tins of sardines. Behind this the wall was lined with empty, unstocked shelves. Otherwise the shop contained nothing.

'Is this a shop? Boz asked. 'Where's all the produce?'

'That's it, that's all they have.'

'But all these empty shelves. Why?'

'Maybe in the past they did have lots of stuff, maybe in the future they will.'

'These, please.' I pointed at a tin of sardines and a jar of pickled gherkins. 'At least it makes shopping easy. That's the problem with the western world: too much choice.'

'I don't get it,' said Boz. 'Empty shelves. This would never happen in a Scaggs shop.'

While we were sitting in a café in the town square a lean young man with a wide smile and a wispy moustache approached us and introduced himself as Ivo. Despite the heat, he was wearing an ill-fitting camel hair coat.

'German?' he asked.

'English,' Boz said.

'You have seen the walls?' Ivo questioned. Seeing him sweating in his heavy coat made me feel uncomfortable.

'Yeah, you can't miss them,' Boz replied.

'They are good? Yes?'

'Yeah, they are good.'

'I give you a tour?'

I looked across the piazza. Over the terracotta roof tops I could see the city wall snaking up the hillside.

'We can see them from here. They are very good. Thank you.'

'The walls, they are big, they go round the town. I take you.'

'No thank you.'

'But they are tall.'

'Yes, I can see them.'

'The walls are strong. They have stood for many hundreds of years. No army has ever conquered them. You want to see?'

'No thank you. We can see them from here.'

For a moment Ivo was silent. He then gave a sad sigh.

'Okay, for you I drop my price,' he said shrugging his shoulders. 'Special price. Special lucky price.'

Boz was becoming exasperated. He turned to me.

'There's something weird going on in this town. These walls are okay, but they're not exactly the Great Wall of China, or Berlin even. Are we missing something?'

Across the almost empty square an old man was arranging oranges on his cart; a woman, not young, was carrying an oil drum on her head, seemingly oblivious to its weight, and talking to a friend. There was a long and beautiful call to prayer from a minaret. I looked at the ochre coloured gateway, the adjoining fortifications and the fields of lavender in the distance. As a child I'd always enjoyed visiting Windsor with its sturdy stone walls and the changing of the guard every day at eleven o'clock. 'No, they're just walls,' I said.

Ivo continued, 'The walls they go round the town. They are big.'

'Ivo, my friend,' Boz said patiently, 'I can see the walls and yes they are big, and yes they do go round the town. Thank you for your offer, but we do not require your services. Please go away.'

Ivo smiled. 'I take you to the museum, perhaps.'

'No thank you.'

'Folk dancing?'

'No.'

'Ah! Folk dancing with swords! Very good. Yes?'

Boz and I both shook our heads. For the moment Ivo was defeated.

Ivo moved a couple of steps away from our table and stood with his back to us, looking at the square. I didn't feel good spurning his offer. Ivo was clearly an honest man, doing his best trying to earn a crust. We were travellers and by definition had money, even if we thought otherwise. He held his hands behind his back pretending to ignore us.

I started to write a postcard to send to Mum and Dad. The selection on sale had been limited. A man and woman in local costume standing beside a haystack; the head of a donkey with a speech bubble in Cyrillic; and this, a picture looking down on the town taken from the mountains behind, highlighting the gateways and extensive walls.

Ivo discreetly looked at us over his shoulder. I ignored him. He turned back and continued to survey the square with his chin raised in a proprietorial manner. He stole another glance at me. I couldn't help but smile. He walked back to our table.

'Excuse me. I advise you not to let people see what you are doing.'

'What!' I wondered what I was doing that could cause offence.

He nodded at my postcard.

'Not much choice,' I said, unsure what Ivo was talking about.

'The people here are very superstitious. It is a bad sign. The sign of the devil.'

'Postcards! The sign of the devil?'

'No. You misunderstand.'

'What! Do people think I am a spy, writing notes?'

'You are writing with your evil hand.'

Boz gave me a pitying look. 'You've got to do something about that left hand of yours. I can see it's going to get us into a lot of trouble. I don't want you put in a wicker cage by these people, taken up the hillside and burnt.'

'Shut up, Boz. If you must know, some girls find it sexy. It means you do stuff a different way. I had a girlfriend once who called me Left Hand Luke.'

'I don't believe you!'

'I'll introduce you to her sometime.'

'Who?'

'Look out for the girl with the big smile on her face.'

Ivo continued: 'My brother also started to write with his left hand. My father beat him so hard his hand swelled up to the size of a melon. He never again used his left hand for writing.'

'This is crazy,' I protested.

'Maybe, but our people are superstitious. They think you will attract the evil eye. It is best not to upset them. May I have a look at that card, please.'

For a long time Ivo stared at the card with deep interest. He looked at it from different angles.

'It is good,' he finally pronounced. 'You can see the walls, they are big, are they not?'

'They are,' I agreed. 'And they go round the town.'

'That is my job to say that,' he said seriously. And then he laughed. 'Good day gentlemen.'

Ivo walked away across the square.

*

Now this is what travelling is all about. An item on the menu had caught Boz's attention.

'Head Meat Pie, I've got to have a slice of that,' said Boz.

'I wonder if it comes with gravy?' I said.

'When I go back to University I've got an idea for my dissertation,' Boz continued.

'You're intending to go back?'

'Yeah.'

'I thought you were disappointed by the course.'

'It's better than working.'

'I suppose so.'

'Anyway, I'm thinking of undertaking some research on the cross-cultural transmogrification of pastry-based snacks.'

'Meaning?'

'The evolution of pies. I might do this for my Social Anthropology dissertation.'

'Interesting. I didn't realise there was a Darwinian aspect to baking.'

'Not Darwinian. This is for the Food and Culture option. What I'm saying is there are international forces influencing the development of pies.'

'Does that include sweet pastries as well?'

'Good question Felix. Now you mention it, it does. Take, for example, the humble egg tart that is so popular with the Chinese.'

'Is it?'

'Haven't you ever had egg tart with *dim sum*?'

'Not that I can recall.' I didn't think I'd ever had *dim sum*. In fact, I didn't know what it was.

'Well, the development of the egg tart can be tracked across the world right back to England. What do they call custard in France? *Crème anglaise.* The twelfth-century crusaders introduced the egg tart to the Portuguese on their way to the Holy Land. The Portuguese then developed it into their own *Pastel de Nata*. Many centuries later, it was adopted by the Sri Lankans - in the 17th Century Ceylon was colonised by Vasco de Gama and his crew - who, being partial to a bit of heat in their food, spiced it up. Which in turn was passed on to the Chinese indentured labourers working on the tea estates. And so it goes on.'

'Boz, I'm impressed. You know your stuff.'

'So that's why I'm keen to go to Albania. I've done a little research since you came up with the itinerary and apart from the experience of visiting one of the world's most totally totalitarian states, I'm interested to sample their food.'

'Why didn't you say this before?'

'I've only just figured it out.'

'Maybe you're on to something. I doubt anybody else would have come up with such a...' I was choosing my words carefully here... 'with such an unusual idea.'

'Although Albania isn't known to have one of the great cuisines of the world,' said Boz, 'they do have their own version of the pasty. It was introduced by Cornish miners during the Balkan Tin Rush of the

1890s. It's called *bureka*; it looks like a traditional pasty but contains fermented cabbage.'

'That could be a shock. Does it come with anything else?'

'It's an acquired taste. It's particularly popular with Germans. You can have plain cabbage with it as well.'

The head meat pie was served on a plate, *a l'anglaise,* with a garnish of limp lettuce and half a tomato. The pie looked good. It had a raised crust, similar to a Melton Mowbray pie. Boz, however, was horrified.

'Get that off there!'

'What?'

'That lettuce. Get it off there. I'm going to throw up.'

I'd forgotten about Boz's lettuce allergy.

'Just get it off.'

'Okay.' I put it on my plate.

'No, somewhere where I can't see it.'

'I'll eat it.'

'You are disgusting.'

'It's a bit of lettuce, Boz.'

'Oh, man, I'll be back in a few minutes.'

Five minutes later Boz returned.

'Better?'

'Yeah.'

'That's a weird allergy.'

'I once had a bad experience with lettuce. It can send me into an anaphylactic trance.'

'How can lettuce do that? It's a salad vegetable, the most innocuous food stuff known to man. It must be 99% water.'

'I don't know why, but it does. For me it's got all sorts of psychosomatic associations. Sunday afternoons, maiden aunts smelling of lavender, Shipham's meat paste. Just thinking about it is making me feel weird. Can we change the subject?'

'What's the pie taste like?'

'Have some.'

'No thank you.' I didn't want both of us to go down with food poisoning.

Boz took a large bite and slowly chewed. He was silent for what seemed like a long time. He closed his eyes as he concentrated. At last he swallowed.

'So?'

'Good. Yeah,' he said in a surprised sort of voice. 'It's a bit like tongue, it's got an interesting firm texture, with a good amount of meat jelly to lubricate. At first there's a musty taste to it, but you get used to that after a while. I like it.'

'Maybe Scaggs' could develop something similar. You could call it the 'Bolton Howler'.'

'It's high quality, but I don't think the citizens of Bolton are quite ready for this,' said Boz, as he took another bite.

After we had viewed all that Hav had to offer - the tranquil square reminiscent of a town in a Spaghetti Western, the astounding Roman triumphal arch, a ruined merchant's house in the Venetian style, and of course the biscuit-coloured walls, which were indeed impressive - we set off for Dubrovnik. As we climbed aboard the ferry I spotted Ivo. Ivo waved and pointed into the distance. 'You come? I show you,' he shouted.

'You've got to admire the guy,' said Boz.

FIFTEEN

I was woken by the revving of an engine, the slamming of doors and the shout of 'OUTTA SIGHT! WE'RE GONNA HAVE A JOINT.'

This wasn't the sort of cry I expected to hear bellowed across a campsite at 7.30 am, especially in the Socialist Federal Republic of Yugoslavia.

I lifted the side of my tent and looked out. The commotion came from three guys in a VW campervan who had just checked into the campsite. They were the Americans I'd seen in Venice Lido, though they appeared to have jettisoned their women.

'Hear that? A van load of drug fiends,' I said to Boz who was in his tent a couple of feet away, 'we need to check those guys out.'

I couldn't get my head round Yugoslavia. It had a weird feel to it. To be honest I didn't know much about the place; all I knew was that Archduke Ferdinand had been assassinated in Sarajevo, and that kicked off the First World War. Whoops! How did that happen? I was also told that it was a communist country, but not quite. There were lots of police, lots of army and lots of teenage girls directing traffic. Wherever we went there would be some stern hottie blowing a whistle telling us where to cross the road. Hadn't they heard of the zebra crossing?

And then there was Joseph Broz Tito. People said that without him the country would be in meltdown. The states that made up Yugoslavia held deep-seated grudges and hated each other's guts. I remembered the words that I had glanced at in a guidebook in a bookshop: *'The six national republics that comprise Yugoslavia view each other with suspicion and sometimes outright hostility.'* They didn't seem to like strangers either.

Personally, I found them a surly bunch. In cafés we were always the last to be served. And Tito, well, there were pictures of him everywhere. He was tanned and good looking in an eastern European sort of way; certainly not your typical communist leader. And he was pictured wearing, get this, a white suit and a striped old school tie. Not a Mao hat and khakis, but a white suit! He looked like he'd just stepped out of the cricket pavilion. If nothing else, Tito had style. To my eyes he looked about as communist as a Hooray Henry on the playing fields of Eton.

But do you know what really surprised me about Yugoslavia? That it was *in colour*. I'm not kidding! It wasn't black and white. I remember in my school atlas the eastern European countries were all shaded grey. I once asked my teacher about them. 'They're communist countries,' she said in tone that precluded further discussion. This was not helped by the black and white Czech films, usually featuring massive steam trains, that I occasionally saw on a monochrome TV. So I always had in my mind that eastern Europe was cold, colourless and not a lot of fun.

The sun was already heating up my tent. It had that early morning smell of hot musty canvas. I put on a t-shirt and my purple loons and headed to the wash block. The Americans in the VW campervan appeared to be searching for something.

'Good morning,' I said as I walked past.

'Oh I say, good morning,' one of them repeated in a posh *faux* Terry-Thomas accent.

I walked straight on. I could hear them laughing. 'Goddamm Brits. What the fuck is he sleeping in? A Girl Guide tent?'

I walked over to them.

'A bit of advice, guys. I don't know about where you come from, but that stuff isn't exactly legal in this country.' To my surprise I could hear myself sounding like my father.

All three looked up at once. They had the assured look of invincible American youth.

'What are you saying, boy?' I wasn't too keen on this 'boy' business.

'What I'm saying is that you could get banged up. And probably arse-raped. That's all.'

'Don't bug us, man.'

I shrugged my shoulders. 'Okay.'

'We don't give a flying fuck. We don't give a flying fuck about anything.' He turned to his friends. 'Isn't that right, guys? We don't give a high flying fuck with wings. About anything.'

'I was just trying to be helpful,' I heard myself apologising.

'Well, go and be helpful somewhere else. Limey.'

Limey! I laughed. I couldn't believe I was being called a Limey. Did Americans still use that language?

'Forget it.' I said. I shook my head and walked towards the wash-block.

As I moved away one of them shouted, 'Hey, we haven't introduced ourselves.'

I turned round and this time two of them were smiling. I don't know why, but the mood had changed.

'My name's Brad, this here is Parker Boy, and he's Cheddar.' Brad had an *Easy Rider* Dennis Hopper moustache and thick dark stubble; he was the sort of simian guy you knew at school who was shaving every day at thirteen.

'Hi, I'm Felix.' I wondered if I'd misheard Cheddar's name. I didn't want to ask as he was still glowering at me through mirrored shades. They all shook hands with me in the polite way Americans do.

'Hey, we're going into Dubrovnik later on. Have a couple of beers, dig the town. I suppose that's legal, is it? Wanna come along?'

'Sounds good.'

'You wouldn't by any chance,' asked Brad, 'have a roach clip on you?'

'Sorry,' I said.

I'd never seen a roach clip. That's the great thing about travel, it broadens the cultural horizons.

'Are you okay?' asked Boz, who had been listening from his tent. 'Did I hear right that one of those guys is called Cheddar?'

'Yeah, I wonder why?'

'These Yanks have funny names. Next thing you know, we'll meet a Danish guy called Blue.'

'They've offered us lift into Dubrovnik,' I said.

'They sound seriously nuts,' said Boz.

'Yeah, I like them.'

*

The campsite notice board was covered by a mosaic of notes and messages. One of them caught my eye:

Looking for Aussie chick Nicola Eatcake travelling from London overland to India. Last seen in Venice. Tell her I'm sorry and I love her. I'm now heading to Athens. Bruce.

I was about to write a note asking for information on Gloria's whereabouts when I read what had been written in pencil below Bruce's plea.

Hi Bruce, I met Nicola in Sarajevo. She said you were lousy in the sack. I was happy to console her. Errol

I put my Biro away. Perhaps not. I didn't want to give Errol the opportunity of further sex therapy sessions.

*

From now on the sky was blue, day after day. I looked at the shimmering mountains. The violent heat made any sudden movement impossible. Even the cicadas had stopped their screaming.

'Goddam,' swore Cheddar, 'Where's my shorts? I gotta get these pants off.'

We were heading to Dubrovnik.

'I hear it's a mighty fine city,' said Brad. 'Do you know that it was once a nation state in its own right? Makes you think doesn't it?' It was too hot to think.

I was sitting in the back of the van with Cheddar while Brad, Parker Boy and Boz were riding up front.

Hey Jude was playing on the radio. We were all singing along. *La La La Laly La La Hey Jude!*

That was one good thing about my childhood years. I grew up with the Beatles, and they grew up with me. They were always there and we were in perfect syncopation. When I was twelve I was dreaming about love ('She loves you'), when I was 16 I was looking to expand my consciousness ('A Day in the Life'), and as I entered adulthood we were ready to go our own ways ('Let it Be'). They never let me down.

'You Brits and your Beatles,' said Brad.

'What's wrong with the Beatles?'

'"I want to hold your hand." That's so lame.' The Yanks all laughed.

I could see what he meant. 'It's romantic,' I said.

'West Coast Acid, that's real music. American music's got balls. Cheddar used to play in a band. Didn't you Cheddar?'

'Seems like a long time ago.'

'They did well,' Brad continued.

'What were you called?' I asked.

'The Meat Truck Explodes,' said Cheddar.

'Have you heard of them?' asked Brad.

'I think so.'

'The Chicago Plastercasters made a plaster cast of Cheddar's cock.'

'Oh man! I shrank like a wiener,' said Cheddar.

'He's being modest. He's right there alongside Hendrix and Jim Morrison.'

'Do we have to have this conversation?' pleaded Cheddar who looked ever so slightly embarrassed.

Brad continued. 'My point is that The Meat Truck Explodes used to support Jefferson Airplane and you don't hear Grace Slick pleading that she wants to hold your hand. She wants it up against the wall. Ain't that right, Cheddar?'

'I ain't saying nothing, man,' said Cheddar.

'I want to hold your hand was early Beatles,' I said. 'Paul McCartney's doing it in the road these days. He and Grace ought to get together.'

'Grace'd eat him alive. He wouldn't stand a chance.'

It was at this moment that Parker Boy spotted my passport.

'Look at that, WHAT IS THAT? A novel by Charles Dickens? You British and your Kings and Queens and your fancy passports. That's not a passport, that's a goddam library book.'

I liked our British passports. There was something solid and reassuring about the binding and the large coat of arms on the sombre navy blue cover. They were certainly so much better than the flimsy nappy-green Yank passport that looked like a Green Shield savings stamp book.

'I think you'll find that wherever you go in the world that this engenders respect!' I said.

'Respect! My arse!' said Parker Boy. 'I'll tell you what engenders respect. A WINCHESTER M14. A Winchester 14 gets all the respect you'd ever want, buddy.'

'You guys are unbelievable. And you wonder why they won't let Americans into places like Albania.'

'Don't worry. If we want to get into Albania, we get into Albania. It's just that we don't waste our time on such a tin-pot country with a dictator who's loose in the head.'

'What if Albania had oil?'

'Well, now you're talking!'

Cheddar took off his damp t-shirt and then without any embarrassment slid off his trousers. He didn't seem to be wearing any underpants. Even though I was looking out of the window, out of the corner of my eye I couldn't help but notice Cheddar's physique - no wonder the plaster-casters were keen to take a mould.

'Couple of beach bunnies up ahead,' shouted Brad. 'We'll offer them a lift.' I don't think Cheddar heard this.

The van slowed down and Brad leant out of the window.

'Where you going? Wanna ride to Dubrovnik?'

'Sure.' They looked like wholesome Scandinavian girls.

Unaware that Cheddar was sitting buck naked in the back of the van the girls pulled open the sliding door of the van.

'Oh my God!' they shouted.

Cheddar was as surprised as they were. 'Ladies!' Cheddar gasped. He seemed to be frozen to the spot.

'You dirty bastard!' one of the girls yelped. The other slammed the door closed.

'Drive!' shouted Cheddar as he pulled on his shorts.

'What the hell's is going on back there?' demanded Parker Boy.

'Just fucking drive!'

We sped off down the road, leaving the hysterical girls in a cloud of dust.

'Do me a favour, will you,' said Cheddar, 'the next time you turn this vehicle into public transport, give me prior warning? Yeah?'

We were all laughing. 'I've told you before, Cheddar,' said Brad, 'you may be hung like a horse, but it doesn't mean like you have to behave like you're in the rodeo.'

We found a bar just outside the city walls. Through a gateway I glimpsed a long straight promenade paved with white marble polished with age and flanked by elegant stone-fronted classical buildings. Later I intended to take off my plimsolls and feel the warm smooth surface of the stone pavement under my bare feet.

But before that I needed a drink. There were a few people that we recognised from the campsite sitting round tables under a spreading tree. Brad ordered local wine. The waitress brought a two litre flagon of the local Riesling. It was sharp and fresh with a slight bubble to it. You could drink it like lemonade.

It was a good place to sit and watch the travellers. Across the street, behind the bus stop, I was interested to see an illuminated neon sign which said *Club Bristol.*

I was beginning to notice that there was a freak hierarchy. The Scandinavians, with their flawless tans and long blonde hair were effortlessly cool. They were always clean and polite. The Dutch were sensibly radical. They had no hang-ups. To an English person they could be alarmingly straightforward. Politics, extreme drugs, child pornography; they could talk openly about anything. The Americans were loco; too much acid, too much Vietnam. Although if you'd been fighting the Vietcong I reckoned you'd got an automatic licence to be weird. At the top of the freak scale were the French. They were so darn crusty. They had attitude. Often they'd be accompanied by nasty brown hyena dogs. They didn't give a *merde* about anybody or anything; their mission was to piss right off the local straight population. At first I couldn't understand why they were so rebellious; generally the French are as straight as a steel rod. But of course they'd had their own revolution in 1968. They'd really done this stuff. The more rigid the society, the harder you have to work to break the chains. The French freaks had built the barricades and overthrown the government. And President de Gaulle, the hero of the Second World War, had been humiliated and done a runner. You couldn't knock what the French had achieved. And the French girls didn't wear knickers.

'Uh oh!' I spotted the two Scandinavian girls across the square. To my surprise they waved and started walking towards us. Both were blonde, brown and gorgeous. They seemed to have recovered from their shock.

'Hi! I didn't recognise you with your pants on!' The taller of the two said to Cheddar with a smile.

'Sorry. I was hot.'

'I could see that.'

She leant over and whispered in his ear.

'Yeah, that's right, The Meat Truck Explodes,' he said smiling.

The girl giggled and whispered some more.

Cheddar raised his eyebrows. 'Later', he said.

Brad ordered another jug of wine.

'So where you guys heading?' Brad asked.

'Let me show you.' I got out my diary.

'Is that your route map?!'

'My Grandmother gave it to me. It's got everything we need.'

'What's up with you guys? First your kiddie tent and then this? Are you on some sort of Lilliputian re-enactment trip?'

'We're travelling light.'

'I should say so.'

I pointed at a little black splot on the map. 'Next stop, Alb..'

'Albania huh? They boil people alive there. But as you said, they don't let us Americans in.'

'Is that because of the Vietnam war?' I asked.

'Nah, they don't want us to show them how to have a damn good time.'

Boz laughed. 'Coca Cola and Kentucky Fried Chicken! Yeah, you Yanks really know how to party,' he said.

Cheddar slowly stood up from his seat. 'Guys, I need to check my *poste restante* [4] and do a few other chores. Don't wait around for me.

---

[4] I don't like footnotes. This isn't some academic dissertation. But I ought to explain how people communicated overseas before email. In those pre-computer days, traveller's post operated through a system called *Poste Restante*.

You could, of course, use the phone. But it was not always available and it was liable to eat a chunk out of your wallet. There were also telegrams, but they were far too scary. For the recipient, telegrams meant one of two things: bad news, or that you were 100 years old.

So, if your loved ones back home wanted to make contact they would send a letter marked *Poste Restante* to your nearest post office. When you arrived in, say, Venice, you would check out the main Post Office, go to the *Post Restante* counter and ask for your mail. Generally, it was a simple and effective system. Although money was liable to go astray, for a simple onion-skin air mail letter *Poste Restante* worked just fine.

Brad, I'll see you back at the campsite.' Cheddar shook my hand. 'See you later, bud.'

Brad continued, 'So, assuming you get out of Albania without having your head poached, where then?'

'Greece.'

'The land of Socrates and Homer. The cradle of civilisation. Pity about the Generals though.'

I was beginning to like Brad. Apparently he'd studied politics and although his Mid West accent made him sound slow, for an American he seemed to be remarkably well informed about world affairs.

'I hear that they're not a big fan of free speech,' I agreed.

Boz had already told me about the Generals. He had explained that in 1967 there had been a military coup. A group of Generals, the Junta, had sent King Constantine packing and now ran the country as a military dictatorship. It was said, however, that the Junta's regime had recently become a bit shaky.

'Yeah, torture's legal there. Here's some advice. Never talk to the locals about politics. They get kind of edgy. You could get arrested; you could get them arrested. You don't want anybody getting their feet burnt on your account, do you? And of course it's all backed by the CIA.'

'How come?'

'We don't want those commie bastards sneaking into Europe through the back door. If it's a choice between extreme left and extreme right the CIA supports the fascists any day.'

'Rumour has it the Generals' days are numbered,' said Boz.

'Maybe. But there'll be another puppet government funded by the Yankee dollar lined up to take their place.'

'Anyway, we're heading to Crete,' I said.

'I've heard about Crete. At least it's more relaxed there.'

'We're going to a little place called Matala.'

'Neat,' Brad said stroking his unshaven chin. 'Sex-on-Sea, they say. Sounds far out.'

'You've heard about it?'

'Yeah, know all about it. Commune of freaks living in caves. Bit of a hippie vibe going on down there. Like *One Million Years BC*.'

'How do you know about Matala?'

'Met a guy who was heading there. Seemed like he was on a mission. English guy.'

'What was his name?'

'You remind me of him. I can't rightly remember his name. He had a girl's name... Adrienne. No, Adrian. That was it. Adrian.'

'That's not a girl's name.'

'I knew an Adrian in high school. She was certainly a girl.'

'Anyway, Adrian isn't the person I was thinking of.'

'You Brits have some funny names.'

'I suppose we do,' I said, thinking that Parker Boy and Cheddar weren't exactly out of the *Observer's Book of Baby Names*.

'Hey, I've got to apologize for Cheddar. He's a bit edgy at the moment. Good reason for it. He had to leave home in a hurry. He's never going back.'

'Because of the plaster cast?'

'Nothing to do with the size of his cock. He's been drafted.'

'Oh shit!' Back home in England pictures of American choppers and screaming children were on the news every day. During my travels I'd forgotten all about it. Vietnam seemed a long way away. Thank goodness when President Johnson asked for military support, our Prime Minister of the time, Harold Wilson, told him to get stuffed. America may think it rules the world, but we Brits don't just come running when the US wants to start interfering with other countries.

Brad continued. 'Conscripted. Fighting a war we don't believe in. School friends, barely adults, have come back in boxes, come back as quadriplegics. And even those who have survived are messed in the head.'

'What about you? Have you been called up? How do they do that?'

'The draft, it's a lottery, they pick a date, live on TV, as if it's a quiz show. This is a life and death situation yet they're treating it like family entertainment. *The Price is Right!* Bob Barker shouting 'Come on down! So we're all watching the show at my house, we've had a few beers to psyche ourselves up for the moment. Some grease ball puts his hand into the tombola and pulls out a number. The grease ball reads out the date: the 8th March. I watched all the colour drain from Cheddar's face - his birthday is the 21st March, only 13 days away. It's a goddam lottery and Cheddar's got the golden ticket. Unlucky thirteen, huh? I'm okay, my birthday is the 7th December. Precisely two-hundred-and-seventy-four days away. As soon as they announced the date Cheddar was off. He didn't even wait for the official letter.'

'I'd have done the same.'

'That was a couple of years ago. The irony is they've now abolished the draft - but Cheddar is still on the run. So do you Brits get called up to fight your wars?'

'We don't have any wars.'

'Bullshit, man. You're always invading some crackpot dictatorship or remote unprotected island.'

'We're not. Not these days. The days of the empire are long gone. We leave you Yanks to strut the imperialist stuff now.'

'What about Gibraltar? Cyprus? All those Caribbean islands?'

'They love us, they don't want us to leave.'

'That's not what I've heard.'

'They like us, more than they like you.'

'Man, they love the American way of life. Why do so many people want to move to the US of A? You should see the Mexican border, those Chicanos swarm across Rio Grande like rats from the Titanic.'

'Maybe, but tell me this,' said Boz. 'If the US is so great, why are you and your mates on the run?' I could see Brad wince. That hurt.

'That's another thing altogether. So, do you guys get drafted?'

'Why would we have conscription? If you want to join the armed forces in the UK you just sign up.'

'Who in their right mind would want to do that?'

'Some people do. They make it sound like you're going to be a welfare worker.'

I remembered the advertising hoardings, 'Join the army. Go abroad. Meet interesting people.' Onto which somebody would invariably scribble: 'Kill them.'

It hadn't always been like this. I can recall as a kid dreading the thought of conscription. All I knew about National Service came from 1950s black and white films. The hero, invariably some charmer like Dirk Bogarde, would receive his call-up papers the day after he had proposed to his fiancé. The windswept marching, the short back and sides, the gristly stews and the bullying sergeant major, all this was in the back of my mind while I was growing up. And then the relief of hearing that the call-up had been abolished. I'll never forget the moment, I must have been only about five or six at the time, and I was having my hair cut. The barber said: 'It's a pity they've got rid of National Service. You would have had a good time in the army.' In retrospect it was a strange thing to say to a kid; he was a lousy barber yet that was the best haircut I ever had.

'So Brad, what are you guys going to do?' I asked.

'The healing power of water is what we're after. But we made a big mistake. I didn't realise you couldn't surf in the Med.'

'Are you sure?' I'd never thought about this before.

'Your European oceans aren't up to much. You're not going to exactly shred the glass on the beaches round here.'

'The Mediterranean isn't an ocean.'

'We're making the best of a tricky situation. Before we started on this trip we made a pledge to each other. We're committed to having a good time and partying our way round Europe. This is our rite of passage. Nothing's going to stop us. So what if the ocean's as flat as a tortilla, there's still some beach bunnies around. In the autumn, after the Munich beer festival, we'll head back to the US. Sell the van in Earls Court, England, and then catch a flight. Parker Boy and I will be going back to the Mid West.'

Brad shook his head in exasperation. 'The Mid West! Ohio! Did you hear about that? First there were tanks on the freeway in Detroit. And then they gunned down the students at Kent State. They're not just sending their sons to war, they're also shooting them for complaining about it. It's crazy everywhere.'

I nodded. I'd seen the pictures in Rolling Stone magazine of the massacre by the National Guard and the four dead students laid out on the campus lawn.

'Cheddar will join the dodger community in Vancouver or somewhere else in Canada. At least from Vancouver you can look across the border and see the snow on Mount Baker. Must be weird for him to think he'll never again step on home ground.'

Brad was silent for a while. 'I don't want to think about this. Let's have another bottle of wine.'

I had a thought. I should have privately checked this with Boz first, but I was sure he'd be cool with the idea. 'Why don't you guys come along to Matala? We could have a groove.'

'Love to, buddy, Raquel Welch in her beaver skin bikini has a certain attraction. But getting the VW on the ferry would clear us out. The money's running low. The way things are looking we might have to go to Istanbul and encourage Parker Boy to sell a spare body part.'

'You could put Cheddar out to stud,' Boz suggested.

'Now that's not a bad idea.' Brad laughed. 'Anyway, we've got other delights to aim for. Munich. Beer in quart mugs and frauleins with jugs to match.'

We talked through the night. Brad told us about a guy he met whose drink was spiked in Turkey.

'He woke up the next day with a splitting headache and twelve inches of stitches across his abdomen.'

'How did the hospital explain that?' I asked.

'Who said he was in hospital? He was on somebody's kitchen table.'

I didn't believe Brad. 'It's the Greeks spreading anti-Turkish propaganda,' I said.

'I'm only warning you. You've got to watch your back in Turkey.'

'And your front by the sound of it,' I said.

I hailed our waitress. She was a pretty, dark haired girl with high Slavonic cheekbones. She smiled and I thought she winked at me. I was feeling good. I'd noticed how the Mediterranean climate softens the leathery north European skin. All that vitamin D being drawn into my veins made me feel healthy. My hair was now blonde. I'd lost some weight, my fingers had turned from stubby sausages to x rays, and more impressively my stomach muscles were tight. I reckoned this Mediterranean weather was so good it ought to be bottled and made available through the N.H.S. Admittedly, I could do with a shave and a scrub up, but I was ready for action.

Brad pointed at *Club Bristol.*

'I think we need to check out that place. Bristol, Ohio. That's only a couple of hundred miles away from where I was brought up. That's got to be an omen.'

'There's a Bristol in England as well. That's where I come from.'

'No kidding? How did that happen? We've got to get into that club. It's our destiny.'

Brad emptied the last drops of Riesling from the two litre bottle into his glass. 'Thank God this stuff isn't alcoholic,' he shouted. I noticed he could hardly stand up.

Not long after, I found myself walking down steps into a stone-floored cellar bar. The *Club Bristol,* which reeked of tobacco, warm bodies and stale alcohol, was lit by ultra-violet light. It didn't do much for Boz's looks. His face appeared pitted with smallpox scars while the ultra-violet light highlighted the stains and sweat marks on his T shirt. It looked as if someone had thrown a handful of salt in his hair.

'Man, you look a mess,' I said.

'You ain't no great shakes yourself,' Boz replied.

I looked in the mirror behind the bar. A zombie, with matted hair and eyes like hard-boiled eggs was staring back at me.

'Yeah, well this light doesn't do anybody any favours.'

I was pleased to see that the waitress from the bar across the square was already on the dance floor.

I shuffled over to her. The DJ was playing the hit of the summer, George McCrae, 'Rock you baby.' I circled round her, chest out, hand on hips, gurning Mick Jagger style.

She saw me and smiled and then, I don't know how, she was in my arms.

'Woman, take me in your arms, rock you baby.'

'You sexy, sexy man,' she said.

I wasn't used to this. Her breath smelt of garlic and cigarettes.

'What is your name?' I asked.

'Slobena.'

'Slobena. That is a beautiful name.'

'The men in Dubrovnik are not good looking. You are beautiful, sexy man.'

I looked over her shoulder to see if Brad and Boz were watching. Boz gave me a thumbs-up.

Slobena ran her fingers through my hair. 'You need a comb?'

'We're camping.'

'Huh. No matter.'

We were moving in perfect syncopation. Body language. It's the same the world over. I could feel the bones of her thin hard hips pressed against mine. I kissed her.

She was all over me! Are all communist girls like this? I might take those International Socialists a bit more seriously when I get back to Bristol. Her hands were everywhere. In my trouser pockets, even. It was like dancing with Shiva. Somehow I stumbled; an unseen leg had tripped me. The uneven floor had put me off balance and I was on the ground.

I looked up.

'Are you okay?' asked Brad, who was pulling me up from the floor.

'Yeah, fine. I need some fresh air.'

I looked around. Where was Slobena?

I stood outside. The stars were swirling in the night sky. The streetlights were so bright. I had to shade my eyes. The mellow Dubrovnik stone looked so enticing. All I wanted to do was to lie on that warm stone. I lay down. The pavement felt as soft as a cushion. I slept.

SIXTEEN

The yanks were cooking outside their campervan.

'What's for breakfast?' I asked.

'Zucchini. Want some?'

I'd never heard of a zucchini before. 'What's that then? We don't have those in England.'

'You don't have zucchini in England!'

'They don't grow in our climate.'

'How can you live without zucchini? They're a Class A vegetable. What vegetables DO you have?

'Peas, carrots, cabbage.'

'Are they the only things that grow in the English fog and rain?'

'Yeah, proper vegetables.'

'Cabbage. That's disgusting. You Limeys, with your boiled cabbage, you just crack me up. Gawd.'

'Oh, I forgot. And potatoes.'

There was something that Brad had said that I'd been thinking about. 'That guy who told you about Sex-on-Sea. Tell me about him.'

'I told you his name was Adrian.'

'Yeah, but what did he look like?'

'Gawd, I can't remember. We were in a dark underground club in Belgrade. I couldn't see further than the end of my cigarette. Have you been to Belgrade? It's a shit hole. Those communists, they just love their concrete.'

'Was he English?' For one ridiculous moment I thought Brad might have been talking about Plank.

'Yeah, he was English. But Belgrade! Posters everywhere; rules, rules, stupid rules. You cross the road in the wrong place and you get put in a work camp for six months. Imagine a city run by the state welfare office. Well that's Belgrade.'

'What did this Adrian look like?'

'Difficult to say. A rugged face. As I said, it was dark. You Brits all look the same.'

'Which is like what?'

'Where do I start? Bad teeth. Don't you have orthodontists in England? Then there's bad skin. Bad hair, Oh man, Brit hair. Walking Brillo Pads …'

'Not forgetting your sticky fingers,' Cheddar added.

I was beginning to regret this question. 'Is that how we really look to you?'

'… I haven't finished. Most distinctive of all, you Brits have pathetic little kiddie tents.' Cheddar and Parker Boy seemed to find this hilarious.

'Very humorous. But this guy, was there anything distinctive about him?'

'Come to think about it, apart from the bad teeth, the acne and the fuzzy hair, there was one thing.'

'And that was?'

'His jaw!'

'He had a big chin?'

'He had a head like a bucket. Even in the dark I could see that.'

'What!'

'Yeah, a face like a board.'

Of course! Adrian! That was Plank's real name. So Plank had out-foxed us. He was fast-tracking to Greece and had taken the express route through Yugoslavia. Admittedly going by Belgrade and Sarajevo had its risks, but this route could knock several days off his journey. Damn it. I didn't want to think about Plank anymore.

'So what are these zucchini?'

'They're like squash. Like baby squash.'

'Oh good,' I said. I was beginning to realise the limitation of my knowledge when it came to vegetables. I didn't know what squash was either. 'Do you always have this for breakfast?'

'That's all we got, boy. Big box of zucchini. We bought them from a woman down the road. This is what we're going to be eating for the next few days.'

Brad offered me a fork and pointed at the sliced courgette in the frying pan. 'Have a try.' Try everything once I thought. 'Go on, get stuck in.'

I put a slice onto the fork and carefully bit into it. It was fresh and clean and somehow green tasting.

'Good?' Brad asked.

'Very good,' I said. Though it wasn't quite as good as bacon and eggs.

*

'Felix, I think we might have a little problem?'

Boz had spent the last half hour writing figures down on scraps of paper. As time went by he scribbled with increasing intensity, heavily crossing out what he'd just written.

'What problem?'

'I've just been doing some sums and I'm a bit short of dosh.'

'Yeah?' I wasn't surprised. Boz was notoriously profligate with his money. I was surprised, however, that he was running short of cash at such an early stage of our trip.

We were travelling on a budget of about £1.50 a day. Out of this we paid for accommodation and food. We were continually hungry but it didn't matter. Breakfast would be coffee and maybe a bun, for lunch we would share a tin of sardines and a loaf of bread, and for supper we'd buy a kebab of indeterminate meat, again with bread, or occasionally boiled potatoes. If we weren't camping we would stay in basic rooms. The remainder of our cash went on beer or wine. At least in Matala the caves would be free.

'I've got less cash that I thought.'

'Not so much WE have a problem more YOU have a problem.'

'What date is it?'

'No idea.'

'Felix, we need to know the date. We've got some connections to make.'

'Eat less cake, that'll cut your costs,' I suggested.

SEVENTEEN

The little Fiat 500 drove away. We stood under a street light on what I hoped was the edge of town. Bats the size of pigeons were flying round the lamppost picking off moths and other flying insects. I could see their horrible hand-like claws sticking out of their wings. I wished I was wearing a hat.

Okay, I admit it, I'd messed up again. Earlier in the day Boz and I had said our farewells to the Yanks. We'd sworn eternal friendship and hugged like brothers going off to fight. We'd exchanged addresses and I promised if I was ever in Ohio I'd drop in.

To my surprise there wasn't a Dubrovnik train station, so the only way onward was to hitch. So we'd thumbed a number of lifts, mostly short rides. It was now getting dark and I was anxious that, despite our best efforts to keep on the coast road, we were many miles inland.

'So where are we?' asked Boz.

'Dunno. I couldn't read the sign. It was in Greek, or Cyrillic or something.' The local language was incomprehensible and the local scripts indecipherable. Over the last couple of days I had shown several people my little map - the reaction was always the same. They would stare blankly and then laugh. We seemed to have fallen into an Eastern European black hole.

'Felix, what the fook are we doing here?'

'Look, we know where we want to go. Yeah? At the moment we just don't know where we are.'

'So?'

'It's at times like this that we have to trust in fate,' I said.

'Yeah?'

'Basically, we're in a bit of a mess.'

'What exactly does that mean?'

'Okay,' I conceded, 'we're lost.'

'Felix, I don't know if I can trust you anymore, let alone fate.'

'What?'

'Sometimes you take things too far.'

'After all I've done for you. What do you mean?' I was indignant.

'How long have we got? You change plans without letting me know. You take me stupid places. Everywhere we go you let me down.'

'I let you down!'

'Yeah. You get pissed and crash out in a gutter.'

'So?'

'It's not a good thing to do. We're English.'

'English! Who cares?'

'I do.'

'You care? Since when?'

'I do. A bit,' said Boz.

'You're supposed to be my road buddy not my nursemaid. I bet Neil Cassady didn't have this trouble with Jack Kerouac.'

'Hey, I'm Dean Moriarty, not you,' Boz protested.

'No, I'm Dean. You're Sal Paradise.'

'No way! I'm more of a driver than you. '

'Actually,' I said, 'I've always thought of you as more of an Alan Ginsberg figure.'

'Piss off.'

I don't know why but we both laughed.

We started walking along the road.

'First Rule of the Road', he muttered, 'You only get a lift where there are vehicles.'

I could feel that Boz was still narked. We walked in silence. Eventually he said: 'Well if you'd listened to me, I could tell you exactly where we should be.'

'Yeah?'

'Yeah!'

'Where?' I asked.

'St Ives,' he said.

'WHERE?'

'St Ives. Swimming with pilchards in St Ives. Or even Morecambe.'

'Oh I get it. You're pissed off that you haven't had a blow job behind the rocks.'

'I don't know what I'm doing here, Felix? Here I am lost in the middle of Europe. There are places in Bolton that I've not yet been to. Smithall's Dean; The Hall in t'Wood. Legendary sights like that. I don't even know my own town, yet here I am fooked up and far away from home, lost in the middle of God knows where. I keep on asking myself, what am I doing here? Where are we Felix? Look around you. It's dark and we're on the edge of some dusty, dirty shanty town with nowhere to sleep. We don't even know what country we're in.'

Boz kicked the ground creating a small dust cloud.

'We'll find somewhere to crash,' I said.

'I keep asking myself, how come I've followed you all this way when I could be in St Ives. Where are the women that you promised? Where are the pilchards? This is like a bad acid trip. When am I going to come down?'

I could see Boz was panicking. 'We'll get a map.'

'A proper map?'

'Yeah. With roads and stuff on it.'

'And towns?'

'Yeah, and towns.'

'Would it mark churches with spires, post offices and trig points?'

'Yeah, all that.'

'And telephone boxes and footpaths.'

'Probably.'

Boz shook his head, and gave me a sideways look. 'And contours?' he asked.

'Yeah, the full one inch to one mile Ordnance Survey map if that's what you want. Now piss off.'

That's the brilliant thing about Boz: he gets angry for a couple of seconds and then lets it go. His bad moods are over as quickly as his one skin doobies.

'Boz, I promise we'll get something sorted.' I was hoping that when we got to Matala Blodwyn might be able to relieve him of his psycho-sexual tension. The cave would be very dark, that would help.

'Maybe, but I'm still not sure if I can trust you.'

We carried on walking down the road.

'What's the time?' Boz asked.

'Dunno. Late. We can either crash in a field or walk into town and see what's happening.' The night time temperature was dropping and I could smell the damp on the long dusty grass. 'There might be a late night bar,' I said hopefully.

I could hear the high revs of a distant motorbike. And then there was a lonely silence. Even though the temperature must still have been at least 25 degrees, I gave a little shudder. 'Let's head into town.'

The empty streets were dimly lit. We walked past small shuttered houses. A large grey dog, probably wild, slunk across the road and headed down a side street. There was barking from inside a house and a woman shouted.

'I'm not keen on dogs,' I said.

'I'm going to have a dog, a Border Collie, when I can,' Boz replied.

'Dogs like you. They sense the fear in me.'

'What's the problem? You just chase them away.'

'It's not that easy.'

'What you need to do is tickle their arse with a stick. That usually distracts them.'

'Are you sure?'

'If it doesn't, you just shove the stick right up.' He made it sound as easy as pushing a finger into a jar of Vaseline.

'I don't think I want to get that close.'

'If we have any trouble with dogs I think it's best if you leave them to me.'

We were now in a street lined with shops.

'I don't reckon this is the night-club part of town,' said Boz.

'It's difficult to know WHAT part of town this is.'

Boz pressed his face against a shutter and squinted through the metal grille. 'I can see brooms, dustbins and small agricultural implements.'

'Anything else?'

'A picture of Tito.'

'At least we know we're still in Yugoslavia.'

'I reckon this is about as lively as it gets round these here parts. We'd better find a quiet corner to crash.'

'Where do we go?'

'Somewhere quiet. Somewhere where we won't be seen. At least it's warm. There must be a park somewhere.'

We walked about some more. I felt surprisingly depressed; an empty town with no name, devoid of charm and nowhere to sleep.

'At least it's not raining,' I said. 'Think of doing this in England.'

'I've done this loads of times back home.'

'You have?'

'After a lock-in. Sometimes it's easier to crash than walk home.'

'Where do you sleep?'

'St Peter's churchyard.'

'I'm not sleeping in any churchyards.'

We looked in shop doorways and down rubbish strewn alleyways. Eventually we came to a small square in the older part of town. The ground was gravelly and there were some thin clipped bushes. It wasn't secluded, but by this time we were ready to crash anywhere. There were a couple of benches by a drinking fountain. I pulled my sleeping bag out of my bag and lay on one of them.

'It's not a cave, but it'll do,' I said. It was so quiet we were whispering.

'We can even clean our teeth,' said Boz looking towards the trickle that was coming out of the waterspout.

'This is okay, isn't it?' I was so tired I could hardly speak.

'Just right.'

'Your turn to make the tea in the morning.'

'Ha, bloody, ha.'

I didn't sleep well that night. It felt strange dossing in such a public place. All the time I was listening for people. Several times I was woken by dogs. One was so close to my face I could smell its damp meaty breath. After that I pulled the sleeping bag over my head.

I was woken with a jump by the clatter and rattle of a shutter being lifted. Although it was past dawn, I could still see stars in the clear early morning sky.

'Boz! We need to get up. There'll be people around here soon.'

We walked round the square. There was a faint smell of freshly baked bread in the air. I noticed a bent blue pole that might have been a bus stop. It had a faded notice strapped to it. We both looked at it.

'It's in Cyrillic.'

'Bloody hell.'

There was what looked like a municipal office with a red, white and blue flag flying from a small balcony. Otherwise, mostly shuttered shops edged the square. Someone opened a door and threw a bucket of water across the pavement. I hadn't realised that the town was overlooked by a dark granite castle.

'We ought to check that out.' said Boz

'Yeah, and the walls.' We both laughed

The first establishment to open on the square was a bar. Even before tables and chairs were put on the pavement I had noticed men in worn blue overalls going into the building. They entered bent and tired but ten minutes later appeared to leave upright and with a spring in their step. I wondered what they were up to.

We went into a small dark room. It smelt of strong coffee and cleaning fluid. A group of men were standing at the counter discussing a sheet of paper. Without a smile they eyed us up and then continued their heated conversation. Sitting at a table in the corner was a cluster of war veterans, wearing army fatigues, some of whom appeared to have lost limbs. I didn't think it polite to look too closely, but one man in a wheelchair seemed to possess only his upper torso.

The barman ignored us for five minutes and then shuffled over and nodded. We pointed at our fellow drinkers. Without a smile he walked away and pulled two small thick glasses from under the counter and filled them to the brim with a clear liquid from a bottle with an elaborate Cyrillic label. I remembered the guidebook had said that Yugoslavians drank an aqua vita called slivovitch for breakfast. This plum brandy was described as an eye opener. It appeared to improve the posture as well. It sounded just what we needed.

Like the men we'd observed in the bar, Boz and I knocked back our slivovitch in one. The extreme bitterness and high alcohol content had an interesting effect. All moisture evaporated from my mouth while my sinuses felt as if they had been freeze dried. I watched with fascination as Boz's eyes bulged and the blood vessels dilated; simultaneously a dreadful death rattle emanated from his lungs as he gasped for air. He slammed his glass down on the counter. 'Yeah, I'll have another one of those.'

As we walked past the town hall a smartly dressed woman came out of a side door and beckoned us. 'Come,' she ordered.

I wondered what she wanted. Surely it was too early in the morning to be soliciting for sex?

'Nien zimmer,' Boz said, thinking that she was offering us a room.

She pointed to a sign written in half a dozen scripts by the door, one of which said *Enthnographyc Musee*.

'You want to see the trousers of the revolution?'

'We should investigate' I said, 'this is what this trip is all about.'

'Why not?' said Boz.

'Do you speak English?' Boz asked the woman.

'*Rwy'n gallu siarad tamaid bach o gymraeg,*' was the woman's answer. The slivovitch was confusing me.

'Pardon?'

'I speak Welsh.'

I was intrigued. 'You speak Welsh?'

'I speak a little English, but mostly Welsh.'

We entered a gloomy hall that smelt like a dry old attic.

The woman led us over to a grey shop mannequin wearing just trousers and a gold braided military hat.

'See - Tito's trousers,' the woman said proudly. 'The hat is not his,' she added.

The woman stared at me expectantly. I wasn't sure what to say. I wondered when Tito had worn these khaki army fatigues. The hat was certainly more interesting than the trousers.

'Good!' I said nodding knowledgeably.

I looked around. The walls were lined with display cabinets and glass domes containing an unsettling collection of stuffed animals. Closer examination revealed mis-shapen bodies, contorted mouths and squinty eyes making these figures grotesque yet comical. They appeared to be mainly road kill or the maimed victims of shooting accidents mounted by an inexperienced taxidermist.

'We have nothing like this in the Bolton Museum,' Boz said. I could see he was on the verge of laughter.

I moved away from the freak[5] show to a series of flat-topped cases that filled the centre of the room. I studied dusty ancient objects and sepia toned photographs. It was difficult to detect a theme to this apparently random collection of artifacts. There was a pile of cannonballs, a collection of faded moths and a model, seemingly made of matchsticks, of what I guessed was the castle on the hill. There were pictures of peasant women sitting in doorways and of proud hunters with guns. One photograph showed a smiling moustachioed man,

---

[5] This is not a compliment.

blunderbuss on hip, posing next to the body of an enormous bear, several feet taller than him, strung from a hook. There were pictures of bison, wolves and a strange animal that I couldn't identify; it had the body of a human boy crouched on all fours but the teeth and facial hair of a dog. I gazed at a picture of a group of women sitting in a field in their oddly familiar traditional costume of shawls and lace. They wore stove pipe hats and appeared to be drinking out of cups and saucers.

'Here?' I asked the woman.

'No, Wales. A gift. Our town is brother [6] with Machynlleth. A very beautiful town. It has much rain. It is very lucky. Here we have no rain for many months. Every drop of rain is a drop of gold.'

Boz was admiring a large metal-jawed instrument. 'Look at this,' he said in awe.

'It must be a bear trap.'

'No, it's a man trap. I've seen them before. They used them on the Lancashire moorland estates in the eighteenth century. You put your foot on the plate in the middle and wham, that's the end of your poaching days.'

'Are you sure? If you got caught in that your body would be cut in half at the waist.'

'We're not far from Transylvania - this is probably the beginner's model.'

'You like?' asked the woman.

We both nodded. Though 'like' wasn't quite the word that expressed my feeling about this cruel instrument.

'Very good to catch Romany gipsy,' she said approvingly.

I found the museum's ambience strangely unsettling and was glad to go.

As we left the woman said *'Ffarwel,'* with a distinct Welsh accent.

---

[6] I think she meant 'twinned.'

EIGHTEEN

Leaving the squat in Bristol for the early morning shift was an unpleasant jolt to my biological clock. At the thin light of dawn Stoner would pick up Boz and me from the end of our street in the red Transit and take us to that day's checkpoint where we would meet P.C. Bixby. We would set out the cones along the road and by 6.00 am we were ready to stop the traffic. P.C. Bixby would oversee the traffic control while a couple of the team would ask passing drivers where they were going and why. Another task, one of the easier jobs, was to hand out questionnaires to passengers on the green double-decker buses. This involved a journey into town, waiting on the bus as it turned round, and then getting off as the bus passed the checkpoint on its return journey.

I found Stoner to be a considerate and supportive boss.

'I've got an idea,' Stoner said. 'I've been thinking about what you said about earning money for your travels. I'm going to set up a poker school. That'll be an excellent opportunity for you to top up your wages.'

'I know very little about cards.'

'I'll teach you. I'll explain the theory and then you can put what you've learnt it into practice.'

'John, you're too good to me,' I said, flattered by his attention.

'Don't thank me. It'll be a good team-building exercise. We'll start when we're put on the rural patrol.'

Stoner also understood that because of the repetitive nature of the job it was easier for us to work when we were gently kippered. The knack was to get the right balance. Lebanese Gold was a light resin particularly suited to the early morning shift. I felt it helped me relate and empathize with the public even if I occasionally stumbled over my words or lost concentration. Yet I was surprised how up-tight and aggressive some drivers could be. They only had to wait half an hour and they could see we were working as fast as we could. More than once somebody said 'What's this, a pop festival?' The Lebanese Gold could also induce paranoia: I always felt that P.C. Bixby was staring at me. When I looked at him he would smile and give me a cheery wave.

P.C. Bixby's constant presence made it difficult for us to take full advantage of our tea breaks. One of the team would be assigned 'pig watch'; their job was to keep P.C. Bixby under observation in the wing mirrors of the van. P.C. Bixby's every move would be monitored.

'Cool. Cool. Uncool. Uncool. Cool.'

Fortunately P.C. Bixby rarely came near the Transit. During his breaks he would sit in his panda car reading a book and smoking roll-ups. I noticed he never took his peaked hat off.

One day when Boz and I were leaving our house for the early shift Boz said 'I helped myself to a wodge of cake from the fridge for breakfast.'

The cake, which I'd knocked up from a packet of ready-mix and added an extra ingredient that Betty Crocker seemed to have missed out, was kept in the fridge so the mice couldn't eat it. I was rather pleased with my new and adventurous culinary expertise. I planned to take a chunk of this cake with me to the cinema to watch *2001 - A Space Odyssey*. As we caught the Transit to work Boz was uncharacteristically quiet.

'I'm feeling a bit weird,' Boz said as we arrived at our checkpoint. The special ingredient was kicking in.

It was due to be a heavy day. We were interviewing drivers by Horfield Common, on the Gloucester Road, a busy commuter route into Bristol. Interaction with the public would be fast; we'd have to work quickly if a tailback of traffic miles long was to be avoided. We already prided ourselves as a crack team, we couldn't carry lightweights. But by now Boz could hardly speak.

I had a word with Stoner. 'Put him on the buses,' Stoner said. I reckoned Boz could just about handle this.

I'd noticed that Boz had become one of Stoner's favourites. Boz and Stoner had an immediate bond that came from both of them being brought up in Bolton. For hours they would discuss the local football team, The Trotters, or talk about the merits of different late night shebeens, and more surprisingly, fishing, which seemed to be a popular pastime in the north west. They'd reminisce about the iconic clothing emporium Bowe's of Bolton where you could buy the high-waisted, baggy Falmer's jeans that seemed to be uniquely fashionable on the dance floor of Wigan Casino. More than once Stoner asked about Boz's sister.

All morning Boz zoomed in and out of town on double deckers, but he never quite negotiated the right moment to request the bus to stop. Every half hour I would see Boz through the window of a passing bus, his bewildered face increasingly like Munch's *Scream*. He would then continue to the end of the line.

It was obvious that Boz was becoming seriously distressed. I said to Stoner, 'I've got to go in there and get him.'

Eventually, with only a slight scuffle, I was able to escort Boz off the bus and put him in the back of the van. P.C. Bixby meanwhile seemed to have noticed Boz's dazed behaviour and appeared to be laughing uncontrollably. Boz spent the remainder of the day sleeping off his trip among the traffic cones.

*

True to Stoner's word, after a month of gathering urban transportation data our team was dispatched to the Somerset borderlands where we set up surveys in quaint villages with unusual and expressive names like Gurney Slade, Chewton Mendip and Nempnet Thrubwell.

The best days were when we were assigned quiet country roads. There might be a flurry of tractors and farming equipment being transported first thing in the morning and then again at about five in the afternoon, but the rest of the day we were spliffing up in the van or on sunny days crashed out by the roadside.

At quiet moments like this Stoner required the team to play cards. 'You either play or you interview,' he insisted. Cards were a good game as we could drop in or out as required. I was grateful that Stoner didn't let on to the team that he'd set this up to help me raise cash. Instead, he said he wanted to keep the team tight and card games would help the dynamic.

It was early afternoon on one of the quieter days of the survey that P.C. Bixby decided to take a walk.

'Cool. Cool. Uncool. Very uncool. Shit!' screamed Boz.

The back doors of the Transit opened and a cloud of smoke blew into P.C. Bixby's face. We looked at him in silence as he took in the scene.

'What's all this then?' he said in a mocking voice.

Stoner took a sandwich out of his bag. 'Lunch,' he said.

'Not that,' said P.C. Bixby, 'this!' He pointed at a half rolled spliff on my lap.

'Herbal cigarette for my asthma,' I said.

P.C. Bixby climbed into the van and pulled the doors shut. He sat on the bench and took off his hat to reveal a luxurious shoulder length pony tail. I wondered what he was going to do. 'Pass that stuff over here.' I looked at Stoner who was sitting at the front of the van. He had his hand on the door handle and looked as if he was preparing to break the four minute mile. I handed P.C. Bixby a piece of resin the size of an Oxo cube.

P.C. Bixby closed his eyes and sniffed the lump. He then broke off a corner, crumbled it between his fingers and put it in his mouth. He rolled it round his tongue, made a sucking noise and spat it out.

'How much did you pay for this?'

I wasn't falling for that trick. 'I don't know. It's not mine,' I said.

P.C. Bixby smiled. 'A bit of advice, sonny. Ventolin gives more effective relief for asthma than this stuff.'

'Thanks. I'll remember that.'

'Well lads, I think we've got a little problem to sort out.'

This was such a drag. Getting busted would really mess up my summer. I'd got some expensive train tickets to buy.

'The thing is,' continued P.C. Bixby 'this is really low grade shit. Whoever's supplying you is ripping you off.'

'Hang on a moment,' protested Stoner, 'that's quality Lebanese.'

P.C. Bixby looked at Stoner and laughed. Stoner realised he'd dropped into P.C. Bixby's trap. 'Quality Lebanese floor sweepings. Our dogs wouldn't piss on this.'

'It's good stuff,' Stoner protested.

P.C. Bixby shook his head. He felt around the rim of his helmet and produced a giant pack of Rizlas and a lump of something in foil.

'If you want good stuff, if you want a quality high, you want to try a bit of this.'

He unwrapped the foil to reveal a lump of liquorice-coloured resin.

'Now this,' said P.C. Bixby, 'is quality shit.'

'What is it?'

'Nepalese Temple. Made by Buddhist monks in the foothills of the Himalayas. The monks run naked through the fields and the pollen sticks to their sweating torsos. Their bodies are then scraped down. This,' P.C. Bixby held up a lump of resin the size of sugar cube, 'is premier cru. As pure as the minds of the Bhuddhist monks who make it. *Appellation controlee* by the Dalai Lama himself.'

'Yeah, but the sweat...' I wasn't too keen on the sweat.

'There's nothing wrong with that sweat. The monks live a clean life. Every month, at the full moon, during *puja*, they bathe in an ice cold rushing torrent. And do you know what that rushing torrent is?'

'Bloody cold?' I said.

Bixby gave me a pitying look. 'It's the source of the Ganges.'

Boz, who up till now had been unusually quiet, let out a low 'wow'.

'This little lump is distilled spirituality. With this you're knocking on nirvana's door. Take a toke on this and you'll think you're sitting next to God.'

'I've read about this stuff but never thought I'd get to see it,' Boz said. 'Where did you get it from?'

'Our dogs need a regular sniff to keep on form. And every so often I personally have to check that it hasn't reached its sell-by date.'

This was getting even more bizarre. Even Stoner had taken his hand off the door and no longer looked as if was about to make a run for it.

'Perk of the job, son. Mind you I keep clear of the hard stuff. That's left for the higher ranking officers.'

P.C. Bixby pushed open the back door of the van and said to Stoner, 'We'll discuss this again later. I'm sure we'll be able to come to a mutually beneficial arrangement.'

NINETEEN

We watched in silence as P.C Bixby walked back to his van. As he opened the door he turned and gave us a smile and a little wave.

Stoner wasn't impressed. 'I can spot a bullshitter light years away and when it comes to bullshitting Bixby glows like a beacon. No way is that Nepalese Temple. Bixby's trying to trick us.'

'Trick us! He's got us by the balls. Why would he want to trick us?' said Boz.

'There's nothing worse than a bent copper,' Stoner said.

'But he could have busted us there and then.'

'Did you see his pony tail?' asked Jacqui.

'I don't care if he's got an afro,' said Stoner, 'I still don't trust him.'

'It doesn't matter whether you trust him or not. We've got to play his game,' said Boz. 'And I didn't like what he said about the Lebanese Gold you supply us.'

'You haven't complained up until now. Divide and rule. He's trying to stir up trouble.'

So thirty minutes later Stoner walked over to the police van for a discussion with P.C. Bixby. I could see them in heated conversation. More than once P.C. Bixby reached for the notebook in his breast pocket, only to be hastily stopped by Stoner. At one stage I could hear raised voices and shouting. At last Stoner returned to the Transit with a smile on his face. 'Peace in our time, dudes,' he announced. 'I've done as best as I can for you lot. That Bixby drives a hard bargain.' Stoner was reluctant to specify exactly what had been agreed. Beyond stating 'you don't kick a pig to get pork' all he would say was that they had come to a mutually beneficial arrangement and that the team could carry on as before. P.C. Bixby, meanwhile, would be taking off a few extra hours during the day as he had a lady friend in a nearby village who was 'helping him with his enquiries.'

The weeks passed by and we settled into our roles. We'd play cards in the van while Bixby would absent himself on his secret missions. Communications with HQ were regular. One thing was bugging me, however. I'd been working for at least a couple months yet I had still made little money. The cause of the problem was obvious. Rather than giving me an opportunity to top up my wage, Stoner's card school was sucking my wallet dry. Occasionally I'd get an ace and feel that I was making progress. But more often than not my run of luck would be followed by Stoner scooping the board. Sure, we'd all win occasionally, but when it came to pay day and the big money bets Stoner would change gear and sweep the table.

I suppose it could have been worse. Mohan, a sweet trusting guy, was already spent out and was even reduced to borrowing money from Stoner. Stoner was sympathetic, offering wise words of advice. 'Mohan, only bet what you can afford to lose.' This didn't stop Stoner from fleecing Mohan for all he'd got, though.

I had to keep my resolve and remind myself why I was doing this job. The idea was to earn money to go travelling, to hitch up with Gloria, and to live with her in a cave in a state of sexual bliss. Yet at the moment progress was slow and I felt as if I was wading through waist deep sludge.

And then we began to make mistakes. Stoner was concerned the dataheads back at HQ would spot inconsistencies.

It was an early misty morning. I was sitting by a campfire we'd built to keep away the damp. Mohan was strumming gently on his guitar. *'Suicide is painless, it brings on many changes,'* he whispered.

'Felix,' said Stoner. 'I've had a complaint from the data crunchers. Your handwriting is unintelligible. Look at this,' he held up one of my record sheets. 'It looks like a Jackson Pollock.'

'It's the clipboards. We need better clipboards.'

'It's not the clipboards, its Bixby's Nepalese temple.'

'When you're knocking on nirvana's door, in the cosmic scale of things, handwriting doesn't seem that important.'

'Don't blow it for everybody else, Felix. Stick to the Lebanese Gold. We don't want to do anything to attract the attention of HQ. They get a bit twitchy about teams working on the Somerset Levels. They think we're going to sample the local natch and turn feral. I don't want them to pull us back in. I didn't join this company to be a desk monkey opening envelopes. Remember what happened to Sanchez's team.'

We'd all heard stories about Sanchez and his team; crack sociologists who had gone off the rails. The further away they went from base, the more unreliable the data. The strain had been too much. Eventually Sanchez received orders for the team to return to HQ and undertake a month's office duty. The story goes that their van was eventually found abandoned in dense woodland in the Forest of Dean. Apart from a few clipboards and HB2 pencils they had left no trace. Sanchez and his crew were the *Marie Celeste* of the roadside survey world.

Meanwhile, now that Bixby was no longer off bounds, I was interested to know more about him. You don't often see a policeman with a ponytail.

'What are you reading?' I asked Bixby.

'Nothing.'

'I've seen you in the van. You were reading a paperback.'

Bixby opened the glove compartment. From among the usual police paraphernalia of gloves, handcuffs, and Rizlas he pulled out a paperback book with a black and white picture on its cover of an androgynous young man in a high tab-collared shirt.

'*Tarantula* by Bob Dylan.'

'Any good?'

'I've only just started. Like all good literature there are some universal truths in here. They are just a bit difficult to find in this volume.'

We'd talk about books and poetry. Bixby had read Eastern philosophy and some of the Buddhist texts. '*The Dhammapada, The Tibetan Book of the Dead*, they were interesting.' Bixby fancied himself as bit of a philosopher. He pointed out to me the middle two letters of life spell 'if.'

'Can I ask you a personal question?' I said. 'How did you get into this?'

'What?'

'The police.'

'Why?'

'You're the first Buddhist policeman I've come across. If you don't mind me saying, you're not a typical cop.'

Bixby laughed. 'There's no such thing. Look beyond the uniform, we're all different.'

'But all police are bastards.'

'Once I was like you. I was young, I had no particular place to go and fell in with an interesting crowd. In those days we were called beatniks. We liked jazz; this was before the Beatles and the Rolling Stones. I fancied myself as an artist and for a while I went to art school but, I don't know, I couldn't see the point of it.

'I used to go to a snooker club called the *Rue de Bois* above Burtons in Wood Street, not to play snooker, but because it was open for afternoon drinking. The inevitable happened. I got busted for a little bit of marijuana. In those days possession was a very serious offence, you could get banged up for years.

'You'd think I would be freaked. Yet considering the dodgy situation I was in I was surprised how calm I felt. I'd been doing a lot of meditation. As they shoved me into the slammer it was as if I was watching myself through plate glass; I was detached, I felt like I was in a dream, no, it was more like a film. I thought the police were interesting. You know what they say, inside every rebel there's a policeman struggling to get out.'

'I've never heard that before.'

'James Dean said it. Anyway, at that time the police were having trouble with the good cop/bad cop concept. When they dragged me in for questioning the good cop lost his temper and threatened me with a beating. I blame it on *Softly, Softly*. Everybody wanted to be like bad cop Barlow. Good cop Frank Windsor acted like he had a dildo up his arse.

'So I ended up with two bad cops questioning me. I could see they had a problem. This got me thinking. How about a Buddhist approach to police interrogation? I could do the good cop business. So I applied.'

'But you'd got a record for possession, didn't that preclude you?'

'Far from it, it takes one to catch one.' Bixby gave me a knowing wink. 'They must have been desperate, I took the selection test and they offered me the job.'

'But being a cop, how do you sleep?'

'Felix, most of the police are okay. As Laozi says 'There is dignity in all work'. It's only a few that are mean and out to get revenge for their own messed up lives.'

TWENTY

Stoner and I were sitting in the front of the van, Mohan was on traffic duty while the rest of the team were crashed out by the roadside in the thick grass.

'So tell me, what happened to Sanchez? What's the full story?' I asked.

'Ah, so you've heard of Sanchez,' said Stoner gravely.

'Yeah, because you're always talking about him.'

'You don't want to know.'

'I do.'

'It's not something that I like to dwell on.'

'John, it might be good to unload.'

Stoner was silent. He stared out of the window at the flat dullness of the landscape as if he was weighing something up. He twisted the ends of his moustaches. It was a quiet, unseasonably warm yet cloud-laden, afternoon on the Somerset Levels. After what felt like an uncomfortably long time, he took a deep breath and turned to me.

'Sanchez was a good man. We worked together in the early days. You could say Sanchez fixed this whole gig up. He trained as a sociologist at the LSE. He was one of the best transportation theorists in the country; he sure knew his stuff, and what he didn't know he'd find out. He was willing to go that extra mile, ask that extra question. He was always pushing the boundaries. He was a maverick. In the end, that was what did him in.'

Stoner wound down the window of the van and gave a thumbs-up sign to Mohan who had been standing by the roadside for the last two hours. 'It's important to keep staff motivated,' said Stoner.

'Was Sanchez his real name?'

'I don't know. It suited him, he had a big Zapata moustache. I think he came from the West Midlands, Stourbridge, that part of the world.'

'So what did Sanchez do?' I asked.

'Well, first he extended the survey to Forest of Dean. I remember warning him. 'You'll need a different paradigm for the Forest. The figures won't make sense, Sanchez. The long term traffic projections will be too off beam.' But he wasn't having any of it. 'I'll spot the coordinates,' he'd say.

'What's so special about the Forest of Dean?'

'You've never been there have you?' said Stoner. He phrased this in a way that sounded more like a warning than a question.

Stoner continued, 'As luck would have it the coordinates were okay. But Sanchez got greedy. We all got greedy. HQ was impressed by what he was coming up with. You've got to understand, it was at a time when a lot of people were interested in this stuff; the Government, the Ministry of Transport, local authorities. Think about it, Spaghetti Junction, the East Lancs Road, marvels of civil engineering had just been opened. The car was king; they wanted to build urban expressways everywhere. Even in the countryside. Anything was possible. The company had cornered the market. The bosses were making money, Sanchez and his team were racking up bonuses. Why should he stop? So they went a little further, and then further still.

'I remember the day when he told me he was taking the squad up to Cinderford.

'I pleaded with Sanchez. 'Don't do it, man.' I could see the Forest had already taken its toll. I didn't know in what state of health he was going to come back. He'd become obsessed by numbers and their mystical relationships to each other. He'd told me he wasn't sleeping, he had the sweats; I'm sure he was taking medication.

'Even the bosses were worried. In the end they authorised just one team and half a dozen road counters. It's as if they knew.

'Sanchez was adamant, but by now he couldn't see what he was doing, he was strangely obsessed by certain numbers. He wouldn't listen to sense. So they set off. For the first few weeks HQ received regular reports. The usual stuff, just setting the scene and laying down the parameters. But then the intelligence started to get weird. Rumour had it that Sanchez had recruited some native foresters to provide local knowledge. It was a risky strategy. He began to upset an awful lot of people out there. The people of the Forest are unsophisticated country folk, they get suspicious, they don't understand. They taunted us by removing the cones and putting them on fence posts. They were sabotaging some of the roadside equipment. The vehicle counters - those rubber tubes we put across the roads - were being ripped up and used for illicit purposes.'

'Illicit purposes? What sort of thing?'

'Use your imagination.'

I used my imagination and still couldn't come up with anything.

Stoner continued. 'Sanchez was raising awkward questions; the foresters thought he was asking things that shouldn't have been asked. People don't like their movements being mapped. It was none of his business.

'Communications were poor, nobody knew Sanchez's precise location. Most of the public phones were inoperable or had been vandalised. The lines were unclear and likely to cut out without warning. The woodland damp does that. Even so, every now and again Sanchez would register a call from a telephone box in a remote village.

'Nothing made sense. Sanchez must have realised this. He was too far out of the zone for the figures to work. The computer back at base was being overloaded. It was as weak as a house of cards. Valves were blowing all over the place. It was in danger of crashing, and pulling several other projects down with it. It was now the beginning of December. There's a strange micro-climate in the Forest of Dean. A bone raw mistral wind whips along the Severn Estuary and up the Wye Valley. HQ said Sanchez must be back by Christmas.'

Stoner was staring out of the window. I followed his gaze. Mohan was standing with his knees slightly bent - it looked like he was busting for a pee. Stoner looked at his watch and wound down the window.

'Mohan, couple more hours, and then you can change over. Okay?' I heard Mohan give a strangled grunt of acquiescence.

'And that was it. Suddenly it all went quiet. The wire went dead. Nothing more was heard from Sanchez and his little team.'

'Why didn't they just come back?'

'Sanchez wasn't the sort of guy to come back. 'Quitting's for losers,' he used to say. This was his life's work, his whole career rested on it. You're only as good as your last job. At HQ everybody was freaked. They felt responsible. At one stage they sent out a rescue team. But Sanchez was clever. By that time he'd won over the foresters.'

'How did he do that? Was it the rubber tubes?'

'He bought them drinks in the pub. But more important, he showed them things. He broadened their minds; he'd sit in the pub and talk. They'd sit round the inglenook fireplace and he'd talk about what he'd seen and what he'd done. Oh, how he'd talk. Until you've met Sanchez you wouldn't know how a man could talk. He'd tell them about Marx and Engels. The foresters would listen, their heads bowed, hearing about a world they could only ever dream of.

'They'd ask earnest questions about far away places. Gloucester, Cheltenham. He told them about the new overspill town of Swindon. He won them over, they recognised somebody with a superior knowledge. They respected him.

'So he set the locals on the rescue squad. The forest can be a dangerous place. The mists come down quickly. Without warning visibility can drop to nothing and you can get disorientated. You begin to image things - wild boar the size of cattle, web-fingered foresters, eyes in the wood, watching. In that sort of environment you need local knowledge. It was cat and mouse, and the mouse didn't stand a chance. Of course, HQ tried to hush it up.

'But you can't hush up a thing like that. Sanchez became a legend, people admired what he did. Pushing the boundaries! He enlarged people's minds; they saw what could be done.' Stoner threw his arms open wide and stared at me. 'But at what cost?'

'So what had happened?' I'd got a feeling that I'd heard this tale, or something like it, before but I couldn't quite place where.

Stoner gave a dramatic pause and then slowly shook his head.

'God alone knows. Sanchez had looked into his soul and gone mad. The horror, the horror! The Forest of Dean does that to you.'

'It can't be that bad!'

'Ah, the cold heart of Cinderford!' Stoner muttered. 'One by one the team slowly drifted back to HQ. They were pathetic and broken, only fit for desk jobs. But of Sanchez, not a sign. That's the mystery. In the spring Sanchez's van was found hidden in the undergrowth.'

'Is he still alive?'

'There are rumours, of course. Some say he's living as far away from roads as you can get. Others say he's left the country and is holed up somewhere trying to forget that the wheel was ever invented.'

'What do you think?'

'I reckon that's not the last we'll hear of Sanchez. He's out there somewhere, of that I am certain.'

Stoner pointed to Bixby's car. 'Part of his job is to make sure we don't extend the boundaries. He's got nothing to worry about. Felix, I ain't about to do a Sanchez.'

TWENTY ONE

We hauled ourselves off the back of the pick-up. The two guys who had given us a lift from the town-with-no-name pointed down a long straight track to a cluster of huts, the Yugoslavian border post, perhaps half a mile away. They seemed to be in a hurry to leave. They waved and smiled and gave us a thumbs-up. Despite this bravado I could detect a tremor of concern. They swung their vehicle round and disappeared along the road in a cloud of dust.

In the distance I could see a red and white barrier blocking the road flanked by a wooden hut on each side. There wasn't a soul to be seen. We walked through the shimmering heat. Goat bells echoed from the distant hills.

So far our navigation round Europe had been straightforward. My strategy to follow the sun seemed to have worked. Sure, we'd been lost for a couple of days but that happens to everybody. There was, however, a pinprick of concern lurking in my mind. If everything went according to plan we were soon to visit Albania. Yet apart from the risk of getting our heads boiled, and having a dictator that made Uncle Joe Stalin look like a *Blue Peter* presenter, I realised that I knew very little about the country. My diary map wasn't much help. Other than the name - abbreviated to Alb. - not a single thing was marked; no capital, no roads, nothing. I also noted that Albania was shaded in black. I don't know why but I had a bad feeling about that.

We talked loudly as we approached the sheds.

'Hello!' Boz shouted. I knocked on a blue painted door that was ajar. 'Hello, anybody there?' I cautiously pushed the door open. The room contained a stained wooden table with several rubber stamps on it, a couple of metal chairs and a kicked-about filing cabinet. In the corner of the room was a stainless steel wash basin. Looking down from the wall was a gilt framed picture of Marshall Tito.

'I'm worried about that wash basin,' I said.

Boz walked over to it. 'I think you need to be more worried about the rubber gloves in the waste bin.'

'We need our passports stamped. What are we going to do?' I said.

'I don't think we have to worry about our passports,' Boz replied.

'Do you think we can just go on? What about the barrier?'

'We just walk around it. Or if you really wanted to you could limbo under it.'

I liked the idea but thought it could be interpreted as disrespectful. 'Too hot for that,' I said.

We sat for five minutes in the shadow of the hut. For a border crossing it was eerily quiet.

'They must be having lunch,' Boz said.

'I'm getting thirsty,' I said. 'We need to move.'

We walked round the barrier and into no man's land. 'You can't say we haven't tried,' I said. I was trying to reassure myself that this was a sensible thing to do.

Even now I was waiting for a shout. I imagined eyes watching from afar.

'Don't keep turning around,' said Boz, 'it looks suspicious.'

The border must have been about half a mile away. There was nothing to indicate that we were leaving Yugoslavia or that we were entering Albania. The road was a rutted track with dead grass in the middle. There wasn't a tree in sight in this yellow savannah. There was no wind. It was as hot as the devil. I could feel the heavy baking air as I walked though it; I could feel the searing heat of the road through the thin soles of my plimsolls. Why had I got rid of my desert boots? Surely there was a hint in the name that they might have been a better choice for these arid conditions.

'It's quieter than I expected,' I said.

'Maybe it's Sunday?'

'I'd expect more traffic on a Sunday. People visit friends and family on a Sunday.'

'Anyway, I don't think it is Sunday.'

I could see something ahead in the straight road. In the haze it looked like a tin can, but it was moving.

'What's that?' I said. 'A mine?'

'Yeah, a mine on legs.'

I could now see what it was. 'It's a tortoise!'

The Albanian checkpoint was more substantial. The road was flanked by flat roofed concrete buildings while the way was blocked by battered oil drums. A large red flag adorned by a black eagle flapped languidly.

I could see two men talking animatedly. They had rifles, Kalashnikovs probably, slung across their backs. One of them was jabbing his finger at the other. They were standing too close to each other for this heat. As we got nearer I could hear that they were talking in raised voices; they were shouting. I don't think the soldiers had noticed us.

Boz looked at me. 'Don't let them see you're a south paw.'

'Sometimes you don't know when to let up, do you?'

'At least they haven't got dogs,' said Boz.

'You like dogs.'

'Not nark dogs.'

The sight of those rifles made me think. Perhaps this wasn't such a good idea. Perhaps we should have waited at the Yugoslav checkpoint. I looked at Boz. He was gazing ahead, smiling. The white light from the midday sun was making my eyes water. We were now within fifty metres of the guards. I lifted an arm and waved.

'Hi!' I shouted.

'Don't wind them up. These customs people are always on a power trip. Rule of the Road Number Five: respect men with rubber stamps.'

The two men had stopped arguing and were staring at us.

'Hi there!' I shouted again. The soldiers didn't move. 'Is this Alb.?'

'That's a stupid question. Anyway it's Albania.'

'Okay, you say something. Have you got your passport?' I asked.

'Yeah, in my pocket.'

'I think we ought to have our passports ready. No sudden movements though.'

I looked at Boz. 'How's your Albanian?'

'As good as my Serbo-Croat.'

We walked up to them, big smiles, arms outstretched, our passports in our hands.

The sun was nearly directly overhead. The guards had moved and were now pressed against the wall of the bunker standing in the shade. We were in the full blast of the brutal heat. I don't know why but I didn't like the look of them. They were both dark haired: one had a pock-marked face that clearly made shaving difficult. I also noticed that the backs of his hands were matted with black hair. The other was clean cut except for a drooping Balkan moustache.

Boz gave his big charming smile. He pointed down the long road. 'Nobody there.' He waved his hands in front of his chest. 'Nobody there,' he repeated.

The look on the men's faces was not welcoming. I felt like we were intruding on something. The man with the pock marks reminded me of a pineapple. He seemed angry. He shouted at his colleague. It was clear that he was speaking rudely to the other guard. On closer inspection, the rifles were antiques, pre-First World War, the sort of gear I was conscripted to use in the school Cadet Force. There was an odour of cooked cabbage in the air. Balkan moustache took our passports and flicked through the pages. He looked at my photograph and without a smile glanced at me. He then checked the pages again. He seemed to be looking for something.

Balkan Moustache made a deep throated noise, and handed our passports to Pineapple Face. They both stared at us. They then started yelling at each other. Out of the blur of shouting I thought I recognised two words. I'm sure Balkan moustache said 'Dirty Hippies.'

I didn't like the way this was going. Hippie equals drugs equals big trouble equals full body search. I remembered what Plank had said. Was this where I got arrested for looking like a freak?

I glanced at Boz. Almost imperceptibly Boz shook his head. I guessed he was thinking the same thing. They pointed at my passport and jabbered something that I thought might be to do with the absence of exit stamps.

'Nobody there,' Boz said.

'*Niet.*' I added. I though they might understand Russian.

They obviously did. The man stuck his jaw out and through a tight mouth said: 'Weezer.'

I looked at Boz. 'What's he saying?'

'Beezer?' Boz suggested.

'That's just stupid.'

'Weezer,' the man said, loudly and more aggressively.

'Oh visa,' Boz said.

Nobody had asked us for a visa before.

'No visa,' Boz replied.

The guard shook his head and pointed to the shimmering road. 'No weezer.' He was ordering us to go back. There was no arguing with him.

Balkan Moustache strode over to a desk, took a pair of scissors out of a drawer, and started clicking them in a menacing way. I didn't understand. I didn't want him mutilating my passport.

'Let's go,' Boz said.

'Go? Go where?'

'Back to the Yugoslav border.'

'What? We can't go back now.'

'Let's go before something happens.' Suddenly Boz was looking anxious.

'Why?'

'There's no point. We haven't got a visa.'

'Boz, why are you looking at me like that? It's freaking me out.'

'Bad scene, man. Let's just go'

'I don't understand, what's the problem?'

'C'mon Felix, let's just go. It's too hot standing here.'

'But we've walked all this way.'

'Yeah, and we've got to walk all the way back again. Let's get started.'

'Do you think we could ask them for a drink?'

'No!'

'Just some water?'

'No. We need to leave. Now.'

'He's got our passports.'

'Please,' Boz said, pointing to our passports which were still in the guard's matted hand. The guard smiled; but there was no compassion in his eyes. With our passports in our hands we started the long hot walk back to Yugoslavia.

'What's wrong with you?' I said as we moved away.

Boz was silent until we were out of earshot of the guards.

'I think they were getting ready to give us a haircut.'

'You're kidding.'

'And I'm not talking about a trim of split ends.'

'Did you see that guy's hands. I thought he was wearing gloves.'

'I didn't notice.'

'They were the hands of a werewolf!'

'I don't reckon they get much business,' I said. 'They seemed surprised to see us.'

'A haircut or an internal examination - it's not much of a welcome. No wonder Albania doesn't have a tourist industry.'

'It's a pity. I was looking forward to tasting an Albanian cabbage pasty.'

'Fermented cabbage pasty!' I corrected Boz. 'That's a culinary experience I won't regret missing.'

Either the heat was getting to me or Boz's nervousness was catching. As we walked away from the checkpoint I imagined a rifle focused on my back. It might be a blunderbuss, but it could still do collateral damage. I could feel the exact point on my neck where the shot would enter. Even though I was wet with sweat I shuddered. Something in me seemed to have snapped.

'We don't even know where we are. I don't like this, Boz, I really don't like this.' I could hardly swallow, my mouth was so dry.

'Felix, relax.' Boz seemed calmer now.

'It's the heat. My shoes are melting and my bag feels like a lead weight. I should have bought a rucksack and I need a hat. Why haven't we got hats?'

'Hats are daft.'

'There are times when you need a hat. If we ever get out of here I'm going to buy a baseball hat.'

'Yeah, we'll buy hats.'

'If they start firing, you dive to the left and I'll dive to the right. That way one of us should survive.'

'Shut up Felix.'

The land was deserted. Even in the most inhospitable and deserted landscape there was always a young boy looking after a goat or an old man pushing a stick. But here there was nobody.

The cruel heat. The sun was like a sledgehammer. My throat was tight; I could hear the blood in my ears. I was becoming destabilised by dehydration. I could still feel that rifle focused on my back. Never in my life had I felt so vulnerable.

'Out here anything could happen. We're in no man's land. There are man traps out there. Those guards could be bored and take a pot shot at us to liven up the day. How do you know one of them hasn't had an argument with his wife and wants to take it out on two freaks?'

'Why would they do that?'

'You saw them, they were angry. Nobody would find out.'

'GUNNED DOWN IN NO MAN'S LAND.' I could see the headlines. Why had I come on this stupid trip? I never imagined my life ending like this. My body left under the white sun, slowly nibbled to the bone by tortoises, never to be found. Boz was right; we should have gone to St Ives. In St Ives they don't have mad, disturbed snipers shooting at strangers. Right now I could be swimming with pilchards. I was going to die and I hadn't had my squeeze from Gloria. I hoped Mum had got my postcard.

'Get a grip, Felix. The heat's getting to you. This is a border crossing. Not a firing range.'

Half way between the two checkpoints we came across the tortoise walking down the middle of the road. Boz picked it up and rubbed the shell under the tortoise's chin. A dry head poked out; it opened its mouth panting for air. 'Know how you feel little fella,' said Boz, as he gently put the tortoise in the weak shade under a dry shrub.

'Do you know,' I said, 'I never realised tortoises were carnivorous.'

'They're not.'

'That one is. He had a funny look in his eyes. Definitely a meat eater.'

'You need to get out of this sun.'

'I need a hat.'

I squinted through the shimmering heat.

'Boz, can you see what I can see?'

I couldn't be sure. But it looked like there were a couple of people in uniform standing outside the Yugoslavian control post.

'Yeah, two people guarding the control post, when before there were none.'

'Shit! Are you thinking what I'm thinking?'

'What I'm thinking,' said Boz, 'is that nobody, neither Yugoslav nor Albanian, has stamped our passport.'

The two guards stared at us intently as we appeared through the haze. I felt so exhausted I thought I was going to cry. But I didn't have the energy.

'Leave it to me,' said Boz.

TWENTY TWO

This was crazy. After several months working on the West of England Transportation Survey I was beginning to realise what a mug I was. I still had no more cash saved than when I'd started the job. Okay, true to his word, Stoner had supplied some good shit at the end of the month but I was still without any money.

All I knew about poker I had learnt from Stoner. Stoner acted like a Zen Master. 'You must follow my teachings and do exactly as I tell you. Only when you have reached the highest level of cardmanship can you stray from the path of learning and devise your own strategies.' 'When will that be, O wise man?' 'When you play with wisdom and clarity.' 'And how long will that be?' 'Many years, Grasshopper.'

The problem was that I was his disciple and he could read my every move. I needed to break away; I needed to come up with my own strategies. But did I understand enough about the game to do this? I'd only got another couple of weeks on the survey before I was due to leave. I had to get my priorities right and spend more time playing cards.

Meanwhile Boz had handed me five new £5 notes. 'Here's my cash for the Eurorail ticket.'

'I'm going to buy the tickets in a couple of weeks' time,' I said.

'Can you look after the money for the time being? You know what I'm like with cash.'

'Yeah, sure.' I was impressed. Normally, Boz had little respect for the discipline of regular saving and was a frequent visitor with his stereo system to Raselles, the pawn shop in Old Market. I was even more impressed by the fact that he trusted me.

One evening I had a look through *Casino Royale*. I remembered there was a gambling scene featuring James Bond and his arch rival from THRUSH.[7] I flicked through the pages looking for inspiration. Bond had lots of cold baths, something that I wouldn't be doing. I also noticed that he smoked over seventy cigarettes a day. No wonder he needed the baths.

Ian Fleming said the game revolved around luck and that you had to treat Lady Luck like a sexy woman; you had to caress her, cajole her, make her your mistress. This was obviously my problem, so far Lady Luck had proved a reluctant visitor. What could I do to attract her? If she didn't come hammering on my door soon I was going to be in big trouble.

It was at about this time that Boz came up with an interesting idea. Stoner had told us that HQ were hassling again about targets. 'We've got to keep focused,' Stoner kept on saying.

'It's easy, we make the numbers up,' was Boz's response.

'What?'

'Those targets aren't going to just go ahead and hit themselves. We make up those little shit-kickers. We count the cars as they go by and guess where they are going and why.'

Stoner didn't seem bothered one way or the other. 'So long as HQ keep off our backs I don't care.'

'But that's unethical,' I said.

'Since when have you been worried about ethics?' said Boz.

'The British Association of Sociologists has a strict ethical code and I'm sure making up evidence isn't part of it.'

'I didn't know you were a member of the British Association of Sociologists?'

'I'm not a member yet, but one day I will be.'

---

[7] It was actually SMERSH. THRUSH was the arch enemy in the Man from Uncle. (THRUSH stands for Technological Hierarchy for the Removal of Undesirables and the Subjugation of Humanity.) Ed.

'Meanwhile let's make it up, okay?'

'You are such a skiving bastard.'

But Boz was right. It was obvious. In the morning the punters are going to work. At midday they're off to the pub or home for a lunchtime shag. You throw in a few googlies, like hospital appointments, to keep the boffins in the office happy.

'And after a week we don't even have to do our counting.' Boz added. 'By then we have a daily average, we work from that. I don't know what Sanchez was getting so excited about.'

'Maybe that's what happened to him? Maybe he made it up and HQ twigged.'

'Well, if they did, he didn't do a very good job. Look, you're the sociologist, you know about this sort of stuff. Think of this as a challenge: man against the machine. People are so predictable. They think they are free, but like everybody else they are shopping in chain stores.'[8]

---

[8] Many years later I visited the West of England and noticed the idiosyncratic road system. Among sociologists the West of England Transportation Survey has become a *cause célèbre* as a sort of reverse Hawthorn Experiment. While the Hawthorn Experiment showed that people under study work harder and improve their productivity whatever you do to their work environment, due to the very fact that they are being observed and therefore feel special, the message that came out of the West of England Transportation Survey was even more obvious. Namely, never, ever, employ hippies to collect data. They won't give a toss, the results will be unreliable and the consequences could be far reaching. In this case millions of pounds were spent constructing six-lane fastways leading to small villages, while what should have been busy commuter routes were re-designated to single lane tracks. The West of England was soon at a standstill - despite recent corrective measures costing a small fortune the highways around Bristol and Somerset are still today frequently jammed. All due to those months of playing 'let's guess where they are going' in the back of a smokey red Transit van. Yeah, I'm sorry about that. But how were we to know? And as for Sanchez's work in the Forest of Dean, well, have you been there recently? No? My point exactly.

TWENTY THREE

It was an overcast Friday afternoon. In the grey light the Somerset landscape looked flat and featureless. It smelt like it was going to rain.

Stoner handed out our wage packets. I looked in the manila envelope with Felix Radstock written on it in an account clerk's rounded handwriting; in it were twenty unused pound notes. Not bad for a week's work. But I knew I was going to have to put those greenbacks on the line if I was to have a chance of winning back my previous week's wages.

I waited for Stoner to go through his payday ritual.

'Anybody interested in the opportunity to top up their wages?'

'I would like that,' said Mohan. I knew Mohan was desperate for money. He needed to scrimp and save every penny he had to pay for his college fees. I reckoned if his parents back in Malaysia knew Mohan had lost his wages gambling they'd be mighty upset.

'What about you Felix?'

'Nah.'

'C'mon Felix, the more people play the more fun we'll have.'

'Not today,' I said.

'Felix, you know you want to.'

'Not this week.' I was playing hard to get.

'Why?'

'I feel that Lady Luck is knocking.'

'C'mon Felix, let her in.'

'Okay, if you insist.' I said trying to hide the desperation in my voice. 'Don't come crying to me if I whoop yer ass.'

We played all afternoon. I could hear distant thunder rumbling over the Mendip Hills.

Stoner shook his head. 'Why did you do that? I told you bet and raise, don't call.'

'How do you know?'

Yet again Lady Luck was playing hard to get; she wasn't even speaking to me, let alone being my mistress.

'I can read you like a book, Felix, and a pretty simple book at that. Here's a tip: if you've got a good hand you don't need to keep looking back to see what you've got.'

That was my problem. A poker face didn't come easy to me.

'Sometimes you've got to follow your instincts,' I said.

'Yeah, but chasing rainbows, that's not a good idea.' Stoner replied.

By the time we had packed up to leave I had lost my week's wages as well as Boz's holiday money.

'Stoner, you're a bastard,' I said. I couldn't look at Stoner, I didn't want him to see the hate in my eyes.

'Hey, c'mon.' Stoner raised his hands in front of his chest as if I was about to throw a bucket of shit at him. 'This was your idea.'

'My idea? How do you work that out?'

'It was you who wanted to set up a card school.'

'I have absolutely no memory of saying that.' I looked at the empty manila envelope. 'Anyway, I didn't expect to lose all my wages.'

'I didn't expect you to be so lacking in self-discipline.'

'Lacking in self-discipline! You wouldn't know self-discipline if it kneed you in the nuts!'

'If you remember, when you first started working for me I suggested an alternative arrangement for our wages. You should have listened to me then.'

'I may be old fashioned but I like the traditional form of remuneration for work - cash.'

'Where's the fun in that?'

I couldn't be bothered to argue. Rain was now hammering on the roof of the van. We had to shout to be heard. I needed to borrow money to get me through to the next pay day. I couldn't borrow from Boz, I didn't want to him to know that I'd lost his cash.

Stoner was the only person I could ask. 'Can you lend me a fiver to get me through the next week? I promise I'll pay it back.'

'Sure,' said Stoner, giving me a big smile. 'Maybe Lady Luck will turn up next time, huh?'

*

It was my last day at work. Today was the day I had to get my money back. If I didn't, I'd lose my holiday, my tryst with Gloria and probably my friendship with Boz. That morning we were on the late shift so I went to the University to have a bath. I had to be feeling good, I had to be feeling relaxed. As I lay in the bath I thought about the afternoon's card game. I had to come up with a strategy. What would James Bond do? Yet all I could think about was Gloria. I imagined her emerging from the warm Aegean Sea in a white bikini … that was it, Gloria was going to be my Lady Luck.

I pulled my secret weapon from my coat pocket.

'What the fuck is that?' said Stoner.

I put on a green eye shade I'd bought from the joke shop on Christmas Steps.

'It's what professional gamblers use,' I said. It was a bit small but it did the trick.

'Don't be daft.'

'It stops the glare in my eyes. It helps me concentrate.'

'Glare in this van? You're kidding!'

'Let's get on with this,' I said.

'Let me try it on?' Stoner sounded like a child wanting a fancy dress costume.

'Later.' I could see that Stoner was envious. He wanted one.

'I'm the boss. I should be wearing that.'

'You're not the boss of this game.'

Stoner gave a snort of derision. 'Okay, let's play.'

My strategy was to play safe but towards the end of the shift take the game up a notch. One by one the team members drifted back to the van to spectate as they realised that this was more than the usual Friday afternoon game. This was for real.

After an hour I was twenty pounds up. This was high stakes, but not unusual for a Friday afternoon.

'Felix, you're not doing what I've trained you to do,' Stoner said.

I smiled and didn't reply. I was going *off piste* with the rules; I had to unlearn the strategy that Stoner had told me.

Stoner kept on looking at my eyeshade. He couldn't see my eyes. He was losing his concentration.

'I don't know where you're going with this hand? I don't understand,' Stoner protested.

'Don't worry. Go with the flow.' I said repeating what Stoner had said previously. 'Remember: wisdom and clarity.' I could see I'd got Stoner riled.

Stoner rolled a big fat joint, lit it, took a couple of light tokes and passed it on to me. I remembered Stoner once saying, 'If your opponent holds all the aces there's only a couple of things you can do. Kick over the table or roll a big fat jay.' I needed a clear head. Without having a hit I passed it on to Mohan.

By now I was up £40.

The back door opened and Boz climbed into the van.

'How's it going, guys?' said Boz.

'We need a few more minutes,' I said.

'Don't be long. It's Friday evening. I've got some things to do.'

'Another half an hour and I'll be done,' I said. Boz was mercifully unaware that it was his holiday money I was playing with.

I continued working at it. 'Create your own luck,' I kept saying to myself. I looked at Stoner. I could see he was confused. He couldn't handle being mauled by his student.

And then there she was. Lady Luck in all her glory had come knocking at my door. She walked straight in and spread-eagled herself across my bed wearing nothing but a full house: I had three kings and two tens. Stoner had a hand of low numbers that wasn't worth a toss.

I looked at Stoner. He appeared tired; his big smile had gone and his moustache was drooping. I had £60 in my hand; I'd reclaimed two week's wages and most of Boz's Eurorail cash.

'Fair do's Felix. You're a smart player. You've responded well to good tutelage.'

I shook his hand. 'No hard feelings Stoner?'

He pulled me towards him and gave me a hug and patted me on the back.

'You have a good trip. I told you I'd help you get some extra cash.'

'Here, have this,' I said as I gave Stoner the eyeshade.

'I appreciate that, man.'

So that was it, Boz would never need to know that his holiday money had been in jeopardy and I was now on my way to Crete. I swore to myself I'd never play poker again.

TWENTY FOUR

Boz went up to the bar to order more beers. After our abortive attempt to enter Albania we had had to backtrack inland. Contrary to our heat-befuddled expectation the Yugoslavian border guards just waved us through. From there it seemed that all routes led to Belgrade, a soulless concrete landscape of tower blocks, cut by big empty roads, with cramped balconies stuffed with washing.

We were now in a cafe in a small dusty town near the Macedonian border.

An old man at an adjacent table, who had been sitting over a coffee for the last half hour, leant over and asked, 'Are you a student?' The old man's eyes were strong and clear.

'Yes,' I laughed.

'You are very lucky. In this country we have few universities. They are many miles away. Many, many miles away.'

'Oh.'

'Where do you study?' he asked. 'Oxford and Cambridge?'

'Oh, no, another University.'

'It is good?' he asked.

'Very good. The beer is very good.'

The old man smiled 'You study beer? You study to make beer in a brewery?'

'I was making a joke.'

'Ah, to laugh is to be free,' he nodded seriously.

'I'm studying sociology,' I said.

'I have heard of sociology.' He shook his head as if in regret. 'My studies were interrupted by the war.'

I wondered which war he was talking about. There seemed to have been so many wars in Yugoslavia. I nodded.

'Hmm.'

'At first we were neutral. But the Germans invaded nevertheless. At the end of the war many of my people were killed. I never returned to my studies.'

'I'm sorry to hear that,' I said, as if acknowledging bereavement. I guessed he was younger than he looked.

The old man leant forward and in a slow gravelly voice asked, 'What is the purpose of your travel?'

'To visit your wonderful country,' was my patronising answer.

'Yes, Croatia and Montenegro are very beautiful. But what is the purpose of your travel?' This time he emphasised the word 'purpose'. I could see this was a serious question.

'Well, we're travelling.' I remembered my resolve at the start of the journey to visit the finest galleries and soak up the local culture. 'We will be visiting the art galleries to see the best pictures.' I though it best not to mention the anticipated sexual reward from Gloria for my cultural exploration.

'Yes, art is good. It will help you understand the human condition.'

'The human condition. Exactly,' I echoed.

'So tell me, what have you seen?'

'Well, nothing as yet.'

'But you have travelled far, have you not?' He shook his head with disappointment. 'Young man, you have come all this way from England and you say have seen nothing.' He looked at me in disbelief. 'I do not understand.'

I could see that he was disappointed. I should have carried with me the hope of youth. He was keen to speak of great things, to discuss politics. For much of his life he had been denied the freedom of speech, of individual thought and the opportunity to vote. I should have been his link with the outside world. Yet here I was, a product of hard fought democracy, with not a sensible thought in my head.

Pulling on his stick for support the man stood up. 'You are very lucky. You have money. You have education. You have freedom.'

I was beginning to realise how fortunate I was. What was I complaining about? Suburbia is one of the highest forms of civilisation. It means you have a job, an ordered life, food on the table and the opportunity for a good education. You can criticise the authorities without fear. You can vote. You have freedom, you have safety. You can laugh, you can joke, you can talk about nothing. Think about that: how fortunate to be able talk about nothing. These people had none of this. They lived in fear of the Stasi, not knowing where their next meal was coming from. They talked of the big issues, of matters of life and death camps.

I stood up and shook his hand. 'I wish you well,' he said.

I was wasting his time; he couldn't be bothered with me. I had everything, he had nothing. As he shuffled away, I wondered what he thought of me. I felt ashamed, I felt like I'd blown out a light.

Boz returned with two beers. 'What was that old guy saying?' he asked.

'Nothing really,' I said.

TWENTY FIVE

It was 7.30 am and half an hour before we'd arrived in Athens on a bus from, from … I have absolutely no idea where we had come from. All I know is that it had been one hell of a journey. Days and days of local buses and bus stations can do even the sanest person's head in.

How we'd got to Athens is difficult to explain. Details about this stage of the journey are hazy in my mind; times and places became tangled. Areas like Montenegro, Macedonia, Bosnia and Serbia, all states not even shown on my map, blurred into one. Suffice it to say we were tired and hungry and there were too many incidents to relate in detail. We travelled for what seemed like weeks. We hitched rides in big trucks where we had to shout over the noise of the engine, we caught buses, we even sat on the back of a donkey cart. Hitching offers the opportunity to spend quality time with society's fringe elements. After all, who's going to offer a couple of hippie long-hairs a lift, other than someone who is a bit loopy? The dashboard would be an immediate give away. Often blue, brown and yellow wires would sprout from where the radio should have been. Or there would be no ignition key and an ingenious and lethal improvised wiring system would be used to spark up the engine. Several times I wasn't entirely sure whether the driver had permission to use the vehicle. Or indeed, even knew the owner.

Once, during a thunderstorm, the driver of an old Skoda and I had to pull the wipers, which were attached to pieces of string, across the windscreen. When we'd got into a rhythm it was a surprisingly effective system; if the driver needed to change gear he would steady the steering wheel with his knee.

Time expanded into a blur; night and day fused into one long dream. We slept in empty bus stations and sat for hours drinking strong coffee while waiting for the next connection. We sped along the Balkan Death Road, an interminable straight highway that hammered through the middle of nowhere. It was best not to look at the oncoming traffic. The road was metalled in the middle with dust tracks on either side. Drivers would play dare with each other, hand on horn, waiting for the last split second to avoid collision. There were torn and burnt-out carcasses of vehicles all along the roadside.

I remember waking one night to see the silhouette of the coach drivers changing places as the vehicle hurtled along at eighty miles an hour. As in a well choreographed dance, the driver rose from his seat, all the time keeping his foot on the accelerator, while his colleague slid in behind him. Later, I watched the outline of the demon driver, head tilted backwards, taking long swigs from a wine bottle.

We passed monasteries clinging to precipices; we crossed impossible bridges across deep gorges; we saw massive Balkan castles crowning grey mountains. There was so much to take in: it was so exotic, so different. I kept on thinking 'Far out, we're on the road'. So long as we were moving it didn't matter. The road became our life. I was looking for adventure or whatever came my way. Over the days we adjusted to the irregular rhythm of the highs and lows of travel. My thoughts were focused on the present, undistracted by outside influences. Occasionally I'd glance at a newspaper headline or walk past a television in a shop window, but generally I was living in my own sealed bubble. There were no distractions from the here and now. As far as I was concerned the worlds of Laurel Close and Bristol had ceased to exist. If they were to disappear into a suburban black hole of zero matter I wouldn't know.

As we headed east and south the countryside became drier and less hospitable. At first there were fields of sunflowers, mile after mile. Then rows of ancient olive trees appeared. But this gave way to drier, scorched land. Coarse grass disappeared to be replaced by empty scrub and then bare mountainside. Occasionally, we'd pass a boy, or an old woman, sitting under a makeshift shelter of sticks and animal hide watching bone-thin goats.

And the towns were different as well. They smelt of garlic, herbs and fish. I wanted to look at everything: the whitewashed walls, the blue doors and windows, the terracotta roofs - the details.

I think it was near Thessalonica that we became hysterical. Tiredness and hunger transported us into a state of ecstasy where we laughed and laughed until our jaws ached and our faces were red with sweat and tears. Boz and I pledged our friendship forever.

The uncertainty of travel became addictive. We suffered the despair of standing beside a road waiting for a bus that was never going to come. Then there was the joy of being offered a lift by strangers who would laugh and share their bag of fresh apricots with us, followed by the meditative calm of observing the countryside flow by. I could do this for ever; no responsibilities, no job, no family, no politics, no religion, just watching the world from behind a dusty window.

And then suddenly we were in a large noisy plaza in the centre of Athens. It was as busy as Trafalgar Square. Even at this early hour the heat was hammering out of the sky and bouncing off the concrete pavements. The air was thick and oily; I could feel my chest tightening and found breathing difficult.

Men in pressed suits and smartly-dressed women with brown arms were hurrying to work. The traffic was loud. We weren't used to such activity. A convoy of army trucks filled with soldiers sped down the main avenue. People were shouting and waving at them.

I went into a bank to cash some travellers cheques. Never have I felt so out of place. I sat, unshaven and in dusty clothes, on a leather and chrome chair in the big bright air conditioned room, yet the bank clerk was charming. After viewing my passport he gave a bright smile and asked: 'How do you like Athens?'

'Hot!' was all that I could say. I felt like my brain was closing down; I just wanted to go to sleep.

'Better than Turkey, huh?'

I looked at the coins in my hand. This must have been about the fourth different currency I had used in so many days. I realised that there is something reassuring about the weight and design of British money. These drachmas looked so flimsy. They reminded me of the plastic coins that I used with my red and yellow toy cash register when I was a kid. The money I held in my hand felt like play money.

'Why are we rushing?' I asked Boz. 'No hurry, no worry. I thought we'd agreed not to rush.' After the cool air of the bank I felt like I was standing in a furnace.

'The Heraklion ferry leaves in two hours.'

I glanced down a side street. I was looking for a shop that sold maps. Among the street tat and signs a notice grabbed my attention. I couldn't help myself; I was Odysseus being dragged to the rocks. Flashing in red, white and blue neon the enormous sign simply read 'English Breakfast.'

'Boz, we've got to go in there,' I pleaded.

A minute later we were sat in a cavernous canteen that smelt of freshly shelled hard boiled eggs. The room, which was painted in sea blue gloss, was empty apart from a handful of other back-packers in a similar state of anticipation.

We got talking to a straight looking Englishman wearing voluminous khaki shorts, brogue shoes and brown socks. He had a big round sweaty face with tiny dark eyes. He reminded me of a currant bun. He said he was travelling alone and visiting the classical sights. I think he might have been a teacher, public school probably.

'So where have you travelled?' he asked.

'All over the place.'

'And where is that?'

'We've been on trains, buses, boats.'

'And where have these buses, trains and boats taken you?'

'Oh, and ferries as well.'

'So where have these buses, trains, boats AND ferries taken you? Can you be more precise?'

I couldn't. I was getting annoyed by this man's questioning and supercilious tone.

'Well, Dubrovnik.'

'Ah Ragusa! I have yet to visit. Tell me more.'

'Pearl of the Adriatic. Brilliant walls.' Otherwise I could only remember Slobena and the *Club Bristol* - but I didn't think he'd be interested in that. 'But if you want walls Hav is the place to go.'

'The walls they are big, they go all round the town,' Boz added.

'Oh and Venice, we've been to Venice,' I said.

'*La Serenissima!*' the man squealed. 'You get off the train and it's like walking into a painting. I love Venice.'

'Actually, I reckon it's a bit over rated.' I remembered when we arrived at the station it was more like stepping into a London fog.

'But surely to stand by the Doge's Palace in St Marks Square and look over the dancing waters to St Giorgio Maggiore is one of the most sublime experiences known to man.'

'Yeah, it's okay - if you like that sort of thing.' I said.

'But these buildings are the zenith of human achievement. They rank alongside the plays of Shakespeare, the paintings of Michelangelo and the music of Mozart. They are civilization at its most sublime. They reaffirm humanity.'

'Too many fooking gondoliers for my liking,' said Boz, who had also taken against this creep. 'They get on my nerves.'

'We prefer the less touristy stuff,' I said. 'The teeming back streets, that's where you meet the real people. It gives you a new perspective on life; that's where real humanity is. That is the purpose of our travel.'

Who was I kidding? We'd spent all our time in Venice on a campsite looking in the wrong direction.

The man went back to eating his bacon and eggs.

I pulled a Lipton's tea bag out of the tepid water. I bit into my grey bread roll and looked at the two translucent ribbons of streaky bacon

154

and a cartilaginous egg that had been fried a couple of hours earlier. 'This certainly beats a plate of watery old courgettes.'

'Sure does,' agreed Boz. 'It almost makes me homesick for a Growler.'

We hugged the shady side of the road. As we hurried to catch the metro to Piraeus, I glanced up thin streets that led to a kind of plateau. Stone steps were lined with large cooking-oil tins containing blood red geraniums.

'Why are you walking like that?' Boz asked.

'It's my plimsolls, they're falling apart.'

'I thought they were new.'

'I think we ought to spend some more time here.'

'We've got to hurry if we're going to catch the boat.'

'But this is Athens,' I pleaded. 'I thought we'd agreed to stop bourgeois rushing.'

'I'd love to stay pal, but if we do you'll miss your liaison in Matala. We're behind schedule.'

'It seems wrong to miss this,' I said. 'I need to buy some shoes. Look, there's the Parthenon.'

Through the shimmering heat I could just about make out a mesh of scaffolding supporting a row of massive stone columns. So that's what the cradle of civilisation looks like.

Boz was not impressed. 'It looks like a building site. I'd prefer to visit when I can see it. Anyway the best bits are back in England. I think they've got some of the frescoes in the Bolton Museum.'

The cobblestones of the city streets reflected the sun's heat like a bread oven.

'Boz. Stop. We've got to get a map. I need to buy a postcard.'

We stood on the sheltered side of the street. I was drenched in sweat and panting - the Athens air felt so airless.

'No time to stop now.'

'How behind schedule are we?'

'God knows, I've lost count. Days? Weeks even? Gloria's not going to wait forever, Felix.'

Boz was right, we needed to get a move on. I promised myself I'd check out the Acropolis on our return journey.

I wondered how far Plank had got. Had he really fast-tracked through the Balkans? Yet, there was a flicker of hope. Like a yowling, rutting dog, Plank would be unable to control his baser instincts and would be delayed en-route several times in order to satisfy his carnal needs. I tried to consoled myself with the thought that he was probably far behind us.

'We need hats,' I pleaded.

Boz looked around for a clock. 'Yeah, we'll get hats in Matala.'

At Piraeus, while I was waiting to collect our tickets, I looked at the traveller's notice board in the ferry office. Among the frantic messages of missed connections to the Greek Islands and lifts offered to Belgrade and Istanbul I noticed a plea from Bruce who was still in pursuit of Nicola.

Has anybody come across Aussie chick Nicola Eatcake travelling from London overland to India. Tell her I'm sorry and I love her. Bruce. PS I'm now heading to Crete.

I then saw a note written in thick blue marker pen in capital letters. It had a large arrow pointing to Bruce's message.

Yeah. Hot chick. Met her at Manos Guesthouse. You're a lucky guy.

To which somebody else had added. *Me too!*

Errol's sex therapy session in Sarajevo seemed to have un-leashed Nicola's libido to an appreciative world and she now appeared to be bonking her way round Europe.

TWENTY SIX

I was leaning on the rails watching for somebody I knew to walk up the gangplank. We were on the overnight ferry from Piraeus to Heraklion, Crete. I wondered if I might see Gloria. It's weird; we'd been travelling for thousands of miles, yet we'd see the same people again and again. We all thought we were free spirits doing our own thing, but somehow we were travelling on a predestined loop. We might not have a guide book, but word of mouth ensured that the freak community travelled on the same routes and went to the same places.

I looked down at my plimsolls. They were in bad shape. On each shoe the brown stained canvas was holed and you could see the nail of my big toe. Worse though, the sole on my left foot was now loose. To avoid the flapping sole catching the ground I had to walk like Herman Munster, lifting my foot in an exaggerated manner.

I climbed down a series of metal ladders to find the large dimly-lit communal cabins. Women were sitting on the bunks talking loudly while children rushed about in a state of excitement. The cabin stank of engineering oil mingled with sweat, souvlaki, ouzo and vomit. The deck was a much better place to sleep.

We found a sheltered spot for our sleeping bags and Boz got out his travel chess board. It was getting dark now and we settled down for the overnight journey. We were soon out of sight of any land and the first stars were pricking the sky. The air was fresh, it was good to be away from the Athens smog. I'd bought a bottle of Metaxa Five Star for the journey.

What is it about chess? It's a surprisingly sexy game. For some girls chess can be a real turn on. People make assumptions about chess players. Boz had this pocket travel chess set that we'd set up on long journeys, on trains and at bus stations. We'd sit staring at the board with its little black and red plastic figures, sighing, taking a drink, walking away. We used it as a talking point, a point of introduction. Invariably we'd draw a crowd of onlookers. Old men, young girls, children would stand behind us waiting for one of us to make a move. We were also offered dope. If a freak sees you playing chess he assumes you need some draw. And who were we to argue? We never actually played the game. I'd given up playing Boz a long time ago, he was far too good.

'Felix, you know I said I had a problem.'

'What problem?'

'Remember, in Dubrovnik, I was concerned that my cash was disappearing too quickly.'

'Yeah?'

'My financial situation's not got any better.'

'I told you. Lay off the pies.'

'You said cake. Anyway, it's only eased the situation slightly.'

'I'm not surprised. What about that?' I said, pointing to a pastry Boz had bought in Piraeus.

'That's Baklava.'

'Pies, Baklava, it all costs money, Boz. You've got to economise.'

'I have and it's not helped. My wallet is almost running on empty.' Boz lifted a forkful of syrupy filo pastry to his mouth. His eyes flickered in ecstasy as he chewed. 'Anyway,' he said 'I need to eat these for my dissertation.'

'Downgrade the Metaxa Brandy consumption. There's not much difference between the three and five star stuff.'

'You're kidding! The three star is brutal. It gives me a vicious headache if I drink that stuff all night.'

Myself, I'd worked out a daily allowance and was sticking to it. I didn't see why Boz couldn't do the same. I could guess what was going to happen. Sooner or later Boz would ask for a loan.

'What have you got to sell?'

'Nothing.'

'Boz, you don't get it, do you? This is your problem, not mine. Write a letter to your parents and ask them to send you money. You could pick up a cheque in Athens on the way back.'

'I can't do that.'

'Why?'

'I can't ask my parents for money.'

'Why not?'

'They don't know I'm here. They think I'm in St Ives!'

'What! Why didn't you tell them?'

'I never got round to it.'

'They won't mind.'

'The shock could kill the old man.'

'Don't be ridiculous.'

I looked at the postcard I'd bought while we waited for the ferry. The Parthenon looked so old and venerable. To think I'd been in Athens and nearly visited it. And soon I'd be living in a cave.

I was woken by the boat giving a violent judder. In the first light of dawn I could see hardly anything. There was shouting and the clank of metal against metal. For a moment it felt like we were going backwards. I looked out to see a dusty concrete jetty, a couple of grey warehouses and a rusting crane.

The docks were pushed up against sheer cliffs the colour of amber. They were so tall I had to bend my neck to see where the rock joined the thin morning sky. This must be Santorini.

I dozed in my sleeping bag for another few hours until we eventually docked at Heraklion. As we stood on the quayside wondering where the bus station was, we got talking to a speed-freak Londoner called Keith. With his tie-dye shirt, long greasy hair and Mexican moustache he looked like Frank Zappa's better looking kid brother. He was on his way to sell acid blotters to the sailors of the

Sixth Fleet stationed at the American naval base at Chania. He offered us a lift. He assured us that Matala was in the same direction.

Keith drove with a bottle of beer in one hand and spent more time looking at Boz than the road. I sat in the back and enjoyed the extra ventilation offered by a hole in the floor the size of a dinner plate, below which the ground streaked past in a blur.

'And while you're in Crete,' said Keith, 'you've got to visit the mountains in the south. They are snow-capped even in the summer and they're cut by gorges thousands of feet deep. The deepest, the Samaria Gorge, is like a crack in the earth's crust. At one point it's so narrow you can stretch out your arms and touch each side. It's a long rocky walk, at least twenty miles. I saw a guy trip over and break his leg. They had to send out a rescue donkey with a bottle of Metaxa strapped to its neck. It's best to leave all your stuff behind. You sleep on the beach at the end of the gorge. There's just one house down there, a little taverna that sells bean stew. You can hire a bed, but you have to share your room with the family - and the daughter can get a bit frisky. Otherwise that's it. No road or anything. In the morning a little ferry appears and takes you to Loutro, a village along the coast.'

After travelling with Keith for less than half an hour it became obvious that we were heading in the wrong direction. I knew that Matala was to the east and south; by looking at the sun I estimated we were heading westwards. Boz seemed unconcerned: 'Rule Number 9: a lift in the wrong direction is better than no lift at all,' he said.

'How do you work that out?'

'You need to keep the momentum. You can always double back.'

I wasn't convinced.

So we ended up staying the night in a quirky little town with a crescent harbour that could accommodate no more than half a dozen fishing boats, guarded by a tilting lighthouse, its rickety lantern about to slip into the sea.

'Boz, can you come in here?'

'Why?'

'I need your help.'

There was a little too much movement on the floor for comfort. Why are cockroaches so damn *freaky*? It's something about the way they scuttle and wave their nasty little antennae. They say that cockroaches are the only life-form to have survived Hiroshima. In fact the atomic bomb toughened them up. Japanese cockroaches are radiation resistant. Have you ever tried to squash a cockroach? Me neither. But I've seen one hit fair and square with a mallet and it just waddled away only slightly dazed.

'Sort it out yourself.'

'You are such a wimp,' I shouted. Boz was so lazy.

Boz was still reading *Tarantula* [9]. He would flick the pages back and forth as if he was trying to make sense of it.

---

[9] Seeing as we're talking about *Tarantula* I think at this stage it's time to say some more about Bob Dylan. He meant so much to me. Sure, people said he was the voice of the generation. But he was more than that, he was my voice. Bob and I had a personal bond. He was articulating the thoughts in my head, even the weird ones - especially the weird ones. I thought Dylan's lyrics were the key to something. He knew exactly what was going on. I would play Bob first thing in the morning; he'd set me up for the day. I would listen to him through headphones in bed last thing at night. *Blonde on Blonde* was my lullaby. It was aural psychedelia - it was a dream within a dream.

Of course in the late Sixties Bob was a recluse. He'd had his motorbike accident and there'd be no new music for ages. I went to the ICA in London to see the Dylan film *Don't Look Back* and I heard a guy behind me talking to his girlfriend in hushed tones about an acetate he'd heard. It was Bob Dylan and the Band playing in a basement in Woodstock. Illegal recordings, bootlegs he called them. I turned round, I had to ask.

He wasn't impressed by my interruption but said Kensington Market was the place to find them. But be discreet. These were illegal. Can you imagine it? Illegal Bob Dylan recordings! It couldn't get much cooler.

Anyway, the thing about Bob is that he's always one step ahead and one step to the side and sometimes people don't get what he's doing. One day when I was walking through Leicester Square I saw a black and white fly poster on the wall. *Bob Dylan and the Band at the Isle of Wight*. I couldn't believe it! The recluse was out.

It was August 1969, two weeks after Woodstock (in Bob's home town – but he didn't show), when over 100,000 Dylan freaks descended on Woodside Bay on the Isle of Wight. I suffered for Bob that weekend. Nobody had run a festival on this scale before and they hadn't quite worked out how to do it. I slept in a ditch for two days and all I had to eat was one lousy hotdog without mustard. At least there was no mud. Okay, a guy on a double decker bus on the way to the festival passed me a joint; that was a new experience for me on public transport. But it was worth it to see Bob AND the Band for that sixty-minute set. If you listen hard to the start of *Minstrel Boy*, the

Eventually he threw the book on the floor.

'I give up. This is fooking rubbish.'

'What's up?'

'That Bob Dylan, he's off his trolley.'

'He's the voice of our generation.'

'We're doomed if he is. These are the jottings of a mad man.'

'So what are you going to read now?'

'Brad was amazed that I'd never read any James Joyce. He said I hadn't lived if I hadn't read Joyce. He gave me this, *Finnegans Wake*. It's big but it looks like a good yarn.'

'Yeah, I love Irish writers. Flann O'Brien, J.P. Donleavy, plenty of laughs with those guys,' I agreed.

In the end it seemed it would be easier to sleep outside rather than mess about with cockroaches. I spent the night in a white-washed hut on a flat roof with views across the town. It was a beautiful skin-warm, still evening. As I lay on the top of my sleeping bag I felt a sense of contentment wash over me. Although we needed to be heading towards Matala, somehow it no longer concerned me. We were well behind schedule now, exactly how behind I had no idea. I went to sleep listening to the sounds drifting across the rooftops: laughter and the clack of backgammon; the washing of pans; a dog barking and the distant revs of a moped. I dreamt about Gloria who said she had dreamt about me.

---

worst Dylan song ever, on *Self Portrait* (Robbie, you should have known, never attempt a harmony with Bob), you can hear me in the audience shout *Visions of Johanna!*

But as I walked eight miles to the ferry that night I was bemused. Something wasn't quite right. I should have expected it. Rather than the shades, the polka-dot shirts and the Chelsea boots, Bob was wearing a country and western style white suit. I couldn't tell from the distance but it was probably adorned by rhinestones. He'd also lost his sneering nasal whine and was crooning like Bing Crosby. It was only many years later that I came to realize that that night Bob Dylan had been crap.

That's the thing about geniuses, they go their own way. I wondered if Bob was doing another Isle of Wight with *Tarantula*. Sooner or later one of us should know.

In the morning I was woken by singing. A weathered voice, deep but mellifluous, drifted through the morning air from a room below us. The singer was chanting a song that felt intensely ancient and mysterious. Passed from generation to generation and as old as the psalms. I imagined shepherds had sung this song on the Cretan mountainside for centuries,

I'd noticed the singer the day before, a tall and erect old man with a magnificent curled moustache John Stoner would have been proud of. I was impressed by the Cretan men, they seemed to have a strength and self confidence that I'd not come across before. Statuesque and wiry, they wore with a fierce pride their traditional costume of black knee-high boots, jodhpur-like trousers, white shirt, dark cummerbund, embroidered velvet waistcoat and a fringed bandana headband. Their black boots were always highly polished. Although their clothes were traditional they were a statement about the present: 'This is what we are, we are Cretans, get used to it'.

As we walked to the bus station I had a feeling that something was going on. People were talking in the streets, shaking their heads. Men in cafés were reading the newspapers with unusual attention. I wondered if it was something to do with the Junta but didn't like to ask; I didn't want anybody to get their feet burnt on my account.

We stopped for a small strong coffee.

'Turkish coffee, please.'

'Not Turkish,' the waiter said firmly, 'Greek.'

While eating a freshly baked roll flavoured with what I reckoned was caraway, I studied the dusty pictures on the café walls. There were three faded portraits of members of the military Junta. We'd left the iron hand of Tito behind and were now under the dictatorship of the Generals. They looked more like civil servants at a fancy dress party than the real thing. This military regime seemed so at odds with the relaxed Greek temperament. Along the wall from the Generals there was a framed yellowed cartoon showing a Cretan man pitch-forking a

German parachutist. The waiter spotted me looking at the picture. 'Allemagne?' he asked, with a mischievous smile.

'No, no, English.'

'Ah, good. I give you extra yoghurt.'

'Thank you.'

'Where are you going?' he asked.

'Matala.'

'You must find my cousin Spyros and ask him to take you out in his boat. He will show you interesting things that nobody else knows about.'

'What about the caves?'

The man laughed and disappeared into the back of the shop.

Like Boz, I was also becoming concerned about my finances as it had become obvious I needed to shell out on an unplanned purchase. I was going to have to buy new shoes. I'd already seen a shop in the main street that sold footwear, but the window display featured shiny formal work-type brogues, not particularly appropriate to my current lifestyle, and well out of my budget. As we walked to the bus station I noticed a hardware shop with a collection of brown plastic slip-ons hanging from a pole and decided to try on a pair.

'They'll do,' I said.

Boz was laughing.

'What?'

'Nothing. Plastic, you can wear them in the shower.'

'I can wear them in the sea.'

'Yeah, they remind me of jellies. We had them as kids, at the seaside.'

'I don't remember that.'

'You could buy them in Blackpool, for the beach.'

'I've never been to Blackpool.'

Boz said nothing but gave me a pitying look.

The unshaven proprietor shuffled up to me. *'Hellenoplastica.'* He waved his finger. 'Not good,' he said.

'Not good? Why?'

'Not for tourists.'

'But I like them.'

He shook his head. In Greece I was never sure whether this meant yes or no.

He tilted his head back and made a knife cutting gesture across his throat. He followed this with an exaggerated flicking with his fingers from his neck and then pointed at his shoes. For the life of me I couldn't understand what he meant.

'They are...' he hesitated, '...for killing.'

'Killing!' Surely, something had been lost in translation.

'He probably doesn't like people who are bollock-handed,' said Boz.

'Very amusing, Boz.'

'Wait a moment, I think I know what he means,' said Boz.

Boz copied the shop keeper's strange charade but also added a blood curdling howl. And then pointed at his feet and shook his head in the affirmative.

'Not for tourists,' the shop keeper repeated.

'They're abattoir shoes,' Boz announced.

'Abattoir shoes?' I wasn't sure if I'd heard him correctly. 'What the heck are abattoir shoes?'

'Non-slip, blood proof and washable. When I come to think about it I've seen butchers wearing them when they're delivering meat for the Growlers.'

'Sounds useful.'

The proprietor asked, 'You work in ...' he looked at Boz to see if he was using the correct word '... abattoir?'

'No. But I like them. Good for the beach.'

'Good for the beach,' the proprietor repeated, bemused. 'You want big sharp butcher's knife as well? Good for beach!'

We all laughed.

The shoes may have looked weird, but it was a relief to be able to walk properly again.

TWENTY SEVEN

There wasn't a gasp of oxygen in the air. I leant forward to stop my back sticking to the plastic seat. We were now on the final stage of our journey; at last we were on the bus to Matala.

'Open the window,' I said to Boz

'It's as wide as it can go.'

The woman sitting next to me crossed herself at the more treacherous hairpin bends. Every few miles the roadside was adorned by some sacred decorated relics embellished with plastic flowers. I wasn't sure whether these were local shrines or, perhaps, the commemoration of a horrific accident where a vehicle had failed to negotiate deadman's bend and plummeted thousands of feet down the mountainside.

An ancient man wearing a black-fringed Cretan headscarf turned and stared at me.

'*Allemagne?*' he demanded in a craggy smoker's voice.

'*Non, anglais.*' I said, admiring his yellowing handlebar moustache.

He nodded. And then pointed towards a low roofless stone shack in the corner of a parched enclosure.

'*Allemagne.*' He gestured to his neck, death-rolled his eyes and with a cruel hiss made the now all too familiar gesture for throat cutting.

I was confused. First the brutal pitch forking, then the abattoir shoes, now this. 'Abattoir?' I said. Had he seen my abattoir shoes?

'No! *Allemagne! La guerre.*'

This time I understood; he was referring to the Second World War. I tried to hide my shock but despite knowing there were German travellers on the bus I gave a thumbs-up gesture. 'Good,' I replied.

His smile revealed a mouthful of gold. To make sure that I'd understood the full implication of what he had said he repeated the ghastly mime and then gave a deep throated laugh. He reached over and gave me his hand. It was like grabbing a sheet of coarse sandpaper. He held my hand in a crushing grip. 'English. My friend.'

'Crete. Good.' I replied weakly.

The shadows of the mountains were getting longer. From a burning white they now had the ochre hue of halva. I was feeling sleepy. But then we came over a hill and in front of us was the Mediterranean. I still love that first sight of the sparkling sea. As a child on holiday I would search for a glimpse of it through a gap in the rounded Dorset hills. So big, so blue. To someone brought up in the city suburbs, the sea seemed different, magical, hypnotic even. It offered freedom, an otherness, a contrasting dimension not to be messed with. I sometimes still dream about that sea - but now it makes me feel sad.

I could see, between a break in the cliffs, a strip of sandy beach, a cluster of fishermen's sheds and a dozen or so white and blue houses. Matala at last! I hoped Gloria was ready to be my Wilma.

The bus stopped by a row of low whitewashed houses. 'Here's the plan,' I said, 'we check into our cave, clean up and then we go and find the girls.'

As we climbed down from the bus we were surrounded by a coven of old crones dressed head to foot in black.

'*Zimmer? Zimmer?*' they asked.

'*Non merci,*' I said avoiding eye contact.

We walked past an empty taverna and a couple of tourist gift shops down to the beach.

'Who buys that rubbish?' I said, looking at the cotton kaftans and replica ancient Greek jugs.

'It's tat,' Boz agreed.

For Sex-on-Sea, Matala was smaller than I had envisaged. Through the half-closed shutters of a butcher's shop I could see a man asleep on a marble slab.

'No city walls,' Boz observed.

Not far away, towards the dipping sun, was a big wedge of yellow sandstone. And there they were; scores of doors and windows cut into the shadow of the cliffs.

'There's our *zimmer*,' I said.

'Are you sure? Where are the funny cone people?'

'No cone people. I was thinking of somewhere else. These caves are much better. They've been used for thousands of years. Dug by King Phaistos and his Minoan friends.'

'Why aren't they used by the locals now?'

I couldn't be bothered to answer. At times Boz could be too inquisitive for his own good. Myself, I was looking forward to tuning into the historic vibe.

It was good to smell the sea air again. We walked along an almost empty beach past a row of weather beaten huts the colour of driftwood. There was a group of hippies spread out on the sand. Scandinavian I guessed. They shouted out to us. 'Hi.' I recognised one of the freaks from the campsite in Venice.

We ambled over and shook hands. I'd never before shaken hands with a topless girl. One of them introduced himself as 'Blu.' I was interested to notice that he was wearing a necklace of what looked like human teeth.

'From Denmark?' Boz asked.

'Yes, Copenhagen.' I looked at Boz and smiled.

'Have you seen two English girls?' I asked.

'One English girl?' asked Blu.

'No, two. One blonde, very nice looking, one fair,' Boz said. Although Boz didn't say 'so - so' his shaking hand gesture indicated this was what he was thinking.

The Scandinavians looked puzzled. Then one man nodded his head.

'Ah, two English girls - over there,' he said pointing to the caves.

'Ah, yes, two English girls,' another of the group agreed.

'No, there are three of them,' added the girl.

'Three girls?' I asked. They had probably been joined by a fellow traveller.

'Yes, three,' the girl confirmed. 'Two girls and a man.'

A man? Who was this man?

'No, it was two girls. The guy was travelling by himself,' another of the hippies insisted.

I didn't like the sound of this. I didn't like the sound of this at all. What if Plank's progress through Europe had been quicker than I had anticipated? What if he hadn't got waylaid? Maybe he wasn't rutting like a pig in muck, maybe he was focusing his energies on Gloria.

'What did the man look like?' I asked.

They all laughed.

'Yeah?'

'He looked English,' said Blu.

'Okay.' I didn't want to go into the bad teeth, bad skin, bad hair routine again.

'Are they still here?'

'Yes, they are in the caves.'

'Adolf is wrong,' said the topless girl, 'they left the caves a couple of days ago.'

I was confused. Perhaps we were talking about different people.

'Ask Sanchez, he'll know.'

'Sanchez?' For a moment I thought ...

'He's the Rastafarian in one of the top caves. You need a ladder to get to him. You'll see him floating around.'

'So how do we get a cave for ourselves?' Boz asked.

'There are plenty. Some are better than others.'

'Are you staying in the caves?' I asked.

'Oh, no. We are in the village.'

'Are the caves full?'

'We like a good night's sleep.' Blu gave a questioning look to see if I understood. 'Soft bed and a good night's sleep.'

'I like a soft bed and a shower,' added the bare-chested girl.

We scrambled up the cliff. I stood and looked across a sparse olive grove edged by a crescent bay of white sand shelving into a clear turquoise sea. The village was about a quarter of a mile away. A lizard scampered past my dusty abattoir shoes.

As I stooped through a low entrance cut into the sandstone I was greeted by a black cloud of miniscule flies. The cave felt damp - like my grandmother's larder on a hot day.

'The place needs a bit of an airing,' I said, waving the flies away from my face.

'How do we do that?' asked Boz.

The cave was bigger than I had expected. It was large enough for a family to sit round a dining table. There were niches cut into the rock for storage of plates and cooking implements. Two of the larger alcoves were, I guessed, for sleeping. Single beds; a bit tight for two, though.

'Look at this, it's a maisonette,' I said.

'What about the smell?' said Boz.

'That's the smell of history. It's a tangible link with the Minoans.' I breathed in deeply. I wished I hadn't, it was rank.

'I don't like it,' said Boz. 'History has its place. But not where I'm going to crash.'

'Do you know people would pay good money to sleep in the British Museum? We've got this for free. This is a total experience.'

'I don't know,' said Boz.

'Yeah, you don't know.'

Boz was uncharacteristically quiet as we looked around our new abode.

'So what do you think?' I asked.

'Er, Felix, where's the kharzi?'

'I don't know! Where do you think?'

'There's no toilet.'

Many months ago, when we were planning our travels, Boz and I had agreed that there were going to be times when we would be hungry, dirty, tired and needing a loo. It would be no big deal. It would be part of the trip. We would accept it and move on.

'Of course there's no toilet. That's the thing about cave dwelling; there are no toilets. No bog roll either. No hot and cold running water. No central heating. No bloody stereo system. That's probably why caves went out of fashion. That's why the people moved to the village.'

'So what do we do?'

'Use your imagination: you've lived in a squat. Go over there,' I said pointing to the olive grove behind the beach. Dig a hole. I don't want to talk about it. I don't ever want to talk about it. When we started this trip we agreed on that.'

'Felix, what are you getting so uptight about?'

'I dunno. You just hit a nerve.'

In truth, now I was here, I wasn't so sure about these caves. You know how it is, you build up your expectations and then the reality isn't so good. I'd dragged Boz thousands of miles to be here, and now I was having second thoughts about the whole trip. The cave was creepy and giving me asthma. And where was Gloria? Who was that man with the two girls? In the back of my mind I was wondering about Plank. Had he already settled into one of the caves? Perhaps he'd gone feral. Was he holding court, like some club-wielding caveman? Deep down inside of me I was worried.

'Look this isn't so much a cave, it's more of a duplex.' I said, trying to put a positive slant on things. What surprised me was that there was another dim room at the back. In addition to the door, a hole had been cut through the rock from the front room to allow in light.

'Duplex! What sort of word is that?'

'It's got two rooms! It's a bit like I imagined Plato's cave to be.'

Boz nodded his head towards the back. 'But what's in there?'

I stood in the doorway and stared in. It had the not unpleasant deep earthy odour of a greenhouse. Despite the hole in the wall it took a while for my eyes to adjust to the dimness. There appeared to be nothing in the back cave except for a few old bones. 'It'll be useful, we can store our stuff in there.'

'We haven't got much stuff.'

'I'll store my Tiger Balm in there.'

We both laughed. 'Okay, that can be our Tiger Balm store.' At least Boz seemed to have calmed down.

'But apart from that, what do you think?'

'I don't know, Felix. The night is a very dark time for me.'

'It's a dark time for everybody, you fool.'

'No, not like that. Sometimes I cry out.'

'At least it's cool in here. It'll get the early morning sun and by midday it'll be out of the full blast of the heat. Let's give it a go. If we don't like it, we'll find somewhere with soft beds.'

'And a shower?'

'You are such a wimp.'

TWENTY EIGHT

Insects were clouding round a bare light hanging on a string. Every so often a moth would ping against the naked bulb. Matala felt like the end of the world.

'It's quieter in Matala than I expected,' I said.

Tonight we were the only people in the Mermaid Café. It was strange being in such an empty taverna. Where was everybody?

'Sex-on-Sea, huh?' said Boz.

'Look, are you trying to say something?' I was still feeling defensive about the caves.

'No it's just… Well, I can see the sea. But where's the sex?'

'These places don't kick off till later.'

'I reckon it's at least ten o' clock.'

'I've no idea what time it is.'

'Do you realise that if we were back in England it would only be half an hour till closing time.'

'Unless it was a Saturday.'

'Is it a Saturday?'

'Dunno. We ought to get a newspaper sometime.'

'Nah.'

Boz was silent for a while. I looked around the empty room. There was a mural of a tropical jungle on the wall by the door to the toilet. I could see a big white signature: *Jodie*. There was also a travellers' noticeboard. Perhaps Gloria had left a message. I walked over and scanned the notes. There were the familiar messages about lifts, lost passports, and, more unusually, someone asking urgently for 'Spare johnnies – not used'! There was also a note from Bruce.

If anybody comes across Nicola from Oz tell her that Bruce says get fucked.

Poor Bruce. He must have caught up with reports of his ex-girlfriend's nymphomaniac exploits. There was no note from Gloria however.

I took another swig of ouzo and picked up the menu. It was the standard Tourist Police approved tariff. There were four columns - Greek, German, English and French. At first sight it seemed to offer an extensive *a la carte* selection. But on closer reading there were only two items with a price against them: *Moussaka* and *Sea Fish*.

I signalled to a stout middle aged woman dressed in black who had been watching us from the kitchen door.

'Two more ouzo please.'

'*Zwei ouzo*,' she repeated.

'Where is everybody tonight?' I asked.

'It is the war.'

I laughed, thinking I'd misunderstood.

'You think the war is funny.'

'No, I don't think it's funny.' I was still trying to understand what she meant by 'war'. Had I misheard what she'd said? I looked at Boz. I could see he didn't understand either.

'Excuse me, did you say war?' asked Boz.

'Yes, war. You think it funny also? It is not funny.'

'What war?' I asked.

She looked at me as if I was a moron. 'War with Turkey. Not funny at all.'

'Let's get this straight. There is a war with Turkey?'

'They have invaded our country.'

'A war with Turkey? Now?'

How come we'd missed this? I'd seen soldiers with guns and cannons and stuff but I'd assumed it was the regular paraphernalia of the Generals' regime. Isn't this what Generals do as a matter of course?

175

'It is very serious. The Turks have invaded Cyprus.' Her eyes were becoming moist.

'Well, I'm sorry to hear this. Is there anything we can do?'

'There is nothing you can do. Nobody can do anything. Not even the United Nations.'

She walked away.

'You are such an idiot,' said Boz. 'Is that all you can say? 'Is there anything we can do?' It sounded like you were offering to wash the dishes!'

'Hang on, mate. I'm shocked by this. We came here for a holiday. Not a bloody war. A war is not what I had in mind. I came here to escape the daily horror of pictures on the television of Vietcong villages being napalmed. And now we're in the middle of a war zone. Anyway you weren't particularly helpful.

'This puts a whole new perspective on things,' I continued. 'A war? What's she mean a war? Is it a real war? Bang bang, shoot, shoot? Or is its some sort of cold phony war?'

'The Turks aren't exactly known for their human rights,' said Boz. 'It's not an accident that they invented the kebab.'

'What's that got to do with it? Anyway they didn't invent the kebab. The question is, where's everybody gone? Is it safe to stay here?'

'Let's see what happens. It's at times like this we need to chill out. We don't want to do anything too hasty that we might regret later. We need another drink.'

'Yeah,' I agreed, 'we don't want to get too tense in this heat.'

I stared at the menu and pondered whether to have sea fish or moussaka. I wondered what type of fish the sea fish was. I put the menu on the table face down. And then I saw it. At the bottom of the page was a doodle that featured an ejaculating penis and a scrotum as prickly as Desperate Dan's chin.

'Look! Boz, she's been here.'

'What?'

'This is her sign. Gloria's copralexic drawing.'

'Let me have a look.'

I handed the sheet to Boz.

'That's just some stupid kid messing around. Anybody could have done that.'

'Look at it Boz. That's not just any old spunking dick. It's a stylised image.'

'What do you mean?'

'Look at the flow of the lines. Look at those balls. Perfect circles. Difficult things to do, perfect circles. This is done by an expert. It's like a signature. I tell you this was done by Gloria. Gloria was here, Boz.'

'Why does she do this stuff? She's weird.'

'I told you. She's copralexic. It's an illness. She can't stop herself.'

'Huh, sounds like some middle class excuse for pissing off your teachers.'

'Yeah, well, anyhow she was here.'

'She ought to grow up.'

'You sound like her parents. She's perfectly grown up, I can assure you.'

'She ought to stop it.'

'She can't.'

Boz didn't understand. I needed another drink and some food. I ordered an ouzo and the sea fish.

'No sea fish,' the woman said firmly.

'Moussaka?' I asked.

'We have *omer-let* only.'

The war was already affecting supplies. I remembered what Mum had told me about food shortages and powdered egg in the Second World War. I wondered if the *omer-let* would be made with fresh eggs. Boz and I would probably soon need to get a ration book or something.

Later on, the light flickered for a couple of seconds and then went out. We sat in darkness until the woman wordlessly put a candle on our table. 'Blackout,' said Boz. I looked again in the candle light at the copralexic drawing on the menu. It was unmistakably Gloria's handy work.

*

We walked along the beach back to the cave. After the heat and dust of the Balkans and the oily Athens air it was good to be on the coast again. The sea was as still as mercury. A flash from a soundless thunderstorm miles away over the mountains momentarily lit up the dark sky. I spotted something floating in the water. Boz saw it as well.

'What the...?'

'Bloody Hell!'

'Man, that doesn't look good.'

As we got nearer, I could see that it was a body lying flat across the water. I stood by the sea's edge wondering what to do. How long had the corpse been in the water? I didn't want to touch it. Even from this distance it looked like it had been there a long time. I picked up a branch of driftwood and gently poked the cadaver. Sea-weed appeared to be growing out of the corpse's head. This crazy, bloody war.

And then to my horror the body sat up, long dreadlocks and Ben Gunn beard flailing in the air. 'Shit!' I screamed.

The figure turned round and glared at me.

'What the fuck are you doing?' it demanded.

'I thought you were dead.' I was shocked.

'Do I look like I'm dead? I was floating.'

'You shouldn't be doing that, there's a war on!'

'A war! That's a new one.'

'I thought you were a dead body. You scared me. Are you okay?'

'I was until you came along. And started poking me with a stick. Bloody idiot.'

'I thought you were a corpse.'

'Well, I'm not.'

'Sorry. I was just trying to be helpful.'

'I was minding my own business.'

'You're English,' I said.

I was surprised to hear that he had a hint of a West Midlands accent. I wondered if this guy was Sanchez, though I was expecting him to be Ethiopian or at least Spanish.

He didn't appear to hear me. 'I was enjoying the water. It's a good way to relax. Floating in and out with the waves, buoyed up by the sea. It's a meditation. Sometimes I get an out of body experience. Unless some prat comes along and pokes me with a stick.'

'Are you Sanchez?'

'Depends who's asking.' For a man with a reputation for eloquence he seemed hardly able to put one word in front of another.

'Somebody mentioned your name. The Danish guy called Blu.'

'Huh. Well, don't believe anything anyone says about me. And next time you see me doing this, I'll appreciate it if you just leave me alone. Got it?'

'You gave me a fright. The war makes people act strangely.'

'There's too many people on this beach sticking their noses into other people's business.' Sanchez grunted. 'Now, if you'll excuse me I've got something to do.'

Sanchez leant back in the water, spread-eagled his arms and legs and continued with his floating meditation.

TWENTY NINE

I didn't sleep well that night. The air in the cave was musty, my chest felt tight and I wanted to open a window. I wondered about the smell coming from the back chamber. I'd clean that tomorrow.

I thought about Gloria. I imagined her lying on the beach. I wondered how long ago she'd been in Matala. Maybe we were too late. Had she left already? Where would she go next? What do you do on Crete? Visit Knossos? What about the gorge that Keith, the space cowboy from London, had mentioned? Maybe she'd gone there. Surely she'd come back to Matala. After all, we had arranged to meet, hadn't we?

I thought I heard something scuttle across the floor. I sat up. It was too dark to see anything. Boz was snoring heavily. At least he wasn't shouting in his sleep.

I felt annoyed with myself. This was such a stupid quest. Why was I spending so much time dreaming about Gloria? And worse, there was always the shadow of Plank. I could never think about Gloria without Plank intruding at the most inconvenient moment. This was ridiculous. Thinking about Gloria was taking up too much time. I needed to forget her; I needed to forget Plank.

Stuck in the middle of a war! I lay listening for gunshot. That would be something to write about on a postcard. Though not to Mum and Dad. We'd have to hide in the mountains. Live on the land. At least the mountains would be better than this cave. We'd be safe up there. I resolved to buy a bandana. That would be more practical than a hat.

Was I imagining it, or could I feel those little black insects biting me? My hair was itching. I pulled the sleeping bag over my head. We'd move out of this shithole tomorrow.

I woke late. The sun was already high in the sky. Boz was standing at the cave entrance. It was a clear powder blue morning.

'Wow! This is some view,' Boz said. 'Did you have a good night's sleep?'

'I feel rough.'

When I did eventually drift off, my fitful sleep had been punctuated by hideous dreams of laughing skulls with abnormally large jaws.

'I slept like a dog,' said Boz. 'It was the best night's kip I've had in ages.'

I scratched and could feel some wheals on my back. 'I've been bitten to buggery. Don't insects ever sleep?'

'They do, but in the day. Anyway, there's something about this cave that makes me feel grounded,' said Boz. 'I feel safe.'

'I thought you didn't like the vibe.'

'I've got used to it. Yesterday I was tired, I needed a good night's sleep. As you said, people would pay good money to experience this. And we're getting it for free. It'll be a good place to take it easy for a while.'

I was surprised by Boz's change of mind.

'You've got a better ledge than me. It's by the window.' I said.

'Window?'

'Hole in the wall. You know what I mean.'

'I'm happy to swop.'

'I'd like to sleep in the olive groves tonight,' I suggested.

'What? I though you liked it here.'

'I do,' I said. 'But we can't stay in one place all the time. I've always wanted to sleep in an ancient olive grove.'

'Hang on, Felix. We've come all this way to sleep in these caves and you already want to move on. I'm just getting used to it. We've got security, shelter, and a good view. What more do you want?'

'I could do with a cup of tea.'

'We could make a fire. Have you noticed a fire place?' I wasn't used to Boz being so helpful.

'I think we need to clean the cave out,' Boz said. 'I'm going to buy a candle today and check out what's in the back room.'

*

We were sat inside the Mermaid trying to escape the brutal sun. Outside the street was empty: all the houses had their blue shutters closed, battened down against the burning mid-day heat. It was so hot, the slightest exertion and I was sweating; I was sitting motionless and I was still sweating. I could hear low voices as families ate their lunch and the faint echo of scraping plates and pots being washed.

A girl with plaited blonde hair that went half way down her back and a perfect complexion walked into the room, sat at a table and shouted: 'Hey Demetre! 'Coke and Metaxa Five Star. *Efharisto.*' She looked down at her bare feet and said to nobody in particular. 'That goddam beach tar gets everywhere.'

I nodded at her.

'You guys having a good time?' she asked. She gave us a big confident smile.

'Yeah, we've only just got here. We've been sorting out our cave.'

'Which one?'

'I don't know.'

'Some of them interconnect. Has it got ledges cut into the wall?'

'Yeah, that's it, like bunk beds.'

The woman was silent for a moment, as if she was working out how to say something, but then just smiled and laughed.

'I like your sneakers,' she said.

'Thanks. I got them in Rethymnon.'

'Have you met Sanchez yet?'

'I think so. He was floating in the water.'

'That was him. They say he walked here all the way from Ethiopia. He's on his way to the Caucasus mountains, apparently.'

'That's some journey.'

'Interesting guy,' she said pointing to her head and twirling her finger.

'So where have you guys come from?' the woman asked.

'France, Italy, Yugoslavia, Albania...'

Albania! You went to Albania? Are you insane or something?'

'We got as far as the border. They wouldn't let us in; we didn't have a visa.'

'It's one way traffic from that country. And the direction is out. Most people swim for it across the strait to Corfu. Not many make it. If the currents don't get you the sharks do.'

'You don't get sharks in the Ionian Sea,' I protested.

'Well, you know what I'm saying. You guys had a lucky escape.'

She stared at me and shook her head in disbelief. 'Nobody in their right mind goes to Albania.'

'Yeah, well we were a bit lost at the time.'

'So you guys coming back here tonight?'

'What's going on?'

'Party. Same as every night. Party, party, party. We'll drink retsina, eat Mamma's moussaka and dance 'til dawn. And for breakfast Demetre will serve ouzo slammers. You can then crawl back to your cave and sleep it off during the swelter of the day. How's that sound?'

'What about last night? This place was quiet.'

'Last night was the full moon.'

'Yeah?'

'We were grooving in a cove just down along the coast. Made a big fire. Danced around a bit, got naked. You guys should have come along.'

'We didn't know about it,' said Boz.

'Matala's a cool place; the final destination before who knows where. All good dreamers eventually end up in Matala. You meet everybody here; it's strawberry fields forever.'

For a moment I thought of Plank. I hoped not.

'If you're heading to India you go via Istanbul, otherwise you come here. It's the end of the road, there's nowhere else to go. The locals are very tolerant. We're developing an alternative community here. We're going to ship in some geodesic domes.

'The rule of the Generals doesn't extend this far. The nearest police are over the mountain so you can do pretty much what you want. It's best to keep your clothes on at the town end of the beach. Total nudity is okay by the caves. Are you guys from England?'

'Yeah.'

'Where are you from?'

'Near London.' It was always easiest to say London. Men would also know Manchester. 'Ah, Manchester United' they would exclaim and then slap their head and say 'Bobbie Charlton.' This hippie chick didn't look like she was a big football fan.

'Near London huh? You know the Royal Festival Hall? I've been there a couple of times. Played there. Lousy audience.'

'You played there? What do you do?' I wondered which Royal Festival Hall she was talking about. The one in her druggie dreams, probably.

'Sing a bit, play the guitar a bit. Smoke some weed. Listen to all their pretty lies. Usual stuff.'

She saw me absently staring at the big mural painted on the wall.

'I did that,' she said.

'Oh, you're Jodie.'

'Yeah that's me.'

'I thought Jodie was a bloke.'

'Take a walk! You Brits are such arsewipes. I can assure you I'm 100 per cent woman.'

'I can see that.'

Jodie stared at me, and then Boz, for an uncomfortably long time, as if she was weighing something up.

'Hey, are you guys faggots?'

Faggots! Did Jack Kerouac and Neal Cassady have this problem? That picture of Jack and Neal; two good looking American Joes, arms across each other's shoulders, can't they just be friends? Can't you give a good friend a hug? Or put your arm round their shoulder while you're standing at the bar waiting for a pint? What's wrong with that?

'No!'

'Huh!'

'Why?'

'You've got a kinda faggoty thing going on between you.'

'Like what?'

'It's the way you speak. You Brits all sound like closet queens to me. Look, I've got nothing against gays. I just like to know where we all stand.'

'Well, we're not gay.'

Jodie sipped her Metaxa and Coke and stared out to sea. The air was still and the sea motionless. We were all silent for a while. Boz stretched out in his seat and sighed. 'Oh man, this is a beautiful place.'

Jodie waved at a man in a fishing boat as it slowly chugged across the bay and disappeared round the headland.

'That's Spyros - he's got some groovy stories to spin.'

'Mama was telling us about the war,' I said.

Jodie stared at me. 'Don't get me started. Have you heard about this? They've awarded Henry Kissinger the Nobel Peace Prize. Henry Kissinger, the biggest war mongering bastard on the planet, gets the Nobel Peace Prize! Fighting for peace! Isn't that the most spectacular lie in the whole wide universe? You know what they say, fighting for peace is like screwing for virginity! Fighting for peace. Does that ever work? You've got to be sick in the head to understand that. The Yanks dive in, mess up a country and then retreat. It's all been for nothing. Uncle Sam is going to come away from Saigon with his tail ripped off. All those young men, all those beautiful flowers, sacrificed for zilch. Oh man!' Jodie paused and glared at me. 'I've come to get away from all that. I don't want to talk about the war. I don't EVER want to talk about the war. Vietnam sucks.'

'No. No. No. The war here.'

'The war here? Are you crazy?'

'Turkey has invaded.'

'Oh, that! You don't want to worry about that. That's on a little island miles away. That's just the Generals having a bit of fun playing their games. A little skirmish, it gives them something to do, keeps their hand in.'

'Mama said everybody had gone because of the war?'

'Yeah, well Mama, she gets a bit over excited. Don't worry about that, there ain't no war here. In Matala it's just love, peace and partying.'

'Are you sure?' I wondered how much this woman knew.

'Take it easy. It's too hot to get so uptight.'

'We're not uptight!' said Boz.

'Stop acting like it.'

'We've got Tiger Balm. We're cool.'

'Tiger Balm, huh?'

'What part of the States are you from?' I asked.

'You English are such arsecracks!'

She picked up her glass and headed outside. She turned and raised an extended finger. 'Screw you,' she said.

'What's bugging her?' I said to Boz.

'First you call her a bloke and then you say she's American.'

'So?'

'My guess is that she's Canadian.'

THIRTY

But first I needed to find the girls. I started asking around. Although a number of people swore that they'd met Gloria and Blodwyn I could never be sure that I was getting the real story.

'Sure, I've met them,' said an Aussie. 'I spent an evening drinking with Gloria and Blodwyn in this very bar.'

'Were they with anybody else?'

'Yeah, they had a guy with them.'

'Was he weird?'

'I didn't notice it at the time, but now you come to mention it, he was.'

'Did he have a big head?'

'Yeah, big chin, big nose, the ugliest French guy I've ever met.'

'French? Are you sure he was French.'

'All three of them were French.'

Or:

'Yeah, two pretty English girls.'

'Well, that can't be them,' Boz chipped in

'That's unfair. Blodwyn's not that bad,' I said.

Or:

'Gloria and Blodwyn? Yeah, I met them. They were here for a few days but then they went to explore the Samaria Gorge. They said they were then coming back to Matala.'

'Are you sure?'

'Sure I'm sure. What did you say their names were again?'

'Gloria and Blodwyn.'

'Sounds familiar. But then again...'

'I thought you said you were sure.'

'I was. But the more I think about it... No, they were definitely here.'

'Jesus!'

'Chill out man, if it happens, it happens. There are plenty more chicks on the beach.'

And so it went on. I was still no clearer as to their whereabouts than when I had arrived.

Meanwhile Boz had bought candles and had been exploring. As I clambered up to the cave I could see him leaning against the entrance looking like the proud owner of a new home.

'I've had a look around,' he said.

'And?'

'The cave doesn't go back any further than the back room. There's nothing there. Except for some pottery and other stuff. Come and have a look.'

We lit candles and went through the doorway to the back cave. It took a while to see anything.

'That's all there is. Apparently some of these caves connect to others - there's a whole labyrinth cut into this cliff. But not here. Look at the candle, it's not flickering, there's no draught.'

'How come you're the expert all of a sudden?'

'I'm just repeating what that Canadian woman told us.'

'What do you think they were used for?'

'Storage I expect. It's cool in here. Amphoras of olive oil, I imagine.'

'Look, there's some broken pottery over there.'

Boz walked over to the corner of the room and held his candle over a shattered urn.

'Boz, what's that sticking out of the floor?'

'Looks like a bone.'

Boz pulled the object out of the dust.

'Just a bone.'

'It's not just a bone, Boz, that's a human bone.'

'How do you know?'

'I do. Rib bone, I reckon. And look, there's another one.'

'Where?'

'Now that definitely is a human bone. No doubt about it.'

'Do you think so?' Boz seemed unconcerned. 'I reckon it's the bone of a sheep or a goat.'

'They must have bloody big sheep round here. That's a human leg bone.'

'How do you know?'

'Look.' I held the bone against my thigh. 'Perfect match.'

Boz looked at me quizzically. 'Anyway, so what?'

'So what? We're sleeping in a graveyard. Doesn't that freak you out?'

'Not really. Haven't you slept in a graveyard before?'

'No!'

'I've already told you, in Bolton we do it all the time. On a warm summer's night, after a blinder, there's nothing better. Those grave stones retain the warmth. It's like sleeping on a night storage heater.'

'How often do you get a warm summer's night in Bolton?'

'It's not that infrequent, actually.'

'Sleeping on gravestones freaks me out.'

'Better than being under one.'

'It's not natural.'

'Felix, as much as you might like to deny it, death is all part of living. It's about as natural as you can get.'

'Don't get all metaphysical with me. Remind me never to walk through a grave-yard in Bolton on a hot summer's night. It must be like zombie land.'

'Well, this isn't Bolton.'

'It's definitely my turn to sleep by the window tonight.' I said.

*

189

I lay on the beach and read a book. At last I was able to enjoy the soporific heat - though there was always a soft breeze in Matala that made the stifling Cretan air more bearable.

I looked across the sand. In the distance through the haze I could see the rake thin figure of Sanchez struggling through the olive grove pulling his homemade toboggan with a water container on it. The sledge was the sort of contraption used by North American Indians. Sanchez cut an interesting figure. I noticed people gave him bread and olives. Everybody was fascinated by him; aside from the rumour that he'd walked here from Ethiopia I was to hear other stories. It was said he rarely left Matala and he didn't like going near roads. It was rumoured that he'd got a phobia of wheels.

I wondered if this was the same Sanchez that Stoner used to talk about. With General Franco now on his death bed there were more Spanish travellers on the road and Sanchez wasn't such an unusual name. But then again didn't he have the slight nasal wine of a Black Country accent? If he was the same Sanchez his charisma seemed to have faded.

It was so hot I could feel the thick air rippling over my body. Kristina, a honey-tanned German girl who I'd spoken to in the Mermaid, walked by and smiled.

I squinted at her. Her silhouette showed a slim but curvy body. 'Hi there,' I said.

'You better watch out, you're going to burn.'

'It's okay, I've rubbed on some olive oil.'

'You want to fry yourself or something?'

'It keeps the skin soft.'

'Soft red skin. Not good.'

I was getting pissed off by this. She was the third girl to warn me I was going to crisp up like bacon. 'Thanks for your concern - I'm sure I'll be okay.' I went back to reading *The Magus*.

I thought of Gloria. I remembered our evening together in Bristol listening to Cat Stevens. Despite what Boz had said I was certain the copralexic doodle was hers and she had already been in Matala. But would she return? I was sure she would.

I woke from my slumber in the sun with my heart pumping. Why hadn't I thought of this before? The first thing anybody did when they arrived in Matala, and the last thing they did when they left, was to have a drink in the Mermaid. It was obvious; the person to ask was Demetre. Demetre knew the comings and goings of everybody in town.

'Yes, of course they were here,' he said. 'Two lovely English girls - two beautiful English roses. They said they were meeting somebody from England.'

'Did they say who?'

'I cannot remember. What is your name?'

'Felix.'

'Yes, Felix. It was you they were waiting for. Definitely Felix. You are Felix?

'Yes, I'm Felix.'

Demetre shook my hand. 'Felix, I am pleased to meet you. These girls, they spoke about you a lot. You are from ...?'

'Ruislip.'

'Yes, they speak about Ruislip and how beautiful it is.'

I didn't know Gloria knew anything about Ruislip.

'Felix, you must stay here till they return. Stay in this bar. You come here every day. They will return and find you. No problem. I promise. And while you wait I will introduce you to Spyros my cousin. He will take you out in his boat and show you special things. Secret things.' Demetre tapped his nose conspiratorially.

Demetre was right, I had to wait. I had all the time in the world. It was just a matter of hanging around until Gloria and Blodwyn turned up. Meanwhile there was nothing else to do but relax.

THIRTY ONE

The bar was filling up. All the beach bums were there. Out of the kitchen came the warm smell of moussaka. Thank goodness rationing hadn't yet kicked in. I recognised several people; the bare-chested woman I had spoken to when we first arrived was now wearing a white t shirt while her guy had put on turquoise Navaho love beads and a clean head-band. Everybody in the Mermaid appeared to know each other. And soon, so did we.

After travelling for so long Matala was a good place to stay for a while. The azure sea was warm and the air smelt of eucalyptus. As we settled into a routine of doing very little, the pace of life slowed to a beatific calm. I'd get up when I felt the rays of the sun on my face, and go to bed when the ouzo ran out.

During the day we'd lie in the sun reading. A book and a beach; I could do this forever. Some people say they become bored on the beach, but not me. I enjoy the wonderful feeling that you can lose yourself in a novel and read a whole story in a day or two. I love to live in another world, to be energized and immersed in new ideas, new concepts and different perceptions; and to be reassured that the weird stuff in my head is thought by other people as well.

To read, swim in the warm sea, doze, go for a beer, read some more - this was heaven. We'd eat yoghurt for breakfast and watermelon for lunch. In the afternoon we'd sleep under the olive trees, hiding from the burning heat. We'd wash under a rusty shower on the beach with an erratic trickle of water. And before we knew it, the sun was dipping into the sea, it was time for another beer and we were ready to hang out in the Mermaid and chill with the freaks and listen to the battery powered record player or Jodie strumming her guitar. After a while

Mama and Demetre addressed Boz and me by our names. We were no longer just holiday hippies; we were proud to be part of the Matala freak community.

There was a floating population of people coming and going. We were the global village. We'd all hang out and shoot the shit. We'd talk about the bars we'd got drunk in and the characters we'd met. We discussed the cultural icons of the age: Timothy Leary; Carlos Castaneda; Schumacher; Buckminster Fuller; Marshall McLuhan, and the universal message of harmony, understanding and tolerance advocated by *The Clangers*. I learnt about astrology, tarot cards, the I Ching. We argued about politics and the imminent uprising of the oppressed. Though I never could get my head round the shape of the revolution that people said was in the air - it seemed to me more like straightforward revenge. And after the revolution, what next? Ah, the hallucinations of anarcho-hippie ideology. 'What do we want? The World! When do we want it? We want it now!'

And so time drifted by, long and slow. There were no markers to tell me the day of the week; no Thursday evening *Top of the Pops*, no weekends. Since we'd been in Crete I'd lost track. Time merged blissfully into a blur. I was calm, I was living in the present.

'Can you do this?' A German guy sitting nearby threw a silver puzzle ring onto our table.

'Yeah, sure,' I said.

I looked at the four intertwined rings. I wasn't sure how they fitted together. Boz watched me fumble with the pieces. After five minutes he said, 'You have no idea, do you?'

'I'm not familiar with this version.'

Boz took the ring from me. With the flourish of a magician he gently lifted, dangled, turned and lined up the pieces so thirty seconds later he was holding a completed ring in his hand.

'Impressive!'

'There's a technique, a little Turkish girl in Bolton showed me. I'll teach you sometime.'

Boz handed the ring to the owner. The German shouted to Demetre. 'Two Ouzos for my English friends.'

'Where'd you get the ring from?'

'Istanbul.'

'What about the war?'

The German grimaced.

'The war with Turkey,' Boz added quickly.

'Ah! No problem. We left Turkey two weeks ago. I think it's a local disturbance.'

Bouzouki music was playing now. People were shouting. I spotted Jodie, carrying a guitar. She joined a group of freaks drinking Retsina at an adjoining table.

Boz and I got talking about the caves to an English hippie called Rollo. I'd previously seen Rollo at the nudist end of the shore, away from the town. I'd noticed that he was invariably sitting cross legged in deep conversation with one of the more attractive girls.

'No watch, eh?' said Rollo.

'When you're living in a cave who needs one?' I said.

'I find I have something in common with people who don't wear watches.'

'Yeah, they're always late,' Boz whispered.

'Over the millennia the caves have been used for different purposes,' Rollo said, 'some have been used for storage, others for family homes.'

'How can you tell which are the family ones?' I asked.

'A good question, my friend. You have to connect to the vibe. This is a sacred landscape. Some caves have a good heart. You can tell that straightaway. Others, well, they're unpredictable, you've got to tune into the spirit of the place. A couple of days of spiritual transfer and meditation usually does the trick.'

'You seem to know a lot about them.'

'I've been researching ley lines for years. Do you know people have tried to count the caves but nobody has ever come up with the same number.'

'We've been in ours a while, it seems okay,' Boz said.

'Of course some of the caves were used by lepers. People tell this story about a man who woke up with what he thought was a furry animal on his sleeping bag. It turned out it to be his hair. His hair had fallen out in the night. He must have been staying in one of the leper caves. Something to do with the arsenic they used. He ran screaming into the sea. Never to be seen again.'

'Heavy!' I said as I put my hand up to my head, half expecting to feel a porcelain smooth skull.

'Don't worry,' Rollo said, 'That particular cave has been blocked up. I'm also studying the ceremonies they were used for.'

'Ceremonies? What type of ceremonies?'

'Initiation ceremonies. Sacred circumcision and all that stuff. Young men had to live in them while they were instructed in the rituals of manhood. And of course the Minoans also used the caves for funerary purposes.'

'Burials?' I said.

'Many generations of one family would use the same caves.'

'Not our cave, I hope.'

'Probably not. There are a number of tell tale signs to look for.'

'Like?'

'It's obvious. Pots and skulls and bones.'

'Pots and skulls and bones!'

'If there are skulls and bones the cave is a funerary cave. You don't have to read the runes to understand that.'

'What if there are bones but no skulls?' Boz asked.

'The same thing. Somebody has nicked the skulls. The craniums are sold in Athens as novelty ashtrays while local people turn the teeth into necklaces. It's shameful.'

'That's disgusting.'

'Aside from the skulls and bones,' Rollo continued, 'there is one other definite marker ....'

But Rollo never got to finish his sentence. At this moment our conversation was interrupted by a commotion at the door.

'The Junta has collapsed,' somebody shouted. 'The Generals have been kicked out.'

Everybody in the bar gave a cheer. There was hugging and shouting and chanting. Rollo disappeared in the mayhem.

'Holy shit!' I had to raise my voice to be heard. 'First a war, then the fall of the Generals.'

'It's all happening!' Boz shouted.

'It's been a long day, I need to order a Metaxa.' I was still thinking about what Rollo had said about the caves.

'Make it a double,' Boz said.

'I think we need the high octane seven star,' I yelled.

'Yeah.'

'Do you know what?' I said to Boz, 'I think we've experienced enough of the cave dwelling vibe. Why don't we stay in the village?'

'No. We need to save money.'

'But I could do with a shower.'

'Felix, the vibe in our cave is fine.' Boz put his hand on my arm in what was meant to be a reassuring gesture. 'Don't worry, that guy was talking a load of guff.'

'Do you think so?'

'Long hair halfway down his back and an all-over sun tan doesn't mean he's an expert.'

Boz was right. Gloria would be disappointed if she found us lodging in a *zimmer*.

*

There was only one speck of disquiet during those long idyllic days: Boz's dwindling finances. I knew exactly what would happen. At the last possible moment, when Boz was down to his final bean, and we were buying a ferry ticket or something crucial like that, he'd turn his bearded face to me and, like a saucer-eyed Oliver Twist on mescaline, plead for a loan. For his own self respect I needed to avert this embarrassing situation. I remembered our conversation many months back in Bristol. Perhaps now was the time to find out the price of blood on the open market.

'Have you seen a hospital on this island?' I asked. I thought it best to approach this topic in a roundabout manner.

'Are you feeling ill?'

'No, I'm just interested.'

'Is your sun-burnt back okay?'

'It's just that...'

'Oh, man. I know what you are going to say.' I saw Boz's eyes light up as if wires had sparked from a battery. 'Don't even go there, Felix.'

'You don't know what I'm about to say.'

'I do. I know exactly what you are about to say, and you are a sick bastard'

'What was I going to say then?'

'That I ought to check out the price of blood. You want me to sell a pint of my own precious blood. How could you?'

This was frightening. We'd been travelling together for so long we were able to read each other's minds. We'd be finishing each other's sentences next.

'If you want to know, that wasn't what I was going say. My asthma inhaler is low.'

'Liar! You told me you didn't need an inhaler in this climate. You said this Mediterranean weather is so good it ought to be available on the National Health Service.'

'Have you got anything to sell?' I asked. 'What about those bones? Did you find any teeth? Have you got any craniums you could hawk on the beach?'

'That's not funny, Felix.'

'What about busking? Jodie earns a few free drinks with her strumming and wailing.'

'You know I can't play an instrument.'

'For purely academic reasons it would be interesting to know how much they pay for blood.'

'No.'

'You need to do something about it.'

'What?'

'Your lack of money.'

'It's under control, I promise.'

Boz pointed at my sun-burnt shoulders. 'You need to watch yourself.' He made a sizzling noise like a drop of water falling on a hot plate. 'The last time I saw anything like that it was covered in gravy and there was a Yorkshire pudding next to it.'

'Stop changing the subject,' I said.

*

Despite his empty wallet I was surprised to notice Boz taking an interest in the tourist gifts on sale in the main street. One afternoon I watched from a distance as he furtively entered a shop. Through the window I saw him examine a tiny scent bottle decorated with silver filigree. He then inspected a white cotton kaftan. Even from where I stood I could see that its collar was embroidered with gold thread.

'What are you doing, Boz?'

Boz jumped. 'I thought my Mum might like this?' he said as he quickly put down the kaftan and grabbed an ashtray decorated with a picture of a Greek windmill.

'I thought you said she doesn't smoke.'

'She could put peanuts in it.'

'I didn't know she was a nut freak.' I didn't like to mention that they'd get stuck in her false teeth.

'What do you know about my Mum? You've never met her.'

'You said she was like Hilda Ogden.'

'I said she wasn't like Hilda Ogden. Anyway, you never know, do you? She might suddenly get a taste for them. A 'certain age' and all that. I could buy her some pistachios. She'd like them.'

'I thought you hated all this stuff.'

'I've always liked nuts.'

'Not nuts, this tourist crap.'

'Yeah, it's a rip off,' Boz conceded. 'I don't know how they get away with it. Who buys this rubbish?'

*

One afternoon Boz made another of his interesting suggestions. He thought we ought to get closer to nature. I didn't think that was possible; living in a cave was about as stripped back as it got. But Boz said that the cliff face was getting crowded - we now had neighbours on both sides and it felt suburban. I assured Boz that this was far from suburban. But Boz said we could go one step further. For a moment I thought this might involve wearing a loincloth like Sanchez. But what Boz had in mind was to head for the mountains and go wild camping.

'I'm feeling the call of the wild. I think we ought to find that gorge that's like a crack in the earth. We'd light a fire at night to scare away the wolves.'

'But I like it here.'

'We'd spend no money.'

'We've got to wait for Gloria,' I said.

'Give her a few more days, and if she doesn't turn up, I think we ought to try it.'

It did seem an intriguing idea, though I wasn't too keen on the wolves.

THIRTY TWO

S pyros turned off the outboard motor. The sea was flat; I enjoyed the early morning quiet. Apart from the water lapping at the bows, we were surrounded by silence. Spyros pointed at the deep lucent water. 'There. See it?' he said.

I squinted, shading my eyes from the reflection.

'What?'

'There,' he repeated, jabbing his hand towards the water.

My eyes adjusted to the shimmering light. It felt like looking into some great aquarium. Deep down below us, on the sandy seabed, was the skeleton of a boat.

'Oh!'

'That boat is Phoenician.'

'Wow!' I'd heard of the Phoenicians but didn't know much about them. 'How old is that?'

'It sunk over two thousand years ago.'

Boz and I silently stared through the bottle-green water. I wanted to jump in and swim down and examine the bones of the boat. I'd no idea how deep the water was. But it was deep; probably just about reachable by a sponge diver. That the wreck was out of reach made it even more poignant.

'The people who sailed in that boat may well have lived in our cave,' Boz said in a hushed voice. 'Makes you think, doesn't it?'

'This is our secret,' said the boat man.

'I feel privileged to see it,' I said. 'It's fantastic.'

'How can this be secret?' Boz asked.

'Few people know about this,' Spyros repeated. 'Just you. And my family.'

'People OUGHT to know about this.' Boz was about to spoil it. I liked it being a secret. 'They would come miles to see it. It ought to be brought up from the sea bed and put in a museum.'

'That would not be good,' said Spyros.

'Why?' Boz asked.

'It belongs here.'

'But people would pay to see it.' Why was Boz saying this?

'No.'

'Spyros, you could be a rich man,' Boz insisted.

'People like me don't become rich. The director of the Museum in Heraklion, maybe. But not Spyros Christopoulos from Matala. It is best that it remains here. It is our history.'

'You could build a museum in Matala.'

'Why would I do that?'

'It would be good for the town. You'd get more visitors. God, if we had something like this in Bolton.'

Spyros puffed and shook his head. It was clear that he didn't want more visitors.

'You could earn loads of money.'

'I have a nice house, I have my family, we eat good food. I have a car.' Spyros laughed. 'Maybe a better car, a Mercedes perhaps, would be good. But look around you. It is beautiful. There are fish in the sea and over there, olives on the trees. I am content. Change is not always a good thing.'

I could see what he meant.

Spyros stood square-footed at the back of the wooden boat. Something had caught his attention.

'What's that? Sharks?' Boz asked.

Perhaps a hundred metres away the early morning calm sea had been disturbed. I could see sinister black fins cutting the water, and then diving out of sight. Whatever they were, they were swimming towards us.

'Mermaids!' laughed Spyros.

As they got nearer I could see that they were dolphins. They clustered around the boat with their mouths in the air. Spyros threw them some small fish that he had in a wicker basket.

'I've got to get in there,' said Boz.

'You're mad.'

'Can't you hear them?'

I listened. 'No.'

'They're calling me. Listen. You promised.'

'I promised? What did I promise?'

'Pilchards!'

All I could hear was a clicking, like somebody flicking a Zippo lighter. 'I can't hear anything.'

'They're saying come and join us. Can't you hear the clicking?'

'Yeah, I can hear that.' I put my hand to my ear. 'They're saying come on in, the water's lovely.'

'Stop taking the piss.' Boz was taking off his T shirt. Before I had a chance to warn Boz that dolphins can give a nasty bite he had jumped in.

'Whoa!'

The dolphins crowded round Boz like kids in a playground. They didn't look like fish. They had smiles on their faces.

'Oh man!' Boz was laughing hysterically as if somebody was tickling him. The clicking was getting louder. I'm sure the dolphins were laughing as well; they were whistling. And then, to my horror, they pushed him under the water. They had clustered round so tightly that he was held down. All I could see of Boz was a hand sticking out of the water, waving desperately.

'Spyros,' I shouted, 'they're drowning Boz.'

Spyros was unconcerned. 'They like him. They're playing with him. They'll let him go in a moment.'

I grabbed an oar ready to smack the biggest dolphin on the head. But then Boz resurfaced. He was gasping for air. But to my surprise he was smiling. He grabbed one of the dolphins and kissed it on the face. 'You guys!' he shouted joyously. The clicking was even louder. A couple of the dolphins were swimming on their backs waving their fins in the air.

'Felix, you've got to do this. It's incredible. Come in and join me.'

'Frolicking with fishes – it's not really my scene.' I didn't want to. But how often do you get a chance to swim with dolphins?

'Don't call them fish. You'll upset them.'

'It's too deep.'

'Don't worry, they'll look after you.'

'This is mad.' I said as I lowered myself into the water.

I wondered what they would feel like. I reached out and stroked a head. It wasn't scaly; its flesh was firm and toned, it was like stroking a watermelon. I'd never experienced anything like this before - or since. They gave off a vibe. I felt like I was with old friends. I know this sounds nuts but I felt I was communing with a higher order of being. It was as if the dolphins were reading my mind; like they had a sixth sense. Can you feel love? I wanted to hug them.

It was over all too quickly. After about five minutes the dolphins swam away as suddenly as they had arrived. I'm sure I saw one of them wave a fin as a gesture of goodbye.

'That was quite something.' Boz said.

'Yeah. Far out. Better than those little pilchards, I bet.'

'I think that would be another experience. It's the difference between being in a group and a crowd. I'd like to contrast and compare.'

'Next summer, maybe.'

Spyros tied his boat alongside Matala's small jetty. We shook hands.

'How can you keep this a secret?' I asked.

'Just my family… and the people I bring here.'

'Well, I feel privileged to have seen it. How often do you take people here?'

'Not often.'

'Once a month or something?'

'No. A little more than that. Twice a day perhaps.'

Suddenly membership of the dolphin club didn't seem so exclusive.

As I clambered off the boat I turned and said, 'Our little secret then.' Spyros gave a knowing wink. I was now beginning to wonder if the wrecked boat really was Phoenician.

THIRTY THREE

There was still no sign of Gloria and Blodwyn. During my first few days at Matala I'd been in a state of edgy anticipation but as time went by I could feel the tension loosening. If only Gloria would arrive soon and we could share this paradise together. But then again I wondered, perhaps she'd burst the bubble, perhaps this blissful melancholia was as good as it got. I'd spent months shaping Gloria into the woman of my dreams and through no fault of her own she was bound to fall short. Deep in the recesses of my mind I discovered a surprising thought. Maybe it would be for the best if Gloria didn't turn up.

Boz and I were sitting on what Demetre grandly called the *Terrasse Panoramique*. I ordered a Greek coffee and sat looking out to sea, enjoying the cool of the early hours.

'Excuse me,' said a girl who was sitting at the next table. 'Can I ask you something?'

'Sure.' She could ask me anything.

'I'd like to take a photograph of you.'

'A photograph?' Is that all it takes? After a few days sunning myself on the beach French chicks were queuing up to take my photograph.

'Okay,' I said with a world-weary sigh, as if this sort of thing happened all the time.

'Turn round and lift up your t-shirt.'

I winced. I couldn't see it, but I realized I had overdone the sun bathing. It hurt to twist my neck and look over my shoulder. I could see that my once milky skin was now a fiery pink.

The girl laughed. 'You are the colour of your roast biff.' She licked her finger and stabbed it at my back and made a hissing sound.

'Ouch!'

You are hot stuff!' she said as she took a photograph of my back.

'Yeah, very funny.'

Boz continued reading his book but after five minutes slammed it on the table.

'This is even worse than *Tarantula*! James Joyce is a raving lunatic.'

'I thought he was a genius.'

'It's incomprehensible, the words are made up. He must have written *Finnegan's Wake* when he was drunk. This is the voice of a bar room pisshead.'

'I'll lend you Jan Cremer.'

'It better be good, I think I'm getting reader's block.'

I looked at the sea. That was some sea. Today it was as flat as oil. It looked so welcoming. Its colour was grades of deep blue broken by patches of ice green. I could swim to the horizon, no problem.

Until this summer I'd only been as far away from home as Cornwall. The sea had appeared different there; a darker colder blue. Now as I looked at this flat sea I could hardly tell where the milky horizon ended and the hazy sky began. The sky and sea were all one tone. I watched a boat *put-put* across the bay; it looked like it was hanging in the air.

'Do you know what's over there?' I asked Boz.

'Africa?'

'Egypt.'

'Egypt!'

Sitting in Matala, Crete felt so exotic. Yet over that horizon was another continent. We were only a short way away from the Orient: pyramids, camels, hot orange sunsets, harems and hashish.

' "Much have I travelled in the realms of gold",' I said to myself.

'What are you muttering? "Realms of what?",' asked Boz.

"Much have I travelled in the realms of gold." I could remember standing on bare floorboards, waiting for the teacher to mark my exercise book.

'It's a poem I was forced to learn at school. I couldn't understand a word of it at the time. I think it's rather beautiful now.'

'Pretentious git!' said Boz.

I ignored him, but I knew he was more interested than he made out.

' "Much have I travelled in the realms of gold, and many goodly states and kingdoms seen." ' I repeated. I was amazed that these words were still stored in my head.

'That's weird,' said Boz, 'I remember something like that. Stout Cortez standing on Darien looking at the Pacific. Is that the same poem? Chubby Cortez! We used to laugh at that. Who's it by?'

'Shelley, I think.'[10]

We were both silent. I sipped my Greek coffee and stared at the Mediterranean. Being here felt so right. I'd always dreamt of this, even in Dorset, when I used to gaze at the sea. I'd always wanted to go over the horizon. Here was my chance.

'Boz, I could go on forever.'

'Me too. Do you know what, I noticed that there's a ferry from Heraklion to Alexandria.'

'I'd love to hear the call to prayer, echoing across the busy city.'

'We ought to carry on travelling,' said Boz.

'Yeah we need to go further - into less familiar territory.'

'See where the road leads.'

'I don't want to go home,' I said.

'Me neither.'

'We've got nothing to rush back to England for.'

'Apart from University.'

'That doesn't start until October.'

---

[10] He's wrong. It's John Keats (1795-1821): *On First Looking into Chapman's Homer.* Ed.

'We could get somebody to register for us.'

'Or we could take a year off.'

'Another year off.'

'Let's just take it easy.'

'See how it goes.' I agreed.

'Yes. Trust in fate.'

Later that day Boz walked into the Mermaid wearing a white embroidered kaftan.

'What do you reckon?' he asked.

I was astounded. 'Where did you get that from?'

'The gift shop.'

'I thought you hadn't got any money.'

'I haven't.'

'Have you lifted it? That's not cool.'

'No, no, no. I've set aside some money for presents.'

'You look like Demis Roussos,' I sneered. I'd never been able to see a kaftan in the same light since I'd seen Demis Roussos on TV warbling like some Greek Womble in a ridiculous golden affair the size of a double duvet.

'You're jealous.'

'Tur!' I clicked in denial.

'At least I'm trying to make the effort.'

'Effort? Shoving feathers up your arse doesn't turn you into a chicken.'

'Felix, have you looked at yourself recently?'

'What are you trying to say?'

'Look at your abattoir shoes. They're ridiculous.'

'I can't help it that my shoes fell apart.'

'I'm speaking to you as a friend.'

'I'm wary when you say that.'

Boz continued: 'Felix, you're looking a bit worse for wear.'

I didn't like this. 'What do you mean?'

'Just find a mirror sometime.'

'Tell me. What is it?'

I stared at Boz, trying to gauge his expression. He scanned me up and down and he gave me the look of a dog licking piss off a nettle. I braced myself: home truths hurt the most.

'Forget it,' he said at last. 'I shouldn't have said anything.'

I suddenly felt alarmed. Was there something I should know?

'Forget it! I can't forget it. Boz, you've got to tell me. If I've got a massive bald patch, you've got to tell me. As my friend you're obliged to tell me.' I gently tugged at my hair, fearing that clumps would come away in my hand.

'Okay...' Boz sighed '...your hair's dirty and knotted, your lips are cracked, your nose looks like it's been dipped in paint stripper, your clothes stink of sweat ...'

'How dare you.'

'You asked.'

'There's ways of saying this. It's called tact.'

'Let me put it another way, the down and out look isn't a particularly good style for pulling the girls.'

'Rollo seems to do okay. And in case you haven't noticed, the avocado bathroom suite in our cave doesn't come with a mirror.'

'When did you last wash your clothes?'

'You don't need to wash your clothes in weather like this.'

'You're even thinking like a dosser.'

'Can't people see the inner beauty?'

'Look Felix, I'm telling you this for your own good. I'm sure Gloria...'

'You keep Gloria out of it.'

'You want to be looking your best for her.'

'Sometimes, Boz, you push the wire just a little bit too far.'

THIRTY FOUR

Boz's attitude to money was really bugging me. I couldn't understand why he'd bought that kaftan. I hadn't even bought my own presents, and I still had some cash. It was essential to confront Boz head-on and get him to take his dwindling reserves seriously. He needed to be shocked into action.

'Boz, you're a healthy guy. You don't need two kidneys.'

Boz didn't even flinch. 'I'm perfectly happy with my two kidneys, thank you.'

If this didn't push him to the edge nothing would. 'Two kidneys is greedy. How can you justify it?'

'How many kidneys have you got then?'

'Two. But ...' I added, ' ... I'm not short of money.' I could see in his eyes I had flicked the anger switch. The adrenaline was pumping.

'Felix, you are one sick bastard.'

'I'm just trying to be helpful.'

'Why are you so concerned about my finances?' he raged. 'You've never worried about me before. You never showed any concern when I had to pawn my Moody Blues albums.'

'On this trip I feel responsible for you.'

'Well, don't.'

'Your financial deficit is going to have a knock-on effect. I have a nasty feeling you're going to ask me for a loan. And that'll mess up my own plans.'

'It won't.'

I looked at Boz. His hair! All the girls loved his shoulder length hair. It was now sun bleached to the colour of Matala sand. He could get some good cash for that. Five pounds at least.

'Stop looking at me like that,' said Boz.

'I was just...'

'No way, pal. No bloody way.'

'You don't know what I'm thinking.'

'I do, and the answer is 'no way'.

'You'd look good with short hair.'

'Nobody looks good with short hair.'

'Steve McQueen?'

'I don't have a motorbike.'

Boz got up and started to walk away. 'Look Felix, just shut up. If you must know I've sent a postcard to my parents asking them to send money to the *poste restante* in Athens. Satisfied?'

'I'm sorry, I ...'

'Back off, you're beginning to get on my tits.'

'... I didn't know.'

At the door Boz turned and pointed his finger at me, 'And I will hold you personally responsible if my old man dies of shock.'

*

The overthrow of the Generals called for a party. The beach bums, the cave dwellers, the righteous hippies, the zimmer lodgers, even the local men were all crammed into the Mermaid intent on celebrating the end of a bloody epoch. The mood was euphoric. Thick blue smoke from cheap Greek cigarettes blended with the rich smell of Mama's cooking and the aniseed reek of ouzo. All evening we drank and talked. Voices were raised higher and higher to be heard over the clamour.

There was a shout.

'Jodie's going to give us a song.' Yells of 'Yeah!' and 'Whoa!'

Jodie strummed her guitar and the room fell silent. She smiled at the audience and then looked down at her fingers. Jodie sang in a clear high voice. When she sang, her face softened, she had a faraway look in her eyes; it was if she had turned into a different person. Even the old men at the back of the room stopped clicking their worry beads. She had a glow about her. She was beautiful. Her first song finished, everybody wanted more. She sang songs of yearning, of lost love, of travelling. I don't know how, but she was tearing my heart out.

'Jodie, I love you,' shouted Boz.

'What did you say that for?' To my astonishment there were tears in Boz's eyes.

'Man, that was beautiful. She is a beautiful woman.'

'She called you faggot.'

'She called you a faggot AND an arsehole.'

'It was arsecrack, actually.'

Jodie gave a bow. 'Thank you. That's it for now.' She raised a glass. 'Time for everybody to dance.'

People were shouting and stamping and banging on the bar. 'More! More!'

'Okay, just one more. This is a song that I learnt from my friend Country Joe McDonald.' Whoops and yeahs. She went straight into it. 'One, two, three, what are we fighting for…We don't give a damn, the next stop is Vietnam!' More whoops and yeahs.

'Time to party!' The volume on the record player was cranked up. Three Greek guys stood up and put their arms on each other's shoulders. The bouzouki beat started slowly and built up and up to a crescendo.

Bottles kept appearing on our table. 'Who's paying for this stuff?' I asked.

'Who knows? Just drink it.'

'C'mon let's get up there,' shouted Boz. Before I knew what had happened I was on the floor dancing with the Greek guys. The beat was hypnotic. Faster and faster. I was smiling and laughing. I was in a trance. I could feel sweat running down my back. I loved these people. This is how life should be: young and old; freak and Greek. I loved everybody. We were united. It was a big Cretan groove-in. Everybody was up now. Even the old boys at the back were standing.

One of the Greek guys grabbed a big white plate off a table and threw it at the wall.

'What the ....'

'That's what they do here,' Boz shouted in my ear.

A glass hit the wall and shattered. Then another.

I looked to the kitchen to see Mama's reaction. She was shaking her head but smiling.

'I bet you don't do this in Bolton.' I said, as I chucked my glass at the wall.

'Fook the Generals,' yelled Boz, as he smashed a plate on the floor.

For a moment I wondered if this celebration was a little premature. Had the Junta really been pushed off its perch? I didn't want my feet roasted, my sunburnt back was bad enough ... but what the heck.

'Yeah, may they rot in hell,' I shouted.

The room was packed: people were standing on chairs and tables, people were crowded at the door, unable to get in. It was dark outside but I could see faces. I was spinning. The room was spinning. I was hallucinating.

For a brief flash I imagined I saw Gloria and Blodwyn! If only... But then they were gone.

The Greek guys were dancing, arms in the air. We were clapping. Faster, faster, faster. Louder, louder, louder....

'Hey!' We were dancing on flames. The floor was on fire! My plastic abattoir shoes were melting. These guys were crazy. Thin streams of flaming lighter fuel were squirted on the concrete floor and the guys were dancing around it.

I had another ouzo. 'I think I'm entering what Buddhists call the final stage of enlightenment,' I shouted to Boz. We could go on for ever. We were invincible. Yeeehaaa!

I could hear the ringing of a carillon of church bells. Someone was shaking my shoulder. I lifted my head off the table. It was Demetre. He was holding a tray of glasses. 'Breakfast! Ouzo slammers!'

*

'Boz, I've been thinking about something.'

Boz looked at me suspiciously. 'Yeah?'

'Last night I thought I saw Gloria.'

'What?'

'When we were dancing. As I was spinning round I saw somebody who looked like Gloria.'

'Oh, I saw *her.*'

'You saw Gloria as well?'

'No. She looked like Gloria. But it wasn't her.'

'Are you sure?'

'Yeah. She was by the door. There was somebody who looked like Blodwyn, standing next to her.' Boz was silent for a moment. 'It definitely wasn't them,' he said.

'And what about all that stuff in the sea. The waves were glowing like neon lights. Was that my imagination as well?'

'That ouzo is strong stuff.'

'No it wasn't them,' I agreed. 'That Ouzo bends your mind. It makes you see what you want to see.'

'Yeah. Definitely.'

THIRTY FIVE

I was sitting in the *Mermaid* with my back to the door looking out to the beach and the sea, when I noticed Boz give a look of surprise - which was then followed by a wide grin spreading across his great bearded face. I turned to see what he was looking at. Standing in the doorway were two girls. Two stray waifs. Their hair was bleached by the sun and their skin was a honey coloured brown. Their lips were cracked. They were both wearing sawn-off jeans and dirty white t shirts. They looked gorgeous.

I ran over to Gloria and gave her long hug. Her body felt warm and she smelt of sun lotion. 'Where've you been?' I said.

'Felix, how super to see you.'

'When did you get here?'

'Yesterday.'

'It WAS you! I saw you when we were dancing. Why didn't you say hello?'

'You seemed to be having such a jolly time.'

'You should have joined us.'

'We were absolutely exhausted after the trip over the mountains.'

I stood back to take a longer look at Gloria. Somehow her pale English beauty had been transformed into something more overt and physical. She gave me a sweet smile. There were so many things I wanted to ask Gloria, there were so many things I wanted to talk about. I just wanted to be with her. I wanted everybody else to disappear. I wanted to take her to the cave and make up for lost time.

But first there was Boz and Blodwyn to sort out. I did the introductions. 'You remember Boz?' I said to Gloria.

Boz shook Gloria's hand and nodded at Blodwyn.

Blodwyn was looking at Boz with interest. 'Hi, Boz. I've heard a lot about you,' she said.

I hardly recognized Blodwyn. The sun seemed to suit her - her caramel coloured tan emphasised her dark violet eyes. She oozed a sleek, glossy healthiness.

'Have you?' Boz sounded surprised. 'Not all good, I hope?'

'I'll tell you later. Hey, I like your kaftan.'

'Thank you,' said Boz, unaware of Blodwyn's snide innuendo.

'Do you really like kaftans?' I asked. Apart from George Harrison anybody wearing a kaftan looked stupid.

'Yeah, I like a man in a kaftan. It usually means they take drugs.'

'Really?'

'Jimi Hendrix wore a kaftan,' said Blodwyn.

I didn't like to mention Jimi also died in one.

'So what's been happening?' I said.

'I never thought you'd really get to Matala,' said Gloria.

'But we arranged to meet.'

'Well, sort of.'

'We did! We agreed in Bristol. Conical hills, with people wearing conical hats. Don't you remember?'

Gloria laughed. 'I DO remember that. Anyway, as soon as we got here I wrote you a postcard. That was before I saw you dancing.'

'I knew you were here,' I said. 'I saw your doodle.'

'What?'

'Your doodle. On the menu.'

'I don't think that was me.'

'An ejaculating penis.'

'That's disgusting.'

'I thought it was your signature. What do you call it, a tag?'

'What are you saying?'

'I recognised the style.'

Gloria gave me a look that was both bemused and slightly alarmed. She was probably travel fatigued.

'Which cave are you in?' I asked.

'You've got to be kidding!' Blodwyn interrupted. 'Those caves are wretched. We're staying in a *zimmer* up the road.'

I looked at Gloria. 'I thought that was the point of this trip.'

Blodwyn continued. 'Have you been in those caves? They reek. They stink of death and decay.'

I wasn't expecting this. She was right though. It had taken me several days to get accustomed to the odour. 'You get used to it. We've got a window!'

'A window! Far out!'

'It's fine.'

'My standards are obviously higher than yours,' said Blodwyn.

I turned to Gloria. 'A cave's as self sufficient as you can get. I was thinking of making a window box from a cooking oil can and growing herbs. We could knit macramé baskets from goat's wool.'

'Blodwyn didn't like the caves,' Gloria said apologetically.

'If you want to be self-sufficient,' said Blodwyn, 'you want to get a geodesic dome. Everybody in California is living in them.'

'Yeah, but we're in Matala. Caves are all we've got.'

'Haven't you heard what the caves were used for?' said Blodwyn. 'Burials, lepers, all sorts of ghastly things.'

'Yeah, but some of them were family homes,' I said.

'We found bones at the back of our cave,' said Boz brightly.

'Yuk!'

'Boz has sorted that out now.'

'You two are weird.'

'The bones are in the back room. Come and see.'

'I wouldn't go in those caves if the police had a warrant for my arrest.'

I could do without this aggro. For months nobody had told me what to do, or criticised my habits. Okay, Boz may have been a bit sniffy about my personal hygiene but he was my travelling buddy, I was okay with him doing that.

I noticed Gloria staring at my plastic shoes.

'Felix, what have you got on your feet?' she asked.

Gloria's comment all those months ago that you can tell a lot about a person from their feet came rushing back to me.

'*Hellenoplastica* slip-ons. They're good. I can recommend them.'

'Good for what?'

'Yeah, I wanted a pair,' Boz interrupted. 'But they didn't have my size.' I appreciated Boz saying this.

'You wanted a pair of those! Why?'

'They're ideal for cave living,' said Boz without hesitation.

'And on the beach,' I added. 'Everybody wears them round here. You need to get hip.'

Gloria shook her head in disbelief.

'Where did you buy them?' asked Blodwyn. 'I might get a pair.'

I don't know why but we all started laughing.

'We've got a lot of catching up to do,' I said. 'Let's get some more drinks.'

We went outside and sat on the *Terrasse Panoramique* overlooking the sea.

'So where do I start?' said Gloria. 'We've seen so much.'

'Yeah?'

Gloria and Blodwyn talked about Florence and Venice and Athens and all the galleries they'd visited and all the sights they'd seen. While Boz and I had hung round bars and got drunk with draft dodgers they'd climbed towers and queued for hours to study great paintings. They'd seen Michelangelo's statue of David; they'd crossed the Bridge of Sighs; they'd stood on the steps where Socrates had taught.

'Ah, Venice' I said. '*La Serenissima*. To stand by the Doge's Palace and look over the lagoon to St Giorgio Maggiore is one of the most far out experiences known to man.'

'Lousy beach though; too many rocks,' said Boz.

'How can you say that?' I said.

'And too many fooking gondoliers for my liking,' Boz added.

Blodwyn laughed loudly. 'Boz, you are so funny.'

Gloria continued. 'And Florence. Did you go to Florence?'

'Unfortunately we never quite made it to Florence,' I said.

'We couldn't find it!' said Boz.

'Florence is amazing. The Uffizi. You missed something there.'

'So did you go to Firenze?' I asked.

'You're kidding?'

'What?'

'Firenze. Florence. It's the same place.'

'Yeah, of course it is. I'd forgotten,' I said, feeling stupid.

'We are such prats!' Boz roared. 'Felix wanted to go to Florence but there were only signs to Firenze. So we didn't go.'

I smiled and tried to laugh.

'Felix, tell them about how you were mugged,' said Boz.

'I wasn't mugged.' Boz was being a bit too candid for my liking. He was making me look like an idiot.

'How would you describe it then?'

'I don't know.'

'You were missing some money the next day.'

Why was Boz doing this? How could he be so insensitive?

'Maybe. A bit. I could have dropped it when I fell over.' I really didn't want him to dwell on my clinch with Slobena.

'And then we got lost for several days!' Boz was laughing. 'Do you remember that night with the bats the size of pigeons. You should have seen Felix, he was so freaked! He was scared of the bats messing his hair.'

'I was not! I was worried about rabies.'

'And THEN we got stuck in no man's land between Yugoslavia and Albania.' Boz was crying with laughter. 'Felix was hallucinating so much he thought a tortoise was a bomb!'

'I never! It was a mirage. Going to Albania was like walking into a tiger's cage. Anyway you weren't much help.'

Gloria and Blodwyn were now laughing as well. I felt so stupid.

'Poor Felix,' said Gloria.

I wanted to change the subject.

'Did you get to Paris?' I said.

'We're going to Paris on the way back. We want to see the Impressionist painters.'

'Yeah, we want to see them,' I said. 'Perhaps we could meet up.'

'That won't be possible,' said Blodwyn.

When Blodwyn went out to the loo I whispered to Boz, 'You're right, Blodwyn's a pain in the butt, sorry.'

'She's got a bit of a gob on her but I don't want her to feel left out,' he said.

'That's thoughtful of you.'

'She told me she comes from Bury, and her old man has a butcher's shop in the market,' Boz said giving me a wink.

'So what about you guys?' asked Gloria.

For a moment my mind went blank. Although I'd got so much to tell her I couldn't think where we'd been.

'Yeah, the trouble is,' said Boz 'for most of the time we didn't know where we were.'

Gloria said, 'Blodwyn's got this book. *Europe on $5 a Day*. It lists all the top sights.

'How much!?'

'Five dollars.' I couldn't believe it. That was about £3 a day. That was a fortune.

'That's double what we spend!' said Boz.

'You guys have gone feral, you've have been living on this beach too long,' said Blodwyn. 'You're virtually cannibals,' she added.

'Blodwyn nicked it,' said Gloria.

'I suppose stealing keeps the cost of travelling down,' I said.

'I'm not keen on the underlying sarcasm in your voice,' said Blodwyn.

'And I'm not keen on being called a cannibal.'

'Anyway, I liberated it. Books should be for everybody.'

'That's one way of looking at it,' said Boz, laughing.

'A book's not property. I don't see why reading should be the prerogative of the bourgeoisie. I think of it as redistribution.'

'You've got to be careful,' I said.

'Don't worry kid, I can handle myself.'

I scanned the book. It was big, perhaps two inches thick, obviously for somebody who didn't have to carry their own luggage.

'We like to go off piste and feel the call of the wild,' I said. 'Away from the tourist traps and souvenir tat. Discover the real country; get the ethnic vibe. Take the road less travelled. That sort of thing. A guide book puts pressure on you to see the top ten sights and you end up going where everybody else goes. If you do that you don't have the time to visit the things you really want to.'

'How patronizing!' snorted Blodwyn.

'The book helps if you're in a hurry,' Gloria said.

'We weren't in any hurry.' I looked at Gloria. 'Apart from meeting up with you.'

'Show them your map, Felix.'

I pulled out my little pocket diary and handed it to Gloria.

'I can't read the name of the countries, let alone the capital cities', she said. 'No wonder you were lost.'

'For a while Felix thought there was a country called Alb. Of course it's short for Albania. Anyway they wouldn't let us in.'

I tried to explain. 'I like the bigger picture. All Europe on one page, you can see how countries interrelate.'

'They cut off your hair in Albania,' said Blodwyn. 'We met a guy who had his sideburns shaved off by the border guards.'

'We had a lucky escape then,' I said. I wouldn't have wanted pineapple face anywhere near me with a razor.

We were soon in the travellers' groove, swapping tales of the people we'd met and the places we'd stayed and all the things we'd seen and done. I loved this twilight hour. The sun disappeared over the horizon leaving an orange afterglow. Sensing the occasion, Demetre put large bowls of olives and pistachio nuts on the table. Gloria spoke of the farming techniques she'd observed.

'They really are self sufficient,' she said.

'Yeah, they're peasants,' Boz replied.

'And did you see the live animals in the markets?' asked Gloria. At first Gloria had thought they were pets, but Blodwyn had explained they were for eating.

We all wondered what had happened to Bruce and Nicola. Were they ever going to meet up? Boz eulogized about the pies and pastries he'd sampled. After eating exotic vegetables like red peppers, courgettes and aubergines, I said I'd never again look at English greengrocers, with their dull display of carrots, cabbages and parsnips, in the same way. Blodwyn gave me a look which I could only describe as pitying.

Blodwyn said how liberated she felt in a foreign country - it made her more confident; nicking stuff was so much easier. She couldn't imagine getting caught. We all agreed the less people have the more generous they are. 'In Crete visitors are viewed as a gift from God.' I wasn't sure about this, though I didn't say anything.

'Hey, what about the war?' Boz suddenly asked. We were all speechless, not quite believing what he'd said. Blodwyn broke the silence by proclaiming 'This Greek wine tastes like toilet cleaner.' Nevertheless she put her head back and drank a tumblerful in one.

Boz raised his glass and proclaimed: 'We are on a righteous journey of discovery. I'm not letting a war spoil my summer. We must travel boldly.'

'Yeah, right on' I added, 'we must travel boldly where no man has gone before.'

I couldn't tear my eyes away from Gloria. I felt like I was being swallowed up by a warm sea; I was drowning. I couldn't help it, I knew this was madness and I was likely to get hurt. But sometimes you have to take risks. Sometimes it is worth it. Just for a moment. For a second a picture of Plank lurched into my mind - I scotched that disturbing image immediately.

We ordered yet more drink. Demetre put another bowl of salty nuts on the table. We agreed that the Greek wine wasn't that bad. We were talking loudly in raised voices. We were talking profoundly; we were buzzing with the drunken comradeship of friends far from home. 'We are ambassadors!' said Gloria. 'Ambassadors of love!' We would be taking love back to our own country. 'If more people travelled there would be greater universal understanding,' I said. 'And no wars,' added Gloria. I thought of the old man on the Macedonian border and realised that this was the purpose of our travel. Man, we were pissed.

It was time to go. We were now the last people in the Mermaid. Demetre was putting the chairs on the tables.

We got up to leave. Blodwyn grabbed Boz and put her arms round his shoulders. 'I'm so tired,' she said. She was hanging round Boz's neck.

'Yeah, well, it's been nice meeting you Blodwyn,' Boz said. I could see he was struggling to decide whether to enjoy the moment or push her away.

Blodwyn gave Boz a big hug. 'I like handsome men - but with you I'll make an exception.' She laughed

'Stop it! I like it.' Boz laughed as well.

Boz turned to me and said, 'Blodwyn and I are going for a walk. Don't wait up. I'll see you tomorrow.'

'Where are you going?'

'Back to her *zimmer*.'

'Do you want to borrow the Tiger Balm?'

'No thanks pal, I'll save that for later.'

I watched Boz and Blodwyn disappear into the darkness. They were leaning against each other, propping themselves up as they walked down the dusty track to a *zimmer* on the edge of the village.

So that was Boz's carnal desires sorted out. It was now my turn to get laid.

THIRTY SIX

Gloria hung onto my arm as we walked slowly along the beach towards the cliff. There was a high clear moon, bright enough to cast shadows.

'I never thought you'd get to Matala,' said Gloria.

'Our cave is over there,' I pointed at the dark cliff where several caves were lit by flickering candle light.

'They look so pretty. Which one is it?'

'The one with the door, and the window to the right. In the dark. I'm sorry they aren't in conical hills.' I thought this was not the best time to tell her what Rollo had said about the caves.

'Don't worry Felix, these are better.'

'We'll light a fire and pretend it's Plato's cave.'

Something had happened. Gloria seemed different. Maybe being away from Blodwyn had helped.

'Felix, I'm glad we've met. Sometimes Blodwyn can be hard work. Don't get me wrong, she's a good friend but she can be a bit unpredictable. Travelling with a kleptomaniac isn't easy.'

Gloria stopped and bent down to take off her sandals. 'Let's paddle.'

We splashed along the shore line. Gloria ran ahead, enjoying the cooling water.

'Look at the phosphorescence,' she said.

The full moon was reflected in the gun metal grey sea. The waves were glowing like neon lights. But then she stopped and gave a muted scream.

'Oh, my God! What is that?' she shrieked.

I ran up to her. She'd raised her hands to her mouth, her knuckles were pressed against her teeth, she was shaking.

'What is it?' I asked, putting my arm round her shoulders.

She pointed. An object the size of a large log was floating in the water, being gently pushed in and out by the slight swell of the sea.

'It's a body!' she said.

Suddenly, like Poseidon rising from the deep, the body sat up in the shallow water. Gloria gave a yelp of terror.

'You again!' roared Poseidon. 'I've told you before. Bloody well leave me alone.'

I had to grab Gloria's arm to stop her from running away.

'It's Sanchez,' I explained. 'He lies in the water to cool off. Apparently, it's very therapeutic.'

'Excuse me,' I said to the dripping figure. 'You ought to warn people what you're doing. Why don't you put up a sign or something?'

'What is it with you? Why can't you leave me alone? Go and poke somebody else.'

'I didn't poke you. I haven't got a stick.'

'Huh!' I was surprised that for a man with a reputation for eloquence he seemed hardly able to put one word in front of another.

'You've just scared the shit out of my girlfriend.'

I could see Gloria look at me; I'd called her my girlfriend.

'I'm sorry, it was me who screamed,' said Gloria.

Sanchez wiped his eyes. Until now he didn't seem to have noticed Gloria.

'Yeah, well, I'd appreciate it if you'd leave me alone.'

'Excuse me,' asked Gloria, 'but what were you doing?'

'Before he came along,' Sanchez waved an accusing finger at me, 'I was floating in and out with the waves, buoyed up by the water, meditating.'

'Somebody said you walked here from Ethiopia,' I said.

'Who told you that?'

'Somebody on the beach.'

'Did Jodie say that?'

'I think he was called Blu - from Denmark.'

'If you must know I came here via Birmingham Airport. And next time you see me doing this, I'd appreciate it if you just leave me alone. Got it?'

'This floating looks lovely.' Gloria seemed to have recovered.

'I can recommend it. I let go of my senses and mentally drift out to sea.' Sanchez seemed calmer now.

'Can I have a go?' Gloria asked.

'Feel free,' said Sanchez patting the water next to him. 'Clear your mind - imagine your body suspended in space. And as you breathe out, count from one to seven. When you get to seven, start at one again.'

Before I could say anything Gloria had taken off her shorts and t-shirt and was lying on her back in the shallow water in only her skinny white knickers. Her arms were spread out and her eyes were closed. Her tanned body looked even more alluring than I remembered.

I really didn't want to be messing around in the water with this wacked out Brummie. Meditation was the last thing on my mind. What I needed was some intense loving activity.

'Why do you count to seven?' Gloria asked.

'I use base seven. Number seven rules our lives.'

'Oh?'

'It is the perfect number. Seven days of creation, seven colours of the rainbow, seven seas, seven holes in the body, seven deadly sins ...'

'Seven dwarves,' I added, laughing.

'What's so funny?'

'I prefer the decimal system.' I said. 'It's more natural. Ten fingers, ten toes, the Top Ten ...'

'Ah, but is it? There are seven bones in the neck. And...,' Sanchez retorted in an incontrovertible tone, 'that also goes for giraffes.'

'This is super,' said Gloria. 'It's like a warm bath. I'm floating, looking at the stars. Come on Felix, come and join me.'

I lay beside her. The water was warm but with Gloria floating next to me, arms and legs stretched out like an offering to the gods, I found it difficult to clear my mind. I counted my breath as Sanchez had suggested but my thoughts kept returning to Gloria. I was struggling to keep my body under control. I tried to think of Ruislip; it seemed so far away. In my state of heightened awareness calm breathing was not possible. I wanted to turn my head and look at Gloria in the moonlight; her body was submerged apart from her face, her toes and two perfect breasts emerging from the sea.

After fifteen minutes I admitted defeat. I was far too distracted by Gloria's curvaceous body to concentrate on my breathing. It felt like there was too much blood in my arteries. Rather than slowing down, my heart rate seemed to be getting faster.

I sat up. 'It was good, wasn't it?' I said, trying to keep calm. My pulse was racing. We needed to get to the cave quickly. I felt so full of lust I feared I'd spring a leak.

Gloria smiled. 'That was fabulous. Do you know, I think that was the deepest relaxation I've had in a long time.'

'Me too,' I agreed.

'Were you okay?'

'Yeah.'

'You were making a funny noise. A whimpering noise.'

'I was fine.'

'My mind feels so clear and uncluttered,' she said as she pulled her t-shirt over her wet body. 'It was like a floating meditation.'

'A floatation.'

'What a good name, Felix. We need to work out how to do this on our farm.' I was pleased to hear that I was still included in Gloria's plans.

'Let's go,' said Gloria, 'We need to warm up.'

'Good idea.'

As we left, Sanchez was stretched out in the water as flat as a board.

'Where's your conical little hat then?' she laughed.

'I'll put on my party hat later.'

Gloria leant softly against me as we walked across the sand. She had goose bumps - I could feel the tiny blond hairs on her arms standing up. At the bottom of the cliff I kissed Gloria's sweet salty lips.

While Gloria was getting ready for bed I quickly searched for my tin of Tiger Balm and held it up against the candle trying to read the instructions. The only thing it said was 'For external use only.' I guessed there should have been an accompanying leaflet. I thought tonight was probably not the night to have such a powerful ejaculation that I'd rip my penis apart.

We laid out our sleeping bags and made love on the moonlit ledge. Oh Gloria! Hallelujah!

THIRTY SEVEN

The next morning Gloria got up early.
'I'm going back to my room. I'll see you later for breakfast at the Mermaid,' she said.

I drifted in and out of sleep serenaded by erotic dreams. Far away I could hear the sounds of the early morning. On the cliff-top above, a goat herd was shouting; further away a donkey was braying. I had a horny dream about Gloria. I wanted her back in the cave now. This trip was turning out to be even better than I had imagined. The happy glow was back. Gloria was so sweet. Last night we laughed so much: about Sanchez, about the caves; she didn't even mind the peeling skin on my back.

I pulled on shorts and a t-shirt and clambered down the rock face. I thought about Boz and hoped he had had a good night with Blodwyn. The empty beach was still in the shadow of the cliff. I was in no hurry, I just wanted to enjoy the moment so I lay on my back in the shade and spread eagled my arms and legs, making a sand angel. I looked up at the pale blue early morning sky. I realized I hadn't seen a cloud for weeks. I turned over and dug my feet into the moist grains below the surface. I put my ear to the sand and could hear the gentle pushing and sucking of the waves. I was looking forward to a long, lingering breakfast with Gloria. I slumbered, drifting in and out of sleep, wallowing in this moment of contentment.

I dozed. I wasn't prepared for what was to happen next. Shortly, I was aware of somebody walking nearby and standing close to me. I was now in the full sun and could feel a shadow across my back. I turned my head to see sandals, black woollen socks and pale skinny legs covered in blond fluffy hair. My heart jumped as a surge of adrenalin pumped into it. I raised my eyes and saw a familiar and grotesque silhouette blocking out the sun. For a second I felt like I was falling into a dark hole. The hour I feared the most had come. Having rutted his way round Europe, Plank was now in Matala.

'Hey! Felix! I thought it was you.'

I sat up. 'You made it then,' I said. I wasn't ready for Plank, least of all now.

'Your back looks painful. You need to put some cream on that.'

I was getting sick of people talking about my back.

Plank put out his hand and gave me a soft handshake. 'Man, am I glad to see you.'

'Did you have a good trip?' I said flatly.

'Is there something wrong, Felix?'

I didn't want to answer. 'What kept you?' I said. 'I heard you were on the express route.'

'I've travelled half way round the world to see my best buddy and you don't appear too happy.'

Best buddy! I wanted to puke.

'It's not my time of day,' I said. 'You surprised me. I'm hardly awake.' I looked at Plank. I was pleased to see he hadn't escaped the ravages of the sun. His face was red and flayed and he had skin flaking off his chin like shredded tissue paper.

'What were you doing squirming around in the sand?'

'I wasn't squirming. I was dozing. I was enjoying the cool of the early morning'

'It looked to me like you were jacking off.' Plank gave a lascivious laugh. It struck me that he always laughed at people, not with them.

'You might behave like that. I don't,' I said. 'I don't need to,' I added.

Plank looked around. 'Nice little place this Matala. So what's the scene?'

'It's quiet here. I'm just hanging out.'

'I was right, then.'

'Right about what?'

'That you'd ditch that dead weight friend of yours.'

'If you're talking about Boz, he's still with me.'

Plank shook his head. 'You have a big heart, Felix. Anybody else would have thrown that freeloader overboard at Dover.'

'We're having a good time.'

Plank shrugged. 'So where's our cave?'

I pointed to the cliff. 'The cave is only for two people.'

'That's fine by me. Has Gloria arrived yet?'

I was vainly hoping that Plank had somehow forgotten about Gloria. 'She's spoken for, if that's what you're thinking.'

'That's a pity, she's currently number one on my 'To Shag List.'

''To Shag List!' Is that how you think?'

'I expect she's fallen for the charms of some smooth talking Greek stud.'

'If you must know, Gloria's fallen for the charms of a smooth talking English stud.'

'Not Boz surely?'

'No, not Boz. Me.'

Plank looked at me in astonishment. 'You?'

'Yes, me.'

'I didn't think you were her type.'

'I am. Very much so. And she's my type as well.'

Plank stared at me for a moment and then laughed.

'Good for you Felix, I didn't think you had it in you.' He punched me on the shoulder like an ingratiating sixth form prefect.

Plank lay on the sand and closed his eyes.

'Anyway, I'm off sex at the moment. I tell you, this is turning out to be some trip. Quite arduous at times. It's as if these Mediterranean senoritas have never had a shag. Have you found that? They like the English physique; they get bored with toned Mediterranean bodies. Too muscley they say. It's as if they view me as a sex machine. Is that all they ever want? Sex, sex, sex. Sometimes I feel abused. And then there was this Aussie chick Nicola in Sarajevo. She'd split up with her boyfriend in Venice. She banged like a door on a windy night. Frankly Felix, I could do with some time off.'

Why did Plank say this stuff? What sort of fantasy world was this toss-pot living in? I didn't believe a word of it.

'I should warn you they're not like that here. We've got a bit of a commune thing going on Matala. The women are more liberated. They like to be on top.'

'Don't get me wrong. That's all part of the service.'

Plank stood up.

'I'll see you for breakfast in half an hour. Then we'll sort out the sleeping arrangements. Now I'm here Boz might like to take the opportunity to move out. He could get a *zimmer* in the village. He'd probably like that.'

'Boz hasn't got any money.'

'There are always ways and means.'

'Look, Boz is my friend.'

'Felix, I know it's difficult being a double-agent but eventually you have to decide whose side you are on.'

'I don't think he wants to move out.'

'I bet he hasn't got one of these.'

Plank reached in his trouser pocket and pulled out a shiny black torch, the sort of torch I'd seen in glass display cases at Millets.

'You're right he hasn't.'

'It's a Magilite. It'll be very useful in the cave.'

'So.'

'It's not only a torch,' Plank pulled the top off, 'see, you can also use it for non-directional lighting.'

'We use candles.'

'Well, think about it, Felix.'

'And they're not senoritas.'

THIRTY EIGHT

I was dripping golden honey into my yoghurt. A cat was dozing in the early morning sun on top of the next table. In the distance I could see an old man walking along the road leading a donkey laden with firewood. I then saw Gloria coming down the street. For a moment I admired the beauty of her walk. I waved.

'Hi! Breakfast,' I shouted.

But Gloria was walking too quickly for this time of day. Even from where I was sitting I could see something was wrong.

'We've got to go,' she said.

'What's the hurry? Take it easy. It's too hot to rush. Have some breakfast. Yoghurt and honey. Your favourite.'

'Felix, we're leaving.'

'What?'

'We're leaving. We've got to go.'

'Where are we going?'

'Not you. Blodwyn and I are leaving. We've got to get out of here.'

'What! I thought you were going to stay in Matala for a while. Last night you said you were going to move into the cave.'

'Sorry Felix. Another time.'

'I don't understand. Is it the cave? We don't have to stay in a cave if you don't want to.'

'It's not the cave, Felix.'

I looked at Gloria. Last night in the cave she'd been so different. It was me. I was the problem. I knew it.

'Another time Felix, I promise.'

'But when?'

'Look, we've got to leave. Blodwyn's packing her bag and then we're out of here.'

This was happening way too fast. I wasn't used to this sudden turmoil. No worry, no hurry was the travelling mantra.

'Boz'll be upset,' I said.

'Yeah, well I can't help that. We're all upset.'

'You're leaving because of me. It's because of me isn't it?'

'Felix. It is NOT because of you.'

I didn't believe her. Of course it was because of me. She'd sobered up and realised she'd spent the night with some dirty faced hippie creep.

'What is it then?'

'Boz will tell you.'

'What's Boz know about it?'

'He was there.'

I knew I shouldn't have let Boz out of my sight.

'What's Boz done? He's a liability.'

'Boz has done nothing wrong. He's trying to calm down Blodwyn.'

I was panicking. I was feeling sick. I couldn't lose Gloria now. Sure, I was never expecting our relationship to be happy-ever-after but for it to finish within… within a couple of hours, that was just too fast.

'I've messed up, I've messed everybody up,' I said.

'Felix, I don't need this. It's because of Blodwyn. We've got to leave because of Blodwyn.'

'What's happened?'

'I just came to say goodbye.'

'Say goodbye! I can't believe this. You've got to tell me what's going on.'

'I haven't got time.'

'Please, Gloria.'

'I shouldn't be here, I don't want Mama to see me.'

She glanced at her watch. 'Okay.' She sat at the table. 'Last night Blodwyn broke into the Mermaid and stole a bottle of Johnny Walker Red.'

'Why did she do that?'

'She's like that. She was drunk. You saw her.'

'But … but… why?'

'You know how Blodwyn is. She goes nuts.'

'I've heard she once stole a duck from Gateway.'

'Fine Fare, actually.'

'Why a duck? She's crazy.'

'Yeah, the thing is, last night she was caught. Mama must have been woken by the sound of breaking glass.'

'Was Boz with her? He's such an idiot.'

'No, he was back at our *zimmer*. Blodwyn said he was unconscious or something.'

'So Blodwyn broke into the Mermaid? She broke a window?'

'She knocked over a pile of glasses. She'd already climbed through a window. It was open.'

'Oh, that's alright then!'

'Stop being sarcastic Felix!'

'Sorry, carry on.'

'When Blodwyn heard Mama coming downstairs she tried to hide. She hid in Mama's little office. So when Mama found Blodwyn she thought she was stealing money. Then Demetre appeared. According to Blodwyn, Mama and Demetre handled the situation very badly and made Blodwyn panic.'

'So?'

'Blodwyn punched Demetre on the nose. What else could she do?'

'Theft AND assault!'

'The policeman is coming in on the noon bus. We've got to leave before he arrives.'

'But where are you going?'

'Blodwyn knows.'

'What about the war? You'll get caught up in it.'

'I don't think the war's happening here.'

'When the fighting starts Boz and I are planning to hide in the mountains. Look,' I pulled a scarf out of my pocket, 'I've bought a bandana.'

'Do you think red with white polka dot is a good idea? It's like putting a target on your head.'

I ignored this. 'They'll catch you?'

'They won't bother.'

'You're in big trouble. Theft AND assault.'

'Stop saying that. How do you think I feel?'

'Sorry, I didn't mean it like that. So where are you going?'

'Blodwyn said we're going over the mountains. To the north coast I think.'

I noticed Plank lurching down the street. I hoped he wouldn't see us. I could really do without Plank at this moment. But he'd already spotted us.

'Gloria! How are you?'

'Gloria's leaving,' I interrupted.

'Adrian! How nice to see you,' Gloria said politely.

Plank gave Gloria an overlong hug; his hands wandered over her body and rested on her bottom. Gloria seemed too agitated to pay any attention. I did, however, notice that Gloria gave Plank's peeling chin a double take. Plank pulled up a chair, oblivious to the tense situation.

'So what's on the breakfast menu? I've got a big appetite. Gloria, what are you having?'

'I'm leaving,' said Gloria.

'You can't leave. I've only just got here.'

'Sorry Adrian.'

'Gloria's a bit upset at the moment,' I said.

Plank looked at me over his sunglasses and gave me a 'what have you done to her?' look. 'Oh?'

'A little difficulty.'

'Yeah?'

'With the police.'

'Oh?'

'And they're coming to arrest her and Blodwyn. So they've got to leave. She's fleeing to the north.'

'I'm very sorry to hear that.'

Gloria stood up, ready to go.

'I could come with you girls,' said Plank.

'Thanks for the offer but there's no need.'

'No. I'm geared up to leave anyway. I've seen all there is to see in Matala. I was thinking of heading up to the northern part of the island myself. There's a forest of palm trees I want to see.'

'We're absolutely fine. Don't worry about us.'

'But I've got one of these.' To my astonishment Plank got up and pulled out of his pocket his Magilite torch.

'Oh!' Gloria looked bemused.

'When are you off?' asked Plank.

'Now,' said Gloria.

'Okay, give me five minutes.'

'But Adrian,' I said, 'you've only just arrived.' It felt strange calling Plank Adrian. 'I thought you were going to stay with us in our cave. I'm sure we can find space; we could clear out the room in the back.'

Plank got up from his chair. 'Have a good rest of your trip, buddy.' He offered me his hand to shake. 'And send my regards to that freeloader Boz.'

'He'll be devastated. He was looking forward to that game of backgammon. '

'I wish you the best of luck on your travels, Felix.'

'Will I need it?'

'I think it's best that you have it, mate.'

Plank turned to Gloria, and with an unmistakable tone of triumph in his voice said, 'I'll go and collect my bag and see you outside the bakery in five minutes.'

'Don't worry,' Plank said giving me his vile leering smile, 'I'll take care of them.'

That's exactly what was freaking me out.

It was now just me and Gloria. If only I could have more time, more time to sit with her, order a few coffees and maybe a couple of Metaxas, and talk this through. Then, I knew, everything would be alright.

'Felix, I'm sorry about this,' said Gloria.

'This is the last thing I'd expected.'

'Me too. You and I, we were having a good time. Now I'm on the run. I don't want to leave, Felix. Bloody Blodwyn!'

'You don't have to go.'

'I do. Anyway, I'll see you back in Bristol.'

'Yeah, maybe.'

We hugged. I didn't know what to say. I was feeling mixed up and confused; I was lost for words. This was no way to say goodbye. I stared at her as she walked away. This was the woman who was going to save me. How had this happened? Shit, Shit, Shit. Fuck, Fuck, Fuck. HOW HAD THIS HAPPENED? I watched her beautiful sexy body, and my dream, disappear down the street. The girl I'd been fantasising about for months was walking away with that horse-faced loon Plank. And I'd not stopped her. I'd just sat eating yoghurt and honey and let her go. As she reached the corner at the end of the street I expected her to turn and wave. But she didn't even look back.

A couple of minutes later I heard the rasping bray of a donkey echo across Matala. I gave a shudder as I thought of that primeval howl bawled by Plank in Bristol all those months before.

THIRTY NINE

'How did you sleep, Felix? Did Gloria like the cave? No nightmares? Still got a full head of hair?' Boz was acting as if nothing had happened.

'The cave was fine, thank you. I slept like a dog and my hair is as thick and lustrous as ever.'

I looked at Boz. 'Why didn't you stop them?'

'What?'

'Why didn't you stop them, you idiot.'

'Oh, Blodwyn and Gloria. They had to go! The police are after them.'

'You were supposed to be looking after Blodwyn.'

'That's the first I've heard about it.'

'I'd set you up with her.'

'I don't think so, Felix. I make my own choices about who I sleep with, thank you very much.'

'I hear you were aiding and abetting a break-in.'

'I was asleep.'

'Tell that to the police when they're toasting your toes! Anyway, Gloria said you were unconscious.'

'She wasn't there. She doesn't know.'

'They've gone, Boz.' I couldn't believe it.

'Yeah I know. They've both gone.'

'With Plank.'

'You've got to be kidding! Plank was here, huh? How is he?'

'Yes, he went with them. He was in here for only a morning and now he's run off with both of them. Mission accomplished for Plank.'

'Is he a fugitive from the police as well?'

'No, he's just got one more tick on his 'To Shag List'. Two ticks, probably.'

'Sorry about that Felix.'

I put my head in my hands and stared at the plastic table cloth. Hell, I could still smell her scent on my fingers. I didn't know what to do. Why hadn't I gone with Gloria and Blodwyn? I was the one who was prepared for the mountains. I was the one who had the bandana. Maybe I should have bought a kaftan as well? Or a bloody Magilite. It was too hot to think.

'I'm sorry it didn't work out for you, Felix.'

'Thanks. What about you?'

'Blodwyn was fun. Maybe a bit too much fun.'

I groaned. I needed time by myself. There was a big white space in my head. I needed to think this through.

'We need a change of scene,' said Boz, 'It's time you and I sought the call of the wild. We need to pack our bags and find spiritual refuge in the mountains.'

'Maybe. I'm going for a walk. I'll see you later.'

'Take it easy, Felix.'

'Yeah.'

'Oh I forgot,' I said, 'Plank sends his regards.'

FORTY

I looked up at the mountains. They were solid slabs of rock the colour of dried blood.

'Look at those rocks,' I said to Boz.

'What about them?'

'Look at them.'

'They're just rocks.'

'I'm not used to rocks.'

'It's no different from the Peak District.'

'I've never been to the Peak District.'

'The Peak District is like that, but with rain.'

Boz didn't get it. These were the sort of rocks eighteenth century travellers came to see and admire on their grand tour of Europe.

'Those rocks are SO solid,' I said.

'Yeah, that's what rocks are about. There's an expression, you might have heard it. Solid as a rock.'

'I'm being serious, Boz. Where I come from you don't see landscapes like this. London isn't exactly known for its mountains. The nearest hills are the Chilterns and they're only chalk. Soft and rounded chalk. Rocks are supposed to make us think about our mortality.'

'How?'

'They're big and old. In comparison we are transient.'

'You are weird, Felix, very weird,' Boz said, shaking his head.

We scrabbled down a dry watercourse through spiky brittle scrub to a small cove.

'I'm going to get some wood for a fire,' Boz said.

'Good idea.' I was happy to let Boz show off his outdoor skills. The mid-day sun was too hot for me to help.

While Boz rooted about in the bush collecting firewood I sat at the top of the beach and picked up a flat pebble to skim across the water. The topside of the stone was wrinkled like a walnut, while the underside was as smooth as an egg. It took me a moment to understand the significance of this. I looked around. How long does it take for rain to cut through stone? Hundreds of years? Thousands of years? I was sitting on a beach that had been undisturbed for millennia. I tried to put the pebble back exactly where I had found it.

The cove was filled with an absolute tranquillity that I'd never experienced before. I leant back trying not to disturb the stones. The atmosphere felt flat and serene. I unrolled my bandana and placed it over my face and closed my eyes. The sun made the cloth smell of freshly ironed pillowcase. I could hear the sea fizzing as it swept up and down the pebble incline. Behind the beach there was the distant rustle of some animal, a lizard or a snake perhaps, and the popping of seed pods in the heat.

Night time. A log burst and sparks shot into the darkness. I lay in my sleeping bag, warm and safe, and looked up. The mountains were just visible, a charcoal mass, silhouetted against the starlit sky. We didn't get stars like this in the orange night of Ruislip. The sky here was lit by so many stars it was blue. I looked for the North Star. I hadn't done that for years. I remembered an August evening while on holiday when Mum and Dad drove us to Egardon Hill. It was warm and we lay on our backs in the slightly damp grass and Mum showed us how to find the North Star by lining up the Big Dipper and Cassiopeia. 'You'll never be lost, now you know how to do that,' Mum had said.

Lying on this beach I felt like some watcher of the skies. I could sense the world spinning, I could hear the stars. My arms were outstretched, I could sense the curvature of the earth, I was clinging on, I didn't know if I was looking up or down. I could feel the rocks and stones through my sleeping bag. It was one of the few moments in my life when everything was stripped back to the basics. I was here. Now. In the moment. Part of this planet. What else did I need? This was it. Nothing else mattered. At that moment I didn't want to be anywhere else in the world. I was as near to God as I would ever be.

'Everybody should see this,' I said.

'Yeah, people should be forced to see this,' said Boz.

A thin silk thread cut across the diamond sky. And another. And then another. So many shooting stars. One of them was so bright it lit up the sky, fizzed and left a vapour trail.

'Did you see that?' I asked Boz.

'I've never seen anything like that before.'

'They must be close.'

'Yeah.'

'This stuff's hard to beat.'

'Yeah, this is what it's all about.'

The fire burnt down to red embers. I lay on my back looking at the sky. I felt so heavy. I remembered one frosty winter evening when I was about nine or ten taking a tin box into the back garden. I wanted to capture the essence of the crystal clear night. I kept the box under my bed and would sometimes open a crack and sniff the contents. I thought this is what outer space smelt like.

As I lay on this Cretan beach I imagined I was one of those asteroids in the domed sky. A glorious flash of energy and that was it. And do you know what, that streak of light put things into perspective. Okay, a bit of angst could be a good thing now and again. But too much and you're wasting your precious time. Gloria had gone. For a while I'd been in a state of shock. But so what? Why was I putting myself through this pain? I was concentrating on the wrong things. All this, the stars, the mountains, the fragrance of wild sage and thyme, this was life distilled to its finest essence. This was what travelling was about. I needed to appreciate it. I was always thinking about what had happened, or what I was going to do. Yet on this beach I felt at peace with myself and at peace with the world. What was it Bixby had said? 'Be here, right now.'

I tried to stay awake and watch for more shooting stars but sunk into a deep sleep. Later, I awoke to the velvety darkness. The fire was almost burnt out. I heard a nearby owl give a *tuok-tuok*, and then far away on the mountain, a lonely shepherd's dog let out a long mournful howl. Or was it a wolf? I gave a shiver and fell back to sleep the most content I'd ever been.

*

In the morning I watched the sun coming up over the mountains and felt its rays warming the night chill away.

Shhhhhhurbang!

'What the heck was that?'

The peace of the mountains had been ripped apart by the bang of a fighter plane flying low along the coast.

My heart was thumping dangerously. I looked at Boz. We were both shocked.

'The war?' I said.

'Not here, surely?'

The roar had come without warning. It was such a vicious unnatural sound. For perhaps thirty seconds afterwards there was a clamouring of bells as the mountain goats fled in aimless panic. And then the flat silence came down again and calm was restored.

'I'm sure I read that Crete was once part of the Ottoman Empire,' said Boz. 'Although that was a long time ago, the Turks still think they rule Crete. After Cyprus this is going to be their next target.'

I wanted to ignore this interruption to our blissful time with nature. I tried to blank out the memory of the noise and concentrate on the quiet. Boz and I didn't speak about it again. But that terrible roar, and all that it stood for, had lodged itself in my head.

*

Back in Matala I could hear the distant sound of Leonard Cohen singing 'So Long Marianne'. Somebody had bought new batteries for the record player in the Mermaid. Tonight, for the first time, from its usual warm faded purples and reds, the colour of the evening sky had changed to slate grey. The leaves on the olive trees were flickering from green to silver in the breeze. Ripe olives were dropping onto the ground. As we sauntered along the beach, waves were breaking and our bare legs were blasted by little pin pricks of sand. The wind was in from Africa. Boz and I agreed it was time to move on.

As we waited for the bus, I spotted Rollo ambling down the road.

'Are you guys leaving?' he asked.

'We've got to head back,' I said.

'Maybe I'll bump into you again some time.'

'Yeah. Take it easy.'

The dusty blue and white bus to Hania pulled up. There was a scramble of hippies and locals to get seats.

I turned to Rollo and shook his hand.

'We never did get to finish our conversation about the caves,' he said.

'No, another time, maybe. Good luck with your studies.'

We grabbed a seat on the shady side of coach. Rollo was outside our window standing in the shadow of the bus. The vehicle started to move. After weeks of travelling away from England, we were shifting the arc of our journey homeward. Despite the trauma of the last few days I was sad to leave Matala. I gave Rollo a goodbye wave.

'I meant to tell you,' Rollo shouted, 'the funerary caves are the ones with the ledges cut into the rocks.'

I could have done without knowing that.

FORTY ONE

We'd been standing on the quayside in the hammering heat for about four hours. For some inexplicable reason the ferry to Piraeus was full. Was it because of the war? Or the fall of the Generals? Maybe, as Boz suggested, the workers were rising up and taking over the means of production, or in this case transport?

On the bus over the mountains I'd felt a tinge of sorrow. I'd loved the sense of constant movement, the feeling of an endless summer. Although it would be ages before we would see the grey cliffs of Folkestone, this change in direction had taken some of the lustre off that sense of freedom.

The waiting crowd was shouting *'Ella, ella, ella.'* I'd no idea what it meant, but I joined the shouting anyway. It felt surprisingly good. As a linguistic mechanism for conveying frustration it seemed to do the trick.

I was hoping that we might be squeezed onto the ferry at the last moment. But the boat already appeared to be dangerously over-crowded. Even from where we were standing I could see people packed on the decks and waving out of portholes.

'Hey,' Boz nudged me. 'Look at the back of the boat where the flag is. Isn't that them?'

I squinted. It was. Gloria and Blodwyn were leaning on the ship's railing, looking down, watching the activity on the quayside.

I couldn't understand it. I thought they would have left Crete days ago.

I shouted. 'Gloria! Blodwyn!' They didn't seem to hear me.

Ever since that numinous moment on the beach watching shooting stars I felt I'd managed to get some sort of control over my emotions for Gloria. But even the sight of her from a distance brought back all those annoying and useless feelings of love, lust and jealousy.

She'd left deeper scars than I realized.

'We've got to get on that boat.' I said. I shouted again. Gloria must have heard her name, for she turned and looked in our direction. I waved and yelled. But she didn't spot me in the crowd. She turned back to Blodwyn.

We squeezed forward. I pushed past old ladies with baskets and stout men carrying wooden boxes. We were pressed against a tall metal railing.

'Gloria. Blodwyn,' I shouted.

They were still on the deck. They were talking to somebody standing in the shadows who had given them drinks. I could see Gloria press the cold bottle against her forehead.

'GLORIA!' I shouted.

Gloria moved again and this time she saw us. She held her arms in the air and gave a big sweeping wave. She pointed us out to Blodwyn. Who waved and jumped. I could see Gloria cup her hands to her mouth and shout.

'What?' I yelled. I couldn't hear her above the dockside clamour of revving vehicles and banging metal.

Both Gloria and Blodwyn shouted again.

And then the figure in the shadow stepped forward. It was Plank. Standing behind the girls, he slowly raised his arms and gave a triumphant thumbs-up sign. What did that mean? What did that gesture mean? I felt sick to the stomach and defeated. Is this what he does? Travel across Europe like an avenging devil stalking innocent girls? Relentlessly wearing them down until they don't have the energy to resist? Two thumbs? What did that mean?' Had he ticked both of them off on his 'To Shag List'?

'Oh look, there's Adrian,' said Boz.

'He's just screwed your girlfriend.'

'Who?'

'Plank has fucked Blodwyn.'

'Do you think so? How do you know?' Boz didn't seem that concerned.

'I can tell.'

'I can hardly see him. I didn't really think of Blodwyn as my girlfriend. Anyway I thought he was after Gloria.'

'Gloria's got more taste.'

Boz looked at me quizzically.

'Well, good luck to him,' said Boz.

I looked at Boz aghast. 'How can you say that?'

'We're on holiday. Easy come, easy go.'

'You are so superficial.'

The crowd was squashing us against the railings. *'Ella, ella, ella.'* I tried to turn round.

A woman in a headscarf with a live lamb held to her chest was standing directly behind me. I could feel the lamb's little hooves pushing and kicking against my sun-burnt back.

'Back off,' I shouted. I didn't want the lamb to get crushed.

Boz continued. 'What's the problem?'

'Boz, you have no idea, do you?'

'I know you like her. But I just thought she was like all the others. A quick wham, bam, thank you, m'am.'

'What others?'

'I don't know.'

I'd spent the summer with my best mate, living with him as close as we could decently get, yet he had no idea what was going on.

'There aren't any others.'

We were now squashed against the iron railings in the sizzling heat. I could hardly move. It was like a football crowd pressing forward after a goal. I felt as if the life was being squeezed out of me. I tried to turn my head to face Boz.

'So how do you feel about her?' Boz asked.

It wasn't the best place for this conversation.

'I can't stop thinking about her.'

'Yeah?'

'And there's a funny feeling in my stomach.'

'That could be a number of things.'

We both laughed.

I continued. 'There's an electricity. When I touch her, something happens. I can really feel a surge of something. Little darts of electricity. Have you had that? Do you know what I mean?'

'Yeah, I've had that. Just before an orgasm.'

'It's more than that. At other times as well.'

'You've got it bad. Sorry pal, I didn't realise that you're such a hopeless romantic, I didn't understand that Gloria meant that much to you.'

'How do you think Gloria feels about you?' Boz asked. Sometimes he could be lousy at reading the situation.

What do people think of you? That's not the sort of question you ever want to ask. Not even of your best friend. Do you really want to know what they say behind your back? That route leads to self doubt, insecurity and madness. But what did she think of me? I didn't want to ponder this, I didn't want to know.

'Boz, that is such a shitty question.'

But I knew in my heart I meant very little to her. I was a laugh, I was kind, we'd had some good sex, but she wanted more than this. I knew that. She wanted some big hunk who could build geodesic domes, rig up windmills and muck out the pigs. What use was I with my windowsill of herbs?

Stop that right now! See what I mean about self doubt? What sanctimonious rubbish! What bollocks! Stuff Gloria. Stuff Blodwyn. Stuff Boz. Stuff the lot of them.

'Do you want to know what I think of you?' I said to Boz.

'Not really. But I've got a feeling that you're going to tell me anyway.'

'I am going to tell you. You are an award-winning arsehole.'

'Felix, I was only trying to help.'

We were silent for a while.

Pressed against the hot metal railings I could hardly move. I was feeling faint. My brain was being boiled like an egg.

Boz was looking at me with concern.

'Are you okay?' he asked.

'Yeah. I'm okay. Sorry Boz, I don't mean it. The sun's too hot, I could do with a hat. This bandana's no good at all. Are you okay?'

'I'm fine, pal.'

'What about Blodwyn? Was Blodwyn okay?'

'She's a very giving person. She's keen to share her love. Which is fine by me. She told me she once had sex with five different people in one day.'

'That is a lot of love.'

'These railings are baking.'

I felt like a sardine on a grill. For a moment I didn't think I could take much more. I felt like my chest was being squeezed in a vice. Every last molecule of oxygen was being pressed out of my lungs by the crush of the crowd. With all the energy I could muster I shouted, 'Back off!' But nobody understood.

And then, at about four o'clock, as the sun was turning the dockside buildings to a butterscotch yellow, the ferry whistle gave a long low hoot. The cry of 'ella, ella, ella' increased in intensity. There was a rush of activity as ropes were unfurled; the ship belched a puff of black smoke and then, to my dismay, it slowly slipped away from the quayside.

The pressure of the crowd eased as if a clamp was gradually being released. I could see Gloria and Blodwyn waving. Plank was standing behind them with his arms crossed. Although I couldn't see it, I imagined he had a smirk of self satisfaction slapped across his great bucket head. 'Never give a fucker an even break,' he was probably thinking.

I turned to Boz. In the absence of anybody else to blame I said 'You fucking idiot.'

Boz obviously felt the same way. 'No, you're the fooking idiot. There isn't another ferry for days. We're stuffed.'

We stared at each other. Standing all afternoon in the heat had mashed my brain to pulp; I hadn't got the energy to argue.

'Let's go to a bar and discuss what we're going to do next,' said Boz.

'Yeah. That sun was hot.'

'Don't worry pal, we'll catch up with her.'

'Do you think so?'

'Of course. We keep meeting the same people all the time, don't we?'

'I suppose so.'

'We'll meet her again, I promise.'

That was a big promise. I didn't see how Boz could say that, but I was grateful anyway.

FORTY TWO

We had one last thing to do.

'Let's get straight to the Louvre,' I said.

'Yeah, we've saved the best for last.'

'What better way to end our journey than with the Impressionists?'

'The search for culture, that's what this trip is all about,' said Boz.

'It's a pity we missed Venice,' I said. 'And Athens.'

'We were there. What more do you want?'

'I'll go back one day.'

'It was you who was always in a hurry to get to Matala.' Boz had a point, I suppose.

'At least we went to that ethnographic museum in the town-with-no-name.'

'That was interesting. Do you remember the Romany mantrap and the woman who could only speak Welsh?' We both laughed.

The journey from Crete to Paris had been gruelling. After our attempt to catch the Hania ferry we'd hitched along the Cretan coast to Heraklion and from there hopped onto a boat going to Piraeus. In Athens Boz picked up a cheque from *poste restante*. As far as I know his postcard hadn't resulted in a fatality in the Scaggs household back in Bolton. Meanwhile, I calculated I had enough drachmas to buy a puzzle ring as a memento of our trip.

We planned to travel by night so that we could save on the cost of hotel rooms. To our dismay all trains from Athens appeared to lead to Belgrade, the last place on earth we wanted to pass further time. At Belgrade, such an unlovely city - harsh, angular, and unforgiving - we spent several miserable hours in the early morning in a rancid waiting hall watching cockroaches skitter over our bags. A long while later we rolled into Munich. Boz was keen to move on quickly as, he said, a sombre post Olympic Massacre vibe hung over the city. I did get the opportunity, however, to use my last pfennigs on a shower in the station restroom. From Munich it was a long slow journey, delayed only by a stray cow on the line outside Stuttgart, to Paris.

We walked from the Gare de l'Est down to the Latin Quarter. After the intimate narrow streets of our recent travels, Paris's wide boulevards and cobbled squares made me feel small and insignificant. South of the river we saw a coachload of armed riot police ready for action parked opposite the street cafés of the Boulevard St Michel. We eventually found accommodation, many floors up, in a dull pension in the Rue Git le Coeur. There were time switches controlling the feeble landing lights.

Our lodging was furnished with a vast ornate wardrobe and twin beds with enormous sagging horsehair mattresses. The room smelt of bitter Gauloises and wasn't the sort of place you wanted to spend much time in. As we unpacked our bags we heard muffled shouting from next door, soon followed by the rhythmic judder of a bed. If I leant out of the window and craned my neck I could see not walls, but the embankment of the Seine.

We went into the Louvre gift shop.

'There don't seem to be any postcards with the Impressionists on them.'

'*Avez-vous les van Goghs?*' Boz said to an attendant who with his lofty stature bore a striking resemblance to General de Gaulle. The attendant stared down his nose at Boz with a disdainful look, shrugged his shoulders, and then fixed his gaze on an item of great interest in the far distance.

'Are you sure the Impressionists are here?' Boz said to me.

'Where else are they going to be?'

Boz tried again.

'*Excusez-moi, avez-vous les van Goghs.*'

The attendant shrugged his shoulders again - but this time he smiled as he shook his head.

Boz was making progress.

'Excusez-moi monsieur, avez-vous les van Goghs, les Monets et les autres impressionistes?'

The attendant sighed and pulled from his pocket a worn scrap of paper.

He pointed to the words *Jeu de Paume*. *'Monsieur. Voilà.'* He raised his arm and indicated across the wide cobbled courtyard. *'Jeu de Paume. Cinq minutes.'*

'Maybe the Impressionists have a gallery to themselves,' Boz said.

'Why would they do that?'

I had a flashback to the beginning of our trip.

'Hang on, do you remember that guy we met in Soho, the one with the hat and the pink cravat, I'm sure he mentioned the Jeu de Paume.

'I think you're right.'

After walking across grand squares and through formal gardens we were ready for a drink.

'That was a long *cinq minutes*,' said Boz

'You've got to suffer for your art.'

At last we were going to see the finest paintings in the world. We needed to be alert, we needed to be cogent, we needed to be appreciative. All this could be put at risk if our concentration was disturbed by a nagging thirst. We ordered beers.

'This is good,' I said. What could be better than sitting in the Tuileries gardens in the late summer sun, having a beer in anticipation of seeing a collection of the most exquisite pictures ever painted?'

I was excited; over the last few months we'd seen and experienced so much. This was a suitable climax to our grand tour.

'This is a memorable moment to celebrate and savour,' said Boz as he ordered another round.

'We've got to do this,' I said.

'This is what this trip is all about,' agreed Boz. 'Culture with a capital K.'

'Yeah, wake up and smell the …what was it?'

'Patchouli.'

I sat back soaking up the September sunshine. I don't know if it was the onset of autumn or the different latitude but the quality of light was softer and mellower than the searing white of the Aegean. Across the gardens I could see a round pond with toy sailing boats on it.

I wondered what Gloria would visit in Paris? Notre Dame? The Eiffel Tower? Earlier, near the Sacre Coeur, we'd walked past the Musee de l'Erotisme. Boz said it looked interesting, but I didn't reckon I'd find Gloria there. Blodwyn maybe, but not Gloria. Quite honestly, despite Boz's promise on the Hania quayside, I'd given up any hope of seeing Gloria again on this trip.

'Boz, can I ask you something?'

'Yeah.'

'That Tiger Balm, what exactly do you do with it?'

'Just put a dab on your forehead. Where your third eye is.'

'Oh!'

'The third eye is the gateway to your inner consciousness.'

'Is it?'

'Don't put it anywhere else.' Boz looked at me in horror. 'Oh man, it's not a sex lube.'

'I know that, I'm not daft.'

Boz drained his glass and picked up his beer bottle. 'There's nothing sadder than an empty bottle.'

'We'd better do something about that,' I said, hailing the waiter.

'Do you know what?' slurred Boz. 'I could murder a joint?'

'A big fat joint before seeing a collection of the finest pictures ever painted would be excellent. If only we had Bixby with us now.'

Boz looked around. 'Perhaps not here though. It's a bit obvious.' We both laughed.

We were silent for a while. There was a distant roar of traffic. I thought about Gloria; the next time I'd see her would be back at

University. By then our summer of love would be over and things would be different.

'Hey, we've got something to do,' I said.

'What's that?'

'The gallery.'

'Do you know, for a moment I'd forgotten about the gallery,' said Boz.

'Me too.'

'I'll let you into a little secret. I reckon those Impressionists aren't all they're cracked up to be.'

'Don't say that Boz. You can't judge them until you've seen them.'

'I've seen them in calendars. Definitely over-rated.'

'You haven't seen a picture until you've seen it in the flesh. The best pictures, the really best pictures give off a vibe.'

'I know that only too well. Now the Pre-Raphaelite Brotherhood; they could knock off a good picture. Millais, he's the dude.'

'You seem to know a lot about this.' I was impressed; over the last few months some of my erudition must have rubbed off on Boz.

'Bolton Municipal Gallery, small but perfectly formed. In fact, Felix, I don't think I can be bothered to go into the Jeu de Paume. You go ahead, I'll stay here and look after our things. You won't be long.'

'But we've come all this way. We travelled thousands of miles to see this.'

'Look Felix, we haven't got much money, right? I don't want to waste my limited resources on a load of losers. That's why these guys aren't in the Louvre. The Louvre's got the quality stuff in it. These Impressionists have been relegated to a shed in the corner of a park. They can't be that good can they? They're second rate. I could get all this stuff back in Bolton. And that's free.'

'Boz, believe me, there's more to the world that just Bolton.'

But Boz had a point. We were now both short of dosh and this wasn't the Louvre. So far we'd had a perfectly good time without seeing the tourist sights. But then again we were so near to the gallery. It was just a few steps and we'd be in.

'Maybe I'll wait here and read my book.' At last Boz had found a novel that he liked. *Finnegan's Wake* had been a non starter - he never got beyond the first paragraph. He quickly swapped it for a spiky northern tale about a ruthless social climber dating an heiress and subsequently coming unstuck. To me *Room at the Top* sounded a bit old fashioned but Boz seemed to like it. I wondered if it echoed his relationship with Jennifer Rutley.

'This building's not a shed, it's an old orangery,' I said.

'An orangery full of lemons, as far as I'm concerned,' replied Boz.

We appeared to be the only visitors - all the Parisians were at lunch. Our footsteps echoed on the shiny wooden floor. After the palatial grandeur of the foyer of the Louvre the gallery felt small and provincial. Perhaps Boz was right and this was the annexe for the rejects.

It took a while for my eyes to adjust. There were so many paintings that were familiar - most were smaller than I had expected. Apart from a thin knee-high wire acting as a reminder for visitors to keep their distance, there appeared to be little security.

The fleshy Renoirs seemed like chocolate-box soft porn; the experimental pointillist stuff, well, it was clever, but soulless.

I was standing in front of a small Monet - depicting an idyllic hot day with a group of figures walking through a meadow. It felt three-dimensional. I could hear the murmur of bees in the wild thyme. It hit all the senses. It emitted a radiance that only a very few pictures do. I stared at it. I felt as if an electric shock had surged through my body; the hairs on my neck were standing on end. I couldn't move. I could feel the Mediterranean heat, I could smell the dry meadow and hear the crackling grass and the metallic scraping of cicadas. For a moment I was back in Crete. Too much booze at midday I thought.

A few feet to my right Boz was staring at a swirling van Gogh. 'Hey Felix, come and look at this.' Boz was swaying dangerously near the picture.

'Oh man. He's lost it,' Boz was saying. 'Van Gogh was one wacked out kind of guy. Totally lost it. Tripping. Look at the way he's painted this. It's as if he's unloading his emotions. Slapping heavy rapid paint on heavy rapid paint. That is a mixed up mind. You're looking at the raw texture of personal pain. Whoa.' Boz was transfixed.

After several minutes Boz moved on to the next picture. 'Oh no! Now look what van Gogh's done,' Boz groaned. 'He's painted his own chair. His own chair with his pipe on it. Isn't that the saddest, loneliest thing you've ever seen? My heart is being torn out by this.'

Boz's finger was half an inch from the canvas. The attendant must have gone for lunch. Boz was rocking on his feet. 'Careful with that picture, Boz,' I warned.

Boz turned to me. He had a blank look in his eyes. It looked like he was having a psychotic episode. It was as if the picture was acting as a conduit for emotional transference. In front of my very eyes Boz was morphing into Van Gogh. Trim his beard and put a bandage round his head and he'd be the spitting image.

'Don't touch,' I warned.

But before I had a chance to stop him, Boz had reached forward to grab the picture. 'I want it, Felix,' he blathered.

I jumped on Boz and pulled him away from the picture. We both fell backwards onto the parquet floor. 'What the hell are you doing?' Thankfully the frame was firmly screwed to the wall. I could hear the sound of somebody running. We were both lying on the floor. 'Get up! Get up quickly!' The attendant skidded into the room just as we were on our feet. 'Over there,' I pointed to the door leading to the next gallery. Without stopping the guard ran past us. There was shouting and commotion, as some innocent art lover, quietly admiring an Impressionist masterpiece, was rugby tackled to the ground.

We sat on a bench in the Tuileries garden in the afternoon sun. It was only September but the leaves were already edged with brown; there was a peppery autumn taste to the air.

'That was quite something,' said Boz. He seemed tired.

'Why didn't you tell me before?' I asked.

'I tried to.'

'When?'

'When we were about to go to the National Gallery. I've tried to tell you loads of times.'

'I didn't understand what you were saying. I didn't realise you were so sensitive.' I was surprised; I was seeing a new side to Boz.

'Sorry Felix, I find this art business powerful stuff. I've got to take it bit by bit, I can't just rush in. Some people get freaked by strobe lighting, I flip out on art. Some pictures can engage at a dangerous level. That's what exquisite art does - it takes me beyond the word and into another dimension rendering me a yabbering wreck. It's like falling in love. I can lose control.'

'Where did you learn about those pictures?'

'I didn't, that's what I see. I can sense the pain, I can feel the grief of the ages.'

'That's impressive.' Boz was behaving remarkably like a soft southerner.

'It's a curse, Felix, I tune into the vibe, I'm hypersensitive to art. The colours, the atmosphere. It's called synesthesia. When I was looking at those pictures I was right there in Provence. Van Gogh was standing next to me. I don't think other people get that. It was pretty harrowing.'

'Looking at that Monet, I felt something,' I agreed. 'But it wasn't enough for me to want to rip it of the wall.'

'There ought to be a sign on those pictures for people like me. *Warning. Emotionally intense.*

'Do you always do that? Grab a picture that takes your fancy. That's a dangerous habit to get into.'

'Oh no! I've never done THAT before.'

'Are you sure?'

'There was a Lowry in Manchester that I related strongly to, but I've never before tried to grab anything off the walls. It was the alcohol that did that to me.'

'Lunchtime drinking and the heat can be a dangerous combination.'

'Especially if it's mixed with art. The emotions come in degrees. It's like a mental tsunami, though I've never felt anything as strong as I did just then. It's not always a good sensation. You know what, I think, in the future, I'm going to stick to the Pre-Raphaelites. They just give me a nice warm tingly feeling.'

I was beginning to feel left out. First Gloria has copralexia, then Blodwyn is a kleptomaniac and now Boz has something called synesthesia. I was such a straight.

'I'm so boring, why haven't I got an interesting psychotic dysfunction?'

'You're a hopeless romantic.'

'There's nothing unusual about that.'

'Don't worry Felix, you're weird enough as it is.'

'Do you think so? Really? How?'

'I'd describe you as a reverse paranoid.'

'I like the sound of that. What's that mean?'

'You think the world owes you a living. You think the world is here to support you.'

'So? Doesn't everybody think that?'

'No. Not to the extent you do. Grants, dole, free prescriptions, travel passes, your Grandmother's purse; to you, it's all one big handout. But you have to pay for everything eventually. As my old man says 'there's nowt free in this life'. In your case you're living on one large social overdraft.'

'I'm not a scrounger. It's my entitlement.'

'I never said you were a scrounger.'

'I think the best of people. What's wrong with that? It's better to be optimistic than cynical, and maybe one day I'll pay back my social overdraft. With added interest. As they say, what goes around comes around.'

'There's a difference between 'thinking the best of people' and thinking they'll give you money.'

'Not that much of a difference.'

'Don't worry Felix, I can assure you, you are as weird as the next man.'

'That's alright then. I'll take that as a compliment.'

'Take it however you want.'

FORTY THREE

With its concrete floor and rows of seats bolted to the ground the waiting room of the ferry terminal reminded me of the Bristol dole office. We were sitting in a secluded corner of the ferry terminal away from the check-in desk.

'I've got a little something for the final leg of our journey,' Boz said as he lifted his rucksack off his back.

'Yeah?'

'Something that I've been saving for the right moment.'

'Huh?'

'And you'll be pleased to know the right moment has come.'

'Really?'

I watched as Boz pulled a protective rubber cap off one of the aluminium tubes of his rucksack frame.

'We need to end this journey with a bang.'

'What are you doing?' I had a premonition that whatever Boz was about to do wasn't going to be good.

Boz gave the frame a shake and knocked it with his fist. A tiny plastic bag, the size of a new penny, fell into his hand.

'What's that? More Tiger Balm?'

He held up the bag in front of me. 'A little present from our old pal Bixby.' I wasn't sure that I liked the sound of this.

'You what?'

'Nepalese Temple, the champagne of shit,' Boz said proudly.

After our travels I thought I knew Boz well, but he had just trawled the lowest level of stupidity yet.

'You daft stupid fucking berk.'

'I thought you'd be pleased. I did this for you.'

'Pleased! We've travelled round Europe with no hassle and now, when we're so near to home, you're about to get us busted. *Pleased* just doesn't sum up how I feel.'

'I thought...'

'Put that bloody bag away, somebody's going to see it. See those mirrors? They're two-way. People are watching us. That's what they do in these departure lounges. They're watching for idiots like you.'

Boz turned his head and stared at a mirror. 'Don't look,' I said, you'll attract attention to yourself.'

I was trying to come to terms with the enormity of Boz's recklessness. 'Do you mean to tell me that you - no, that WE - have travelled round Europe with that stashed in your rucksack frame?' I was sweating at the thought of it.

'Well, I wasn't going to shove it up my arse.'

'How many borders have we crossed? I'm just amazed that you - that WE - haven't been banged up in some Balkan jail house and left to rot.'

'I thought you knew.'

'How could I know?'

'Outside the Jeu de Paume. We almost had a spliff then.'

'I thought you were joking. I didn't realise that you actually had some with you.'

'I was careful.'

'That's not the point. Now I understand why you were nervous of dogs. Why didn't you tell me?'

'Because Felix, I feared that you would act just like you're acting now. Like an ungrateful twat. And this time you're the one drawing attention to yourself.'

I could see Boz was upset. We both needed to calm down.

'Look, Boz, you just freaked me out. This is unexpected.'

'I thought we needed a bit of fuel to keep us going. I was saving this for a special occasion.'

'Okay, okay. So what are we going to do?'

'After what you've said, I'm going to flush it down the loo.'

'That's probably best. We can't smoke it here.'

Boz got up from his seat.

'Wait a moment,' I said, thinking about what Bixby had said about *premier cru* all those months ago. 'It does seem a waste. Let's think about this constructively.'

'No, I'm flushing it.' Boz sounded determined.

'We could eat it,' I suggested.

'After all you've said.'

'It doesn't seem right to chuck it. You've carried this all round Europe. It would be a waste. We could swallow it just before the hovercraft leaves. How long do you think it'll take to kick in?'

'About forty-five minutes, I reckon.'

'That's perfect. The hovercraft takes half an hour. We'll be through customs and into the UK by the time we're knocking on nirvana's door. Sitting next to God will add interest to the train journey to Victoria.'

We waited until five minutes before we were due to board the hovercraft. Boz discreetly broke the lump in two. 'Just swallow it,' he said.

It looked like a piece of black mud.

'Are you sure this is Nepalese Temple?'

'That's what Bixby said. It cost enough.'

'Here goes.' I put the chunk in my mouth. It was disgusting. It tasted organic and excremental; it had the texture of grit and reeked of bitter sweat. I remembered what Bixby had said about the perspiring monks. I could feel myself gagging.

'Don't chew it, just swallow,' said Boz.

'Are you sure you didn't put this up your jacksy?' I asked.

'Stop messing. This is top gear. Get it down.'

But I couldn't get it down. It was breaking up in my mouth; it was like trying to eat a dry cheese cracker. I was swallowing hard but nothing was happening.

I stood up; my mouth was cloyed, I couldn't speak.

I could see Boz looking at me with alarm. 'What the hell are you doing? What's up with your face? Stop drawing attention to yourself.'

I walked across the room as calmly as possible. I swear I could feel the eyes on my back of the hidden watchers behind the mirror. I made it to the toilets. I was gagging. I spat out the mouthful, drank from a tap, and spat again. I swilled my mouth trying to clear the grit from my teeth. The foul excremental taste lingered; I washed my mouth out again.

I walked back to Boz. 'Sorry about that,' I said. 'I had to spit it out.'

'What a waste, that cost over a pound.'

'I don't reckon that was the real thing,' I said. 'The texture didn't seem right. It was like old floor sweepings. I think you might have been ripped off.'

'Ripped off by Bixby? No way. That was the full sweaty Betty McCoy.'

'I don't know.'

'I'll tell you in forty five minutes.'

'Sorry man, I owe you.'

As we got to the ticket gate ready to board the hovercraft there was an announcement over the Tannoy.

'*Messieurs, Mesdames*. Due to technical problems the departure of the hovercraft to Dover has been delayed by one hour.'

Boz looked at me in dismay. 'What am I going to do?'

'Shut up and read your book. If anybody speaks to you be polite.' Boz gave me the look of a dog that had lost its master. 'It's okay, Boz. Sit here and don't move. I'll look after you.'

FORTY FOUR

My heart jumped. Just from the view of her back I knew it was Gloria. She was waiting, by herself, in the queue for the ferry. I wondered where Blodwyn was, I wondered where Plank was. For a moment I wasn't sure that I wanted to speak to her.

I looked over at Boz who was lying on his back on a bench. Thankfully he appeared to be crashed out.

'Hello!' I shouted. Just think of her as a friend, I said to myself. A friend. Nothing more than that.

Gloria turned. Her face lit up, she smiled. She seemed genuinely pleased to see me.

'Felix!' She flung her arms round my neck and gave me a long hug. She'd lost weight.

'I thought you would have been back in England ages ago,' I said. With her warm body pressed against mine memories of Matala came flooding back.

'We got delayed.'

'How?'

'Lots of stuff. It was beastly.' She shook her head.

'Where's Blodwyn.'

'We split up.'

'Are you okay?'

'Blodwyn was such a liability.'

'Boz'll be disappointed.'

'I'm better off without her. She's just too much of a free spirit for her own good. Wherever we went something happened. She attracted problems.'

'What's she been up to now?'

'I couldn't leave her for one minute. We were on a train in northern Italy. I fell asleep and woke to find Blodwyn groping a complete stranger. He couldn't even speak English! She said the carriage had been filled with sleeping gas and he had taken advantage of her. From what I could see it was the other way round, and if there was any gas involved it seemed to be pretty localised. And then she got arrested.'

'So the Greek police caught up with her.'

'No. German police. They were frightening. That's why I'm a week late.'

'What happened?'

'It was so stupid. We were in a supermarket and there were some salamis, bratwurst or something, hanging, above the deli counter. I heard a loud crunch. I turned to see one of these sausages gently swinging in the still air; it had a huge bite taken out of it.'

'Yeah?'

'Blodwyn denied it of course, but as she had a mouthful of bratwurst it was difficult to believe her. They called the police who matched the teeth marks on the salami to hers.'

'I've always thought those salamis are a temptation, but they're normally out of reach.'

'Blodwyn had taken a running jump. When Blodwyn wants something, she goes for it.'

'Wow.'

'By this time Blodwyn was getting agitated and that's when she slapped the policeman. Typical German, he overreacted and she was arrested. So that slowed our progress. Frankly Felix, I'm sorry to say this, but I'm glad to be rid of her.'

Any moment now I was expecting a massive mandible to appear around a corner. 'So what about Plank?' I said, 'where is he?'

'We left Adrian in Athens. He said he wanted to go to Cappadocia.'

Plank must have thought these cave towns were a good place to score. I didn't want to say anything to Gloria; he'd obviously got his ticks on his 'To Shag List' and was moving on to maraud elsewhere.

'Adrian was so sweet.'

'Huh!' However hard I tried I could never think of Plank as being sweet.

'Why are you looking at me like that, Felix?'

'Nothing.'

'You flinched when I said Adrian.'

'I don't know. It's just you could have done better than Plank.'

'What do you mean?'

'Plank: he's a conniving bastard.'

'That's not fair, he's not.'

'And clever with it.'

'You never liked Adrian, did you?'

'I don't like the way he manipulates people.'

'Felix! He was being helpful.'

'Gloria. You have to ask yourself, why was he being helpful? He sees a weakness and he exploits it. He's ruthless.'

'Excuse me, what weakness? I don't think you know what you're talking about.'

'Opportunity, then. I've seen him in action, there's another side to him. He's like a cruel, cunning hunter. You were on his 'To Shag List.' You were in his top five. There's too much of the cave man in him.'

'Adrian would be really upset if he knew you said these horrible things about him.'

I shrugged. So what? 'Yeah, sometimes the truth can be a bummer.'

'And he speaks so well of you.'

'Yeah!'

'He does. Really!' I wasn't sure whether Gloria was being sarcastic.

'What? Of me? You're having me on?'

'He's always talking about you. How funny and interesting you and Boz are.'

'You ARE kidding.'

'No, he likes you.'

'That's just another of his deceptions. He said Boz was a freeloader.'

'He told me that's why he's been travelling round Europe. To hang out with you and Boz. He says you're his best mates. Though he doesn't like you calling him Plank.'

'Best mates! But he's not even a freak! He's a straight. I hate straights.'

'He said you and Boz had arranged to meet him in Matala. He was upset when you said he couldn't join you in your cave. He wanted to do that.'

'He's lying.' I couldn't believe this. It couldn't be true. This was one of Plank's double bluffs. 'Are you sure? Are you really sure?'

'You're a role model for him.'

'Now you ARE taking the piss. Me, a role model for Plank! Tell me he never said that.'

'Well, he might not have used those exact words. But that's what he implied. Anyway,' Gloria continued. 'I like him. He's always been nice to me.'

'He's full of it, and he's full of shit. I don't understand why you can't see through him.'

'Give him a break, he suffers from public school survivor guilt.'

'What?'

'He's a bit damaged. He tries to impress people by exaggerating and making things up.'

'We all do that.'

'No, Felix. Not everybody. Shall I tell you why I like him?'

'I have absolutely no idea why you like him.'

'Because ...'

'I really don't want to hear this. I don't give a damn why you like him. There's nothing to like about him. He's unlikeable.'

'Because... in a funny sort of way he reminds me of you.'

WHAM! I felt like I'd been punched in the stomach. 'What?! What!' I was astounded. This was too much. First Plank was my friend, then I was his role model, and now he was my doppelganger. This was the guy I once seriously intended to mug.

'But I hate prog rock!' I protested.

269

'I didn't say you were exactly the same.'

'And I don't have a 'To Shag List'.'

'Are you sure?'

'Yes!'

'I thought every man has a 'To Shag List'.'

'No they don't. Not like that. Not like Plank's. He methodically ticks off his conquests and gives them a score. I don't do that.'

Gloria looked at me quizzically, blue eyes wide, with a questioning smile on her face.

I continued, 'Let's get this straight. You think he's like me?'

'A little bit. He's a good listener.'

'So, by implication I'm like him.'

'Yes, a little bit!'

BAM! I was like Plank! This time it felt like I'd been smacked in the head. That hurt. I had to hit back.

'Huh! So did you cry out my name when he made love to you?'

'That's such a stupid thing to say.'

'Did you?'

'No.'

'Huh!'

'If you must know, I never slept with him.'

'I don't believe you.'

'He's just a friend. I don't fancy him, Felix.'

'So?'

'That's why he reminds me of you.'

WALLOP! 'Oh.' I didn't see that one coming. That was so unexpected. It was a knock-out hit. The air had been punched out of me, I was on the ropes. A bell was ringing in my ears.

'Felix, I didn't want to say that, you forced me.'

'You never fancied me?'

'Oh Felix, this is so stupid. Let's not hurt each other.'

'But never? What about that wet afternoon listening to Cat Stevens?'

'Yeah, Felix that was fun. But things have changed.'

'Nothing's changed.' I protested. 'What about the cave? We had a good time in the cave.'

'But I was drunk.'

'Oh come on!'

'We did have a good time, Felix. But the summer's over.'

'You said I smelt nice.' Was that it? Just a holiday romance? I couldn't let this slip away. I looked at Gloria's beautiful face. I could see something, a remembrance in her eyes; I knew there was still a glow in her heart. I was back on my feet. SECONDS AWAY. ROUND TWO.

We were both silent for a moment as we gathered our thoughts. I looked out of the large glass window. A grey haze hung over the English Channel. To the right the ferry was being loaded with trucks and cars. Away to the left on a sloping concrete apron I could see the hovercraft with its four bright red propellers on its roof and its deflated and crumpled skirt.

'Where's Boz?' Gloria asked.

'Over there.' I pointed to Boz who was still lying on his back but now had both arms in the air and appeared to be staring intently at his hands. It looked like the doors of perception were just about to open.

'What's he doing?'

'He's feeling a bit untogether. I think he might have had too many travel sickness pills.'

'Some people can be oversensitive to them. Poor Boz, he doesn't look well.'

'He's fine, I'm looking after him.'

Gloria said, 'Look, I've got a boat to board and you've got a hovercraft to catch.'

'Yeah, let's call the whole thing off…'

We looked at each other. I didn't want to be just a friend - that would never be enough. I wanted to be part of her; I wanted her to be part of me. But it wasn't going to happen. I knew that.

'Don't be like that,' she said. 'We've both had a great trip, let's not spoil it.'

'YOU'VE spoilt it.'

'Let's remember the good times.'

'Like going off with Plank. How could you?'

'I promise you, Felix, nothing happened.'

I didn't want it to end like this. I thought of our night in the cave, I thought of Gloria lying in the water. I remembered my resolution under the stars. 'I suppose so.'

We hugged. I was aware of her soft ear against my cheek. She smelt of sun and holidays.

'Friends?' she whispered.

'Yeah, friends,' I smiled. 'We can still have good times, can't we?'

'Will I see you back in England?' she asked.

'Yeah, I've decided to go back to University.'

'That's a good idea.'

'I'll see you around then?'

'Yeah.'

I grabbed her hand. We looked at each other. A silent goodbye. To my amazement there were tears in her eyes.

I watched Gloria walk away. As she got to the corner of the hall, she turned and waved.

FORTY FIVE

We were tired and dirty. As we got off the coach at Victoria and headed to the Underground I noticed a September chill in the air. The first leaves of autumn were being blown along the pavement by a gentle breeze. The streets were busy; everybody appeared to be in a rush. A beggar sitting in a doorway asked me for some spare change.

Boz and I sat silently as the train flashed through the tunnels. It was strange being in this daytime darkness.

In the end we had got out of France and into England with little trouble. I explained that Boz was oversensitive to travel sickness pills. The men with the rubber stamps had laughed. 'Everybody feels sick on that hovercraft,' the official had said.

I thought about Gloria. I didn't know what to feel. I felt sad, I felt happy. I couldn't work it out.

I'd been fiddling with the puzzle ring I'd bought in Athens. I must have lost weight for the ring fell off my finger onto the carriage floor and the pieces fell apart. I picked up the disassembled ring and with a few deft movements put it together again.

As I sat on the train I tried to remember everything I'd experienced over the summer: I had half a dozen currencies in my pocket. I was amazed at the variety of the countries in Europe: monarchies; republics; federations; communist states; military juntas; dictatorships. I'd lived in a cave; I'd slept under the Milky Way; I'd eaten courgettes for breakfast; I'd met people - the memory of whom would stay with me forever; I'd looked through doorways and seen families eating together; I'd seen vagrants sleeping in the street; I'd slept in the street! Though I never did get to jump that freight train.

I had this nagging fear that I'd bang my head, suffer amnesia and the memories of the summer would evaporate like a vast dying lake. They say that you can enjoy a beautiful sunset but you shouldn't try to hang onto it, that you need to live in the present. I don't know about that. I still think of that Perseids meteor shower embroidering the night sky; it was a moment of such transcendental beauty that I have returned to it in my mind many times since.

We'd travelled blindly in our own bubble. I knew so little about other people's lives and the politics that affected them. I'd missed the fall of a fascist dictatorship and hardly noticed the monotony of communist regimes and all sorts of ugly happenings. I'd lain on a beach unaware that the country was at war; I'd danced and partied in a land that twenty years later would eat itself alive.

You could say, and Dad would certainly go on and on about this, that I was unprepared for my travels. According to Dad I had wasted the summer; but then again I'd enjoyed every moment of it. Sure I'd missed St Mark's Square in Venice, I hadn't crossed the Ponte Vecchio, and I'd only glimpsed the Parthenon through a skeleton of scaffolding from the streets below. But Boz and I had explored in our own time and our own pace. We weren't seeing the stuff dictated by guidebooks, but were going with the vibe, trusting in fate, discovering what interested us, interpreting what we saw in our own way. I'd learnt so much: that you can get your head boiled in Albania and your feet roasted in Greece, that there are more vegetables than just peas, carrots and cabbages; and that I needed to go back to Venice and look in the right direction.

Indeed, I was gathering experiences that were to lurk in the shadows for a lifetime; memories ready to be drawn upon at unexpected moments. Was that such a bad thing? Although I didn't know it then, my life was on the cusp of something. The old man in the bar in Yugoslavia had made me ashamed that I didn't value our free education. Thanks to him I realised I needed to return to University - even if the lecturing was a bit too pedagogic for my liking.

That journey was a time of limitless opportunities, remote from the responsibilities of life. I wasn't thinking about the future. For just one glorious summer I was trying in my own little way to be free. I sensed I would never have this opportunity again. I was there, living in the present, in the moment. I hardly ever thought of home, of what was going on back in England. Sheer self indulgence you might say, but I'd argue that in a world of air mail letters, international phone calls and global television news the opportunity to have a time of uninterrupted focus is something that everybody should experience.

Despite my protestations about a monstrously divided Britain and Ted Heath's attempts to break the spirit of the people with rocketing inflation and a three-day week, the journey had made me appreciate the life I lived. We were a lucky generation. No wars (not that I'd been directly involved with, anyway), penicillin, a student grant and the contraceptive pill. We were blessed, and I was going to make the most of these happy times. I wasn't living under martial law; I wasn't living in an artificially-gelled country that would shortly be tearing its soul out; I wasn't being called up to fight in a pointless war. I had freedom to say what I thought, I had freedom to travel: that was worth a lot.

King's Cross. Boz got up and pulled his rucksack onto his shoulders. The doors of the underground train rumbled open.

'See you pal!' he said.

'Yeah, good one. Sorry about the pilchards.'

'The dolphins were good.'

'Hey, thanks for the Tiger Balm.'

The sliding doors started to shut. Boz was standing on the platform.

'Do the same again next summer?' I said.

'You bet!'

The doors closed before we had a chance to say anything more.

'Start with the National Gallery,' I shouted. But I realised that that might not be a good idea.

AFTERWORD

The next day I looked through a pile of letters waiting for me at home. Among the bank statements and *Readers Digest* junk mail there was a postcard. I stared at the picture. It was of Matala. It was taken from a boat; you could see the village and the Mermaid Café and in the distance to the left the yellow cliff. The sender had marked one of the houses with an arrow. I turned the card over. It read.

Felix,
I couldn't wait forever.
I hope you understand.
Gloria X

There was a dark smudge where Gloria had scribbled over what I guessed was one of her obscenities. I angled the card to the light so that I could discern the impression of the pen. I couldn't be sure, but it seemed to say 'wanker.'

THANKS

Thanks to all those people who have told me about their travels in the 1970s. This includes: Chris McCormac, Ian Fryer, Ian Robarts, Jonathon Richards, Julian Brooks, Polly Davies and Ruth Ennols. And especially Pete Bowe with whom I shared three summers travelling the Balkans, Greece and the USA. Though we never did make it to Matala. Also fond memories of a rooftop shed in Rethymnon with Alison Jeffers, Liz Davies, Annie Beatson and Paul Jerome.

Thanks to the late Chris Challis who introduced me, amongst other things, to the works of Jan Cremer.

Thanks to Gillian Marles for the splendid book-cover, Adrian Barclay for the map and Matt Manson for the 'Rules.'

Thanks to Ali Reynolds for editorial support and advice, and Hilary Arundale for her cogent comments and superb editing. Also to Nicky Johns for eagle-eyed proofing. I've been fortunate to have had on-going support from the Bristol Writers Group. My gratitude to Andy Gibb, Emma Norris, Franca Davenport, Gavin Watkins, Gerry O'Donovan, Justin Newland, Louise Gethin, Terry Stew and Tom Sykes, all of whom have supplied ideas and encouragement.

Also thanks to the team at Tangent Books HQ for tea and company: Richard Jones; Jon Lewis; Marc Leverton; Nick Law, and Joe Melia. And an extra special mention to Richard Jones for all he has done to support Bristol writers, artists and cider makers.

And, of course, the biggest thanks of all to Maggie for accompanying me not only through the last 25 years of life but also on the crazy retro trip to Albania without maps or research. If there's one thing I've learnt it's that guide books are a truly great invention!

Also by Mike Manson:

'WHERE'S MY MONEY?'

The cry of 'I want my money' invariably means that something is about to blow.

Max doesn't work. Now he's been offered a job - at the dole office.

The hot summer of '76. Mega-flares. The dole office. Cider. And a riot.

The 1970s. If you were there, you've probably tried to forget it. If you weren't, find out what you've missed.

'I put on a white poly-cotton shirt and my high-waisted mega-flares. I'd also found a tin of blue polish for my platform shoes. The platform was only a centimetre - probably about right for the civil service. I brushed my hair, and with the edge of a comb carefully drew out a centre parting. Then, to create the desired effect, I messed it up again. The finishing touch was provided by a blue kipper tie adorned with a striking green snowflake motif. I looped the tie into a knot the size of a samosa and stood in front of the mirror to admire myself.'

Max is preparing for his next move. He doesn't know what his next move is going to be. But he'll be ready for it when it comes.

The author

For a time in the 1970s Mike Manson worked as a dole clerk. 'This isn't my story,' he says. He has to, he signed the Official Secrets Act.

www.wheresmymoney.org.uk
www.tangentbooks.co.uk